The Last Reich

The Last Reich

Arthur Rhodes

Rutledge Books, Inc.  Danbury, CT

This is a work of fiction. As in all fiction, all names, characters, places and incidents are either products of the author's imagination or are used fictitiously. No reference to any real person is intended or should be inferred.

Cover artwork by John Randall
Cover design by John Laub
Interior design by Al Robinson

Copyright © 2001 by Arthur Rhodes

ALL RIGHTS RESERVED

Rutledge Books, Inc.
107 Mill Plain Road, Danbury, CT 06811
1-800-278-8533
www.rutledgebooks.com

Manufactured in the United States of America
The Last Reich
    Rhodes, Arthur

    ISBN: 1-58244-211-8

    1. Fiction

Library of Congress Control Number: 2001096105

Book One

PROLOGUE

JUNE 4, 1960

The first American attack of the Second American Revolution was scheduled to begin at 1:00 A.M. Central time in Houston, Texas, on June 4, 1960. At 12:55 A.M. Mark Collins, the American leader, leaned back against the seat of the huge oil tanker truck, second in line of the ten trucks waiting on the Herman Göring Highway.

Ten converted oil tanker trucks were seven miles from the fence of the Nazi air base named after the World War II leader of the German air force. The trucks held four men in the cab and inside the converter carriers two rows of men sat on wooden benches.

A special door had been built into the back of the trucks that opened out and would allow thirty men to leave the truck in less than two minutes. Most of the men carried carbines, M-1 rifles and submachine guns. However, the real firepower of the group was four .30-caliber machine guns and a bazooka.

Collins was calm; they had practiced their simple plan many times. On his signal the trucks with lights out and motors idling would move toward the base. The first truck, at a speed of fifty miles per hour, would break through the rusted gate that hung on hinges that threatened to blow over in the strong southwest desert winds. The target of the Americans was the two rows of Nazi jet planes lined up one mile from the gate. Twin runways were not lighted since the Germans never flew at night, but with the light of a full moon they were easily distinguishable to the attackers. Forty jets were the total Nazi air armada in America. Surprising since the Germans had used five hundred jets to defeat America in 1948.

Collins knew there were no guards at the planes. He had driven his small station wagon onto the base every day at noon bringing coffee and sweet cakes to sell to the guards.

Captain Keller had allowed Collins to range over the base selling coffee for twenty-five percent of the profits. Reconnaissance, Collins told his men, dictated that two trucks would destroy the jets and that the remaining eight would attack the air headquarters and barracks of the hated occupation force. During his time on the base Collins could not say which surprised him more—the lack of air activity or the smell of whiskey on the guards' breath during the day.

This would not have surprised Herr General Fredericke, Nazi commander of the base. Morale was low with his men. They, like he, hated the hot humid climate. Unlike the rest of the Nazis in America his men were prisoners on an island in a sea of hostility. Fredericke was an intelligent man and he knew he did not have the resources to subdue the southwest. His uncle, the Reich chancellor, leader of the known world, had sent him to the southwest with five thousand men of which less than one thousand were on the base.

The Reich chancellor thought the people of Houston cowards. They had been taught a lesson in 1953. He was wrong.

At the meeting in Berlin two years ago with one hundred other

Reich protectors his uncle had singled him out as the model for the group. What the leader did not know and no one dared tell him, for it would expose his nephew as the most lax and compromised Reich protector in North America, was that the oil carried by tankers through the Houston ship channel was scheduled by civilian Americans to meet their quotas that were low by Berlin standards.

A rash of killing and riots had greeted Fredericke when he first took control. Quickly he sought out American civilian leaders to end the violence against his outmaneuvered soldiers by the American ruffians. The peace treaty was verbal.

Two of the ruffians, oil workers of Houston, were in the cab of the first truck. The Scanlon brothers were the ruffians of the ruffians.

Collins had met the Scanlon brothers in a high school football game twenty years before.

Collins, a fleet halfback, had swept left and Mark Scanlon had illegally stuck out his leg and tripped him. Collins went down in a tangle, out of breath made worse when the younger Scanlon, Billy, kicked him. The ref missed the first foul but caught the second. When Collins began to recruit members for the underground, the Scanlons were among his first members.

At 1:00 A.M., Collins signaled the first truck to move. By the second mile they were at full speed, four minutes to the gate.

The two Blackshirt Nazi guards were asleep when they were startled by the crash. The gate flew off its hinges and landed forty feet away. Truck one swerved to the left and headed for the planes.

The twin engine ME 262 flew one hundred miles faster than any American plane at war's end. But without proper maintenance and parts fully two-thirds of the jets were not in operational condition. Collins did not know this but even if he had, his dedication to destroy their planes was absolute. Two men dropped off; each carried two

Molotov cocktails—wine bottles filled with gasoline. The truck moved to the next four planes and the first man had set his plane on fire before the truck moved again.

The backup plan was to go down the row, take a U-turn, and be sure they were all destroyed.

Collins had told the other truck, which had a flamethrower, that in the event any ME 262 survived the first attack they must crash into the survivor. They reached the end of the row, made the turn, and could see most of the planes were on fire.

The sound of four .30-caliber machine guns was heard. The driver said, "Those are our guns."

Collins responded, "Just watch the road. Go back slowly." The fourth jet from the end was not burning. A Molotov cocktail had been thrown over the plane and was burning harmlessly on the tarmac.

A small boy next to Collins twisted a wine bottle in his hands and fingered the cigarette lighter in his pocket. Joe Towry, fifteen years old, was the first backup, an orphan since seven when the Nazis killed his parents. He had lived by stealing garbage at night and sleeping in storm drains.

Collins pointed to the jet. "Don't miss."

The boy slid the door open and lighted the wick after he was out of the cab. Moving quickly but under control he reached back and fired the flaming bottle at the fuselage.

The plane ignited quickly and the boy backed away and nimbly jumped back into the front of the cab. With a blank expression he answered Collins, "I didn't." After having to use a knife to make sure he could defend his share of garbage, this did not seem so hard.

The truck moved toward the fight at the Nazi headquarters, and Collins used his field glasses to check its progress.

Most of the German soldiers were draftees, old men and boys who surrendered at the first shots. The barracks building was burning, hit by a bazooka shell, and through the smoke men could be seen coming out of the building with hands up. Collins could see muzzle flashes from the third floor. A hard *core* was fighting back.

The one-story headquarters with the large swastika was quiet, but next door to it and attached, a two-story annex, the Blackshirts had sandbags and two heavy machine guns were firing from good cover.

The plan was to hit the sandbag-protected machine guns with bazooka fire. The crew had done as ordered but in the excitement missed, but thought they had hit and turned to fire at the next target. The mistake cost them their lives and now the German machine gun crews silenced two of the .30-caliber guns.

Collins knew the battle could be lost in the next few minutes. To the right the first oil tankers pulled up with the Scanlon brothers.

Collins saw the door on the driver's side open and the driver fall on the runway. "Was he shot?"

No, Matt Scanlon had pushed him out and was now driving the truck hunched forward picking up speed and heading for the annex.

Collins muttered, "He's going to ram it." The German gunmen realized the danger and tried to transverse the guns to meet the new threat. They fired wild and high. Scanlon at 100 yards pushed the pedal to the floor. The roar of the engine coincided with the Nazi gunners leaving their positions.

At 50 yards Matt Scanlon hit the brake and the truck swerved sideways, rocked, and almost turned over.

Billy Scanlon moved out of the cab, a flamethrower on his back. He did not have to face any gunfire and calmly moved to firing distance and a wall of fire engulfed the top of the annex. The .30-caliber raked the top of the barracks and the battle was over.

7

With less than thirty wounded and ten dead, the Americans had destroyed Nazi air power in America. Events that began June 2 had culminated in the first victory of the Second American Revolution.

It was payback for what happened in Houston in 1953.

Chapter I

On June, 2, 1960, Allen awoke from his dream that America was free again. He often dreamed about the America before the war, especially when he was drinking. He groaned, blinked his eyes to escape from the web of sleep and turned to look at the clock. It was 6:30 and time to get up. He shook his head, sat up, and got ready to face another day. He staggered to his feet still fighting the sleep and went to the window. His small apartment located on the Brooklyn side of New York Harbor faced Staten Island. He peered out, looking across to the Statue of Liberty, now called the Lady of the Torch. From the flagstaff extending from the torch the high flag's red background highlighted the black swastika. Allen put on his glasses and his focus adjusted. In the halcyon days before the war, a clear morning in June would have lifted his spirits as the sun rose over the sparkling waters of the harbor with the sea breeze sending ripples that lapped at the shore.

"Damn," he murmured, hating the black swastika of the Fourth Reich and the arrogance of the Nazis for putting the flag on the statue. The swastika fluttered above New York Harbor, an insult to all Americans.

Allen pulled a page off his calendar—June 2, 1960. Inadvertently he shook his head, another day, a long day of disappointment, would that cursed flag never cease to wave. The flag swirled in the wind and crossed the face of the great statue. A mood of despair and gloom touched Allen. He crossed the small room and sat on the bed. Monday morning was the difficult time; he would have to subsist the full week. The fear and pressure that every subject of the Fourth Reich must face. To Allen it was always the same, the depression of seeing the red and black flag, then a nostalgia for life before the war. His preparation for the week was labored for he hated his job, working in the history section of the state office.

He thought of his supervisor, deputy Codder, the Nazi official in charge of the department. Allen cursed Codder, and slowly the pain shot through his stomach. "Oh God," he muttered, as he doubled over in pain. He bit his lip to alleviate the dull overpowering pressure in his colon. Allen staggered on one knee. If only he could endure the next few minutes. He was forty-one, but looked older bent under the oppression of the Fourth Reich. He staggered into the bathroom, the pressure in his stomach doubling him up in pain.

Allen faced the fact he would never regain his youth. A graduate of State University in 1940, he was a history major in college. When the war broke out, he was drafted and served without distinction in a training battalion in Pennsylvania. When America surrendered in 1950, like millions of others he was caught in the confusion of a defeated major power. He was unemployed and struggled at odd jobs for two years and then took the test for the state history department. The few jobs available required a test. At the department Allen met deputy Codder, a member of the Nazi party. All administrative or management jobs were controlled by party members in America. Codder was a deputy of the Blackshirts, heirs to the dreaded Gestapo.

Minutes later Allen composed himself, shaved, and was ready to leave for work. He dressed in a faded blue suit—threadbare and the cuff of one trouser was dirty. He adjusted his tie before the mirror and then slipped on his armband. The state workers all wore green armbands. He could not leave the apartment without an armband, for to appear on the street without one was surely to be stopped by the Blackshirts. The Blackshirts could stop and search anyone at anytime. If the person resisted or did not pass the inspection, he could be arrested and imprisoned without trial or hope of bail. People who disappeared into the Blackshirt prisons usually did not come back.

Allen despised the regimentation of the armband, but his color green gave him a certain safety. Rarely would the security police stop a green; they would stop an orange occasionally. Orange was the color of most people in the country. The oranges were subject to minor harassment by the Blackshirts. If a line formed in a store or on the subway, the oranges would have to go behind the green. Because the green had this small advantage it was frequently a source of resentment of the rank and file of the people. One day on the subway Allen bumped into a man wearing an orange armband. The man turned, saw his green armband and shouted at him "You lousy turncoat, dirty green."

He punched Allen in the chest and ran through the crowd to escape the bewildered stares of the other subway riders.

Below the oranges were the reds. People who wore the reds were Negros or criminals on parole. They were constantly harassed by the Blackshirts. The work gangs that cleaned the subways were reds. The reds did all the dangerous and dirty jobs. Little safety was observed on construction on the subways and reds were frequently hurt or killed. Lowest of all the people who wore armbands were the Jews, who wore yellow armbands with the Star of David. If a line would queue up for food or transportation the yellows had to go to the back. Even the reds were ahead of the yellows and so when the subways were not working, as they often were not, the yellows had to wait hours after everyone else had gotten on the packed subways and gone home. The Jews could not own a business or work for the state.

All the synagogues were closed and no Jewish holidays could be openly observed. The Jews were not the only people to experience religious persecution—many churches were closed around the country. Still, in New York City, with a large Jewish population, fewer and fewer yellows were seen on the street.

Feeling better, Allen indulged in the practice that was his custom before he left the house. He felt under the bed to see if the packet was still securely tied to the forward slat board. In the packet was his supreme disobedience to the state. For if he was rewriting American history by day, at night he carefully replaced on paper what he had changed during the day. At the commission of the underground his packet was the legacy of almost two hundred years of American history. He would follow other orders from his supervisor, code name Valley Forge, but his main responsibility was the packet. Allen would see Valley Forge every Tuesday before he entered the state office building and on occasion he would be given messages to carry or pass contraband to others, but always the packet was his priority.

As Allen locked his door, his next door neighbor peeked out. She was a Nazi sympathizer and, he suspected, an informer to the Blackshirts. She was friendly to Allen because he was a green. "Good morning, Mr. Allen."

"Good morning, Miss Judkins."

"Heard on the radio, they caught two reds stealing food from one of the warehouses. You can bet some Jews put them up to that."

He ignored her as much as he could, her bigotry disgusted him.

"I think Mr. Williams down the hall is Jewish."

"Got to go, Miss Judkins."

People leaving their apartments began to move to the stairs. The elevator had not worked in years and tired sullen people descended down the stairs. Allen joined the flood of people, pausing at each landing as more joined them. Because all work started at seven-thirty the exodus for buses and subways always began at this time. There would be long lines of people waiting for public transportation. Few people owned or could afford a car.

Allen rode the subway and got off at the stop across from his building, as he always did. He walked up the stairs and blinked as the bright sunlight hit his eyes. He looked across the street and saw the man he knew as Valley Forge. He was startled; never had he seen him except on a Tuesday.

The signal was a folded newspaper. If the agent wanted to talk he would catch his eye, fold his newspaper, and Allen would follow him down the street. If Allen had a message, he would use the same signal to Valley Forge. On many occasions there was no signal and the two would pass uneventfully. Valley Forge folded his newspaper, turned, and walked toward the East River.

Allen slowly moved behind him, perhaps twenty feet, his curiosity making his heart beat faster. Why was he here today? It must be important, perhaps critical. But Allen did not speak to Valley Forge; he knew the discipline of the underground required he wait. Valley Forge was a slight man in his early thirties, always crisp and direct. Allen was taller and heavier, yet he easily deferred to the younger man and was inspired by his confidence. Valley Forge's appearance and personality blended to a low-key relaxed leader. Allen did not know any other members of the Underground. This did not surprise him, the Underground was inactive and the Nazis paid little heed to it.

Allen met Valley Forge because Allen's sister-in-law Heidi needed forged papers. Heidi's mother was Jewish and when the state identification program began and citizens were forced to carry state papers and wear armbands, she was classified a yellow despite her conversion to his brother's church. Allen's brother was afraid they would be separated and since Allen had contacts in the identification department his brother asked him to help. Allen liked Heidi—she was so gay and pretty—and so he bribed officials to get her papers that gave her an orange designation. Since then Allen's brother was killed and he lost touch with her as travel became difficult. He heard later she had a nervous breakdown.

Valley Forge somehow knew about the forged papers and he approached Allen to work for the Underground. Allen hesitated; he did not consider himself a brave man and it all seemed so hopeless. The Nazis controlled the world, and what could a few patriots do against their might? Here events took a somber turn and influenced him. It was Nazi policy to force different ethnic and colored peoples to fight rebellious colonies of the Fourth Reich. Allen's brother was drafted by the Nazis to join their foreign legion in Southeast Asia. At that time both Germany and Japan were trying to subdue the area known as Indochina. Allen's brother was killed shortly after he reached Asia. Allen was heartbroken that his younger brother's life had been destroyed so needlessly. He did not become more optimistic over the chances of the Underground. His hate spurred him to call Valley Forge and volunteer in the cause. Thus Allen, through a series of events not of his making, came to the attention of the Underground and in a moment of grief and despair joined them.

People moved past the two men without notice hurrying to work. Valley Forge signaled Allen to follow him down a flight of steps of a basement store that did not open until noon. It was a familiar spot for them to meet. Allen spoke first "I didn't expect to see you today."

Always direct, Valley Forge said, "Something special, it couldn't wait. Glad to see you spotted me."

"Anything to do with the Houston anniversary?" This week was the seventh anniversary of the Nazi use of an atomic bomb against the people of Houston when they rebelled in 1953. The Underground usually attempted to stage an event during the week to commemorate the victims despite the fact that it was illegal.

Valley Forge shook his head. "No, something even more important than that. I have a special assignment for you."

Allen felt nervous, Valley Forge's deviation from schedule and his emphasis on "special" was ominous.

Valley Forge continued. "We need someone to reach an informant at the Metro Complex. We want you to get into the building and the agent will give you a message and then help get you out of there. Then we want you to carry the message to Long Island."

Allen did not answer. Metro Complex was Blackshirt headquarters; he did not want to walk in that area. To go into the building was unthinkable.

Valley Forge waited. Allen responded negatively, "Valley Forge, I can't do this."

"Allen, besides your green identification, we need you especially for this job. You are the only one we can get into the building."

"I don't know; my job is to catalogue history. I don't know anything about this type of work."

Valley Forge said, "Your Aunt Mary Bee is the person we want you to contact."

Allen knew Mary Bee worked at the Metro Complex, but he had not seen her in years. This was unbelievable.

Valley Forge continued, "You must tell her you're working for State Security, the old Gestapo agency, and that they need to know about the special message received at the Metro Complex. She is the head code clerk so she must know about this."

Allen was stunned. After a long pause, Valley Forge continued, "We can get you into the building and I can get you out."

Allen leaned against the side of the stairwell. His knees were weak. "I haven't talked to Aunt Mary in years. She's a Nazi sympathizer; she won't tell me anything."

Valley Forge grabbed his arm to focus his attention. "Mary Bee has on occasion told people at the Metro Complex that she wished the old Gestapo would come back."

He raised his left hand and with a chopping motion to emphasize the point he said, "She will see someone she knows, you, and you will be wearing a green armband and you will give her a Gestapo countersign. Be aggressive and you can pull it off."

"She won't believe me." Allen lowered his head, a sign of defeat.

Valley Forge decided to change tactics. He must reemphasize there would be a little danger. "The way to get into the building is that we have paid Red Harter, the German supporter, to take you in with his crew. You'll be there a short time and I know you can convince your aunt; she is no brilliant strategist."

Allen nodded, "Aunt Mary was never a deep thinker."

Valley Forge saw him waiver. "We have an agent in the building. She will be there in support. William, this is the most important thing you'll ever do for your country and I know you can help us."

The older man slumped, "I'm sorry I can't do it." Allen looked out into the street, people were going to work as they always did, the world was normal, except for what the Underground wanted him to do. He just couldn't succeed at this.

"Allen, I'm your friend and I tell you we need you."

Valley Forge knew Allen to be an insecure man, but he was honest and had a strong sense of responsibility. He would tell Allen the truth on at least most of it.

"Yesterday the Nazis closed off the Metro Complex. No one in and no one out. We believe a message was received from Germany, an important message."

Allen shrugged his shoulders. "This sounds impossible. You sure you don't have someone else?"

Allen was not as firm in his refusal; the younger man sensed he was waivering. Valley Forge was a leader because he could motivate and direct people.

He said, "I have no one else, Allen." Then Valley Forge played his trump card, "And I think your brother would want you to do this."

Allen thought of his brother. Yes, he was right. "I guess I'll have to try. When do you want me to make my move?"

"Tonight. Right after work."

Allen did not express surprise that it was so soon. The sooner the better. They would meet at Red Harter's bar across the street from the Metro Complex.

Chapter II

Allen could not work. He sat at his desk, thinking of the enormity of what the Underground was asking. What could be so important that the Underground would want him to take such a risk? He speculated whether the Nazis were planning some new form of oppression against the Americans. Could it be the Underground planned a mission pending the interception of the message? He felt alive, excited, not part of the long line of desks in the front of the dreary, ponderous chamber. Allen sat in a row that was charged with rewriting American history from the Civil War until 1900. Other sections were rewriting World War I, World War II, and each decade from the colonization of the New World to the present. People sat in rows according to the period they were working on. They were not permitted to talk during the day. The lunch break was a half hour and Codder insisted that people eat at their desks.

The work made up the textbooks for schools and also the official history for the National Archives. All history must conform to a theme that Americans attacked Germany twice, causing both world wars, that America was a tool of English and French imperialism, mostly Jewish banking interest on the continent. The textbooks were changed at the Nazis direction in 1956; now an even more drastic revision was taking place. The first revision talked of presidents like Woodrow Wilson as warmongers. Wilson was described as a paid hireling of the House Rothchild. The new revisions would delete Wilson's name altogether, for the Nazis' version called the whole American government corrupt and the American president was of no consequence.

Allen's attention wandered during the morning. He could not focus on the Civil War piece he was working on.

"Deputy Codder wants you!" Allen was startled by the message to present himself at Codder's desk at the rear of the room. For an instant he thought they knew, then he relaxed. It would not be pleasant, but they couldn't know of the Underground's plan. Deputy Codder's desk was on a raised platform. He was a small man who was almost lost behind the huge desk. It forced people to look up at him as they stood circumspect before his authority.

Codder was an American, at least he called himself an American, but no one in the room who lived in fear of the deputy imagined him as anything but a Nazi. Codder would have been proud to be considered an equal of the Nazi administration in the building. He yearned to belong to their clubs and be accepted at their lunch tables. They considered him a bore and a fool, employed in a dull and unimportant endeavor. He railed at their contempt and made the lives of the people working for him hell. He was a bully in a situation that did not allow any questions of his judgment. Thus the work dragged and even the destruction of a nation's history became a dull dreary predictable tedium.

Codder peered down at Allen. "You were assigned to write the history of the Civil War and your work is trash." Codder threw the typewritten material on the floor next to Allen. Several sheets slid across the floor to the desk in the back row. People, embarrassed for Allen, pretended to be working and not notice.

"You were told to drop all references to Lincoln. Lincoln is a nonperson in the new order. The reference is to be the American president. The reference to the Emancipation Prodication is to be dropped." Codder frequently mispronounced words as difficult as proclamation. Allen did not speak, for to argue would be fruitless, and to question impossible.

"You are to rewrite the freeing of the slaves in economic terms. The northern American president was destroying the economic strength of the South and for no other reason was he interested in freeing the slaves. I want this rewritten and on my desk by Friday. Do you understand?"

Allen did not speak. Codder raised his voice, "Do you understand?"

Allen nodded and looked at the ground. He picked up the typewritten sheets and returned to his desk. His face was flushed with shame. He would have run to meet Valley Forge when it was six o'clock. He would do anything they asked. Hate welled in his throat and choked him.

While Allen smoldered, Valley Forge waited for him outside. He too hated the Blackshirts, a deep unforgiving laser beam hate, steady and powerful.

He would accompany Allen to the Metro Complex, a center he helped build five years before as a captive. Valley Forge's real name was Michael Ford, an enlistee in the air force in 1943. Sent to England he flew twenty missions in a B-17 as a tail gunner. In 1945 the bomber raids were stopped because of the losses to the new Nazi jet fighters. In 1946 England signed a separate peace treaty with Germany. Ford was interred in a prison camp. In 1950 Michael Ford, with 1,100 other

Americans in the camp, was sent to Germany. They were put to work building the Domed Great Hall in Berlin.

Many died the first year of starvation, cruel treatment, lack of winter clothing, and Michael learned the first first lesson of survival—the will to live. That winter the first glow of the laser beam began for Michael Ford. The work was very dangerous because no precautionary safety measures were used and there were many accidents. With little food and intense cold the weakened men struggled to stay on their feet. Michael worked with a severe case of the flu and frequently with high fevers. He watched as the best stone and materials from other nations were plundered to build the great hall from the blood and tears of the subject people.

The Pantheon in Rome was the model with the area ten times the size of St. Peters. A two-tiered gallery rose to a height of one hundred feet and circled the inside. At the opening stood a giant swastika and 100,000 people could stand at one time inside the hall and listen to the chancellor speak. Vast art treasures were taken from the world museums and decorated the side galleries. Ford hated the building and the Nazi arrogance and power it stood for. He did not see it completed, but he knew from pictures its final form surrounded on three sides by fountains and tiled canals. Someday Ford hoped to be part of the nations of people that would pull down the 130 foot high structure. The name had been changed from Adolph Hitler Hall to the current Reich chancellor's name. This mattered little to Ford. For his abhorrence extended to all who addressed the world's people from its structure.

After the long first winter, when spring came he bribed a guard to register him as a draftsman. Then he was transferred to the huge 250,000-seat Nuremberg Stadium. This stadium was to house the future Olympic Games and the work lacked skilled technicians. The stadium, under the supervision of army engineers, treated the slave labor better. Instantly the officer in charge of his section recognized his lack of drafting knowledge, but protected him and did not reveal his deception.

So he survived three years in Germany and the same officer took pity on his failing health and recommended a transfer back to New York where they were building the Metro Complex. When he left Germany, only two hundred of his former prison mates were still alive. Leaving Germany shackled to a bulkhead on dirty foul-smelling prison ships he vowed he would live to see the Domed Great Hall in rubble.

He worked on the Metro Complex, now his weight forty pounds less than the 160 he weighed when he joined the air force. Two years later the Nazis released him, because they thought he was going to die. He managed to find his brother in New York, who nursed him back to health.

It was a tumultuous time, for Americans were learning the bitter role of the vanquished. The previous year the people of Houston revolted, actually controlling the city for two days. The Nazis dropped an atomic bomb on the city. The atomic blast at Houston convinced the country they must capitulate or resist through the Underground. Ford joined the Underground as soon as his health returned. He proved to be a great recruiter, for he knew how to attract the enemies of the Reich. Michael Ford built his network slowly and surely. Always patient, never doubting their time was coming. For those who urged action, he would say, "We can only kill a few now. Wait—for the day will come," and he would turn a clinched fist with a thumb down.

It was the passive quiet that convinced the Blackshirts that the American spirit was broken. They regarded the Americans as docile, a conquered people with the exception of guerilla bands in the Southwest and Rocky Mountains. The Reich's active enemies were the Australians, Russians, and Greeks. They would not surrender and continued to resist as partisans. The Blackshirts were sure they would eventually destroy all these peoples. As Valley Forge waited for Allen he was not in a docile mood. It was a short distance to the Metro Complex, but light years in importance to the Underground. There was no expression on Michael's face and his intensity remained deep within him; he was confident that Allen would not fail them.

Ford had picked the spot to meet one block from the Metro Complex, and across the street from Red's Bar.

The Metro Complex was all buttoned up but tonight they would take their usual supplies from Red's Bar to the Complex. This would be Allen's entry into the Metro Complex, the price Ford had $20,000 in diamonds in his pocket, the fee to get Allen in and out of the building. Ford had done one other deal with Harter that was for diamonds too. He wondered what share the Blackshirts would take. He knew Red would not renege on the deal; there would be other profitable trades to be made.

Red Harter, proprietor for thirty years of the dark, sparse, and infamous Red's Bar, viewed the establishment as a front for his main business. Red's main business was drugs, corruption, bribing, and theft. He viewed the Fourth Reich as an excellent client and occasional partner. Red started his fortune during Prohibition, but compared to rum running, cheating the Nazis was easy.

Recently Red masterminded a sale of a hundred cases of scotch to Nazi officials, delivered it, and had it stolen back a few days later. Friday a truck full of tank parts was stolen from a few blocks uptown and would be broken up and sold on the black market when it was safe. Red had negotiated the price to the driver to leave the truck where it could be stolen.

So Red prospered under the Nazis and his unofficial partner was Reich Protector Kroft, who shared in the bar and drug traffic. The Reich protector controlled New York for six years and his personal fortune grew tenfold. He longed to return home to Germany, but only if he could leave his wife Helga behind. She was the cousin of the Reich chancellor, ruler of the world and the key to his position as Reich protector of New York. Helga was also the bane of his life. A huge woman, well over two hundred pounds, she hounded and yelled at him in front of subordinates, friends, and all present. He was terrified of her.

Frequently he would hide from Helga in Red Harter's back room, drinking until he passed out and was carried home by his chauffeur. Kroft also depended on Red to service him with ladies. It was easy; the ugliest, stupidest women appealed to him and his escapades were legendary. Once totally drunk, he was driving into the night with a girlfriend until the car reached Central Park. There he insisted on getting out of the car with the woman and disappeared. Next day he was found sleeping on the grass without any clothes.

The incident that scandalized the complex was when Helga found Kroft on his couch with his secretary. Helga had beaten him up.

Harter would have been more concerned about Mrs. Kroft, but on two occasions he had provided her with men. Harter considered the best of the Nazis crooks and the worst of them murderers. If Harter was a beneficiary of the Fourth Reich he hedged his risks by being the largest contributor to the Underground in New York.

It was warm and humid, the heat coming out of the sidewalks

that held it until the sun went down. People began to empty out of the building and head for home. Allen and Valley Forge walked to the street where the Metro Complex was located. Valley Forge explained that Red's bar across from the Metro Complex was an important meeting place for the Blackshirts.

The Metro Complex was three buildings that represented the Nazi headquarters in New York. Closest to Allen and Valley Forge was the five-story communications center. The communications center received messages from Germany and directed orders to local authorities. Next to the communications center was the administration building, ten stories high and the seat of government for the middle Atlantic states. The administration center was one of several in America. Regional Reich protectors did not deal directly with each other, but reported to Berlin. There was much rivalry between them and a constant effort to gain control of additional states. All this was subject to Berlin's dictates. Next to the administration building was the dreaded police headquarters. The Blackshirts held political prisoners and suspected enemies of the state without trial or hope of bail. The complex was the headquarters of various other local government agencies, such as the educational bureau where Allen worked.

In the global network of the Fourth Reich every country had an administrative area comparable to the Metro Complex. In the large countries, like America, there were several such centers and many were huge architectural structures. Even the neutral countries, Switzerland, Iceland, and Brazil, were required to maintain communications centers and respond to orders from the Reich and give tribute. There was no second military power because Japan, Germany's closest ally, had not recovered from the war with America. Japan was attempting to regain the military power they had in 1941, but without the atomic bomb did not pose a threat to Germany. Japan's sphere of influence was Southeast Asia, India, and China. Germany shared in the wealth of Indochina and Korea and frequently drafted troops from other parts of the world to battle the emerging nations in Asia. While they shared in the wealth of the area with Japan, the Blackshirts never committed German troops to Asia. The Japanese did not appreciate having to share the spoils of war while carrying most of the burdens of fighting in Indochina.

Other supporters of Germany, Argentina, Egypt, and South Africa, were in control of local spheres of influence, but all reported directly to the Great Domed Hall in Germany controlled by the Blackshirts. No leader or government instituted a policy without Berlin's approval. The world had never seen such absolute power, and the Reich chancellor and his followers reveled in their power. With the most powerful army, navy, and air force at their command they concentrated on their personal wealth and pleasure. The Reich chancellor had seven homes around the world and was never seen by his subjects.

It was the Nazis' greatest boast that they ruled the world from Berlin and no one moved until the Reich chancellor had spoken. This was true; it was also true that a bureaucratic machine of immense size was built to dominate the world's people. Greater and complete control at the center of Europe meant delay and inaction at the local level on the many problems that arose in the captive nations. So inefficiency and duplication also ruled the world's people. Great agencies existed in Berlin to control world-wide programs.

The energy agency in Germany decided where oil would be drilled and allocated and this gave them immense profits and also a world-wide shortage of oil. The shortage existed because of bad planning and distribution problems. These things fed on themselves; lack of oil not only left the people of Canada and Russia cold, but kept much shipping tied in port. Without shipping, other forms of international trade suffered. America, the land of the automobile, had ten percent of the cars it had before the war because of lack of gasoline.

The allies of the Fourth Reich did not fare better than the local peoples they enslaved. The Japanese, the most industrious people in Asia, lived under a feudal military dictatorship and had little more in food and comforts than the Indians or the Chinese. They were cold in winter from lack of fuel and had little hope that life would improve. The Japanese as victors were responsible for feeding millions of people who produced less as slaves than they did before the war.

The world's gross national product, value of all goods and services produced, dropped dramatically over a five-year period. The world was entering a new dark age where travel was unsafe, infant mortality high, hunger rampant, and unemployment and numbing fear universal. People who remembered the inefficiencies and weakness of the democracies before the war longed to return to such days. The power and complete control of the Fourth Reich produced a stagnation of energy and enterprise.

In Germany, the center of the world, they produced a car that was less fuel efficient, broke down, and was unsafe at speeds over forty miles an hour. The engineers and draftsmen knew the car they made twenty-five years before was a better automobile than the one they built today.

Allen and Valley Forge stared at the complex.

"Are you sure my contacts will be on Long Island?"

Valley Forge replied, "They will all be waiting. After you contact them, they will bring you back to New York. If it works out well, you may be able to write some great history."

"Can you tell me something about the message?"

Valley Forge wanted to tell him, but he couldn't. "Allen, trust us, you'll know in time."

Ford and Allen walked the fifty yards to Red's and entered the bar. Red's was almost empty and Allen seated himself on a stool where he could see the door. It was dark in Red's, the mahogany bar ran in a horseshoe shape away from the door. Behind this was an open area of tables and chairs leading to a back room. Usually at this time of night the place would have been crowded with the Blackshirts from the complex; tonight it was empty.

"What'll it be, gents?" The bartender, bored, was glad to see a customer as he wiped the bar with a rag. It was unusual to see a green armband alone. Usually, a green armband would be accompanied by a Blackshirt.

Allen ordered a beer. The bartender apologized for the television not working. Red's had one of the few televisions in New York City. Like most televisions, it did not work. He turned up the radio and the news.

"Don't mind if I listen to the news? Japanese troops pushed into Cambodia today and destroyed a rebel stronghold."

The bartender sneered, "The Japanese have been chasing them for five years. Those slant eyes can't beat the jungle."

"A riot today in Cleveland resulted in eight people being arrested."

The bartender, a compulsive talker, felt obligated to comment.

"Always food riots in the Midwest. Why can't they get the food to the people?"

Allen turned to the radio as the depressing stories continued—"Two men were hanged in California today for action against the state."

One of the "men" was a twelve-year-old boy.

Red Harter opened the door to his office and waved for Allen and Michael Ford to come in.

After he closed the door he said, "You have a package for me."

Ford handed him the diamonds, which he put in his safe.

Harter explained the plan. "My men will start taking supplies across to the Metro Complex in five minutes." He pointed to Allen, "You stay with me. When it is time I'll knock on the door and you must come out. Only thirty minutes."

Red did not consider this business dangerous. The American Underground was quiet and meek. If there was trouble the Nazi guard knew that the Reich protector would shield Red. Red had not decided if he would give ten percent or twenty percent or the sale of the diamonds to Kroft. Red was not concerned that the Metro Complex was locked up. He had called the day before and was told business as usual. Bring the supplies over and also the Reich protector was short of money, so bring cash.

Red Harter handed Allen a plastic bag. It was full of cash for the Reich protector. Twelve men waited outside. They had hand trucks and dollies loaded with food and liquor for the Metro Complex. The group walked a full block east of the main entrance down a back ramp and finally reemerged at a small door at the back of the communications center. A man peeked through the window and opened the door.

The guard waved the men in. He pointed down the hall to the familiar route they traveled each week to the storage room. The delivery proceeded down the hall and the guard held out his hand. Red Harter handed the man two hundred dollars. He was one of Red's agents at the Complex. Red was usually better informed of what was going on at the Complex than the Reich protector. What Red and the guard did not know was that for once the mysterious message of the day before was treated with top security clearance. Only the Reich protector his top lieutenants and the code room knew the message.

Allen followed them down a long corridor. With the Complex closed, few people were on duty, and they encountered only two Blackshirts in the corridor. The building was like the educational building where Allen worked. The halls were painted a lifeless green and at the end of each hall were directions in English and German.

On the ground floor were the power generator and numerous telephone exchanges. The administration officer and a complex of offices was on the third floor. They moved to the stairs and the second floor past the room labeled "Main Transmitter" and to the code room. Allen could see there was no guard at the door of the main transmitter room. He thought they sure don't worry about security in the Fourth Reich.

The order to close the Metro Complex happened about twice a year, so most Blackshirts were not suspicious.

Interservice rivalry was strong in the Fourth Reich so they believed this was just another feud between departments of the army, navy, Blackshirts, or some top general trying to consolidate his power.

The guard knocked on the door of the unguarded code room.

An attractive girl answered. In her early twenties tall, thin, long hair wearing a black jumpsuit, the uniform of the Blackshirts on duty. On most people the jumpsuit was baggy and lifeless, but on this girl it was taut and streamlined like it had just been pressed and starched.

To Red's question she answered, "No Mary Bee was away for the moment but will be back in five minutes."

Harter took the bag of money from William. "Remember you've got twenty-five minutes." He and the guard left.

William Allen stepped into the code room and watched as the girl deliberately picked up a newspaper and folded it over. The signal! He took the paper from her and folded it the reverse way. The countersign.

She looked at him with intense blue eyes, a thin long nose. She really was very pretty.

"I work for Valley Forge; I sent the message. He said he would send William Allen the historian. I recognize you from your picture." Allen was flattered that she knew him.

Allen questioned her. "Do you know the message?"

"No, I'm not cleared to decode top secret messages; only Mary Bee can do that and she doesn't trust me." The measure of her words told him the girl did not like Mary Bee.

She spoke quickly to lead him to what she knew before Mary Bee returned. "I do know the Nazi jet wing posted in Canada left for Europe yesterday; we had to alert Baltimore so that their jet fuel tankers could refuel the fighters over the Atlantic."

Baltimore was the hub for refueling any fighters or jets that could not reach their destination without refueling. "The message was so important that Baltimore get it right that we sent it in the clear. No code! Something big is happening."

Judy looked at William Allen. He looked much like her father, a kind gentleman. She thought of her father wounded in the South Pacific during the war.

Judy was fifteen when the Nazis pulled down the American flag for good at her school. She told her father that night and for a moment she thought he would cry. He, like many others, took the defeat of America as a personal shame. A year later the Blackshirts arrested their priest and closed the local church because of his patriotic speeches. That night her father gathered her, her sister, and her two brothers together and made them pledge to join the Underground. They were enthusiastic and began with small no-risk responsibilities. It was the Underground way, especially with young people, to require a testing period. Paul, the more aggressive of her brothers, was shot two years later when he tried to help a black man escape from a red work gang. Judy was introduced to Valley Forge three years ago and he directed her to join the code division at Metro Complex. With her good looks and intelligence it was easy to get the position that Valley Forge wanted her to take. In the next three years she passed him many important messages; some were decoded, some were not. Several weeks ago a message was sent to Reich Protector Kroft that was not decoded. Judy was able to get a copy and pass it on to the Underground. Shortly after that Valley Forge told her that an agent would be coming to the Metro Complex soon, and she must help him.

Mary Bee opened the door and stumbled into the code room. Greasy stains were on the front of her black jump suit. Despite the "no smoking" sign on the door, a cigarette hung from her lips. It was her code room. She would do what she wanted. She did not recognize William and dropped a file of papers on her desk. She ignored the two people in the room; she had just had a drink of vodka from the locker in the hallway and she was thinking maybe I'll go back and get another drink.

Judy stood up. "This man has come to see you." Mary Bee looked at William but did not recognize him. Judy knew Mary would not talk in front of her so she went to the door. "I have to check some messages."

Mary Bee was fifty-five, but looked years older, heavy drinking and a life of hating all things American had aged her. She accepted the new world order, especially its racist views.

William spoke. "Mary Bee, it's me, William Allen."

She straightened her glasses, puffed once, and stared at him.

"William. My God, it's William. What are you doing here?" She had not seen him in years.

He answered, "I came in with Red Harter's group to bring supplies."

Now she was alert. "You work with Red Harter? How come I've not seen you before?"

It was against the rules but she had sent messages for Red Harter to various places in America. She was among the many who accepted Red's money. She knew most of Red's men. Now William was part of Red's group. She was immediately suspicious. Like breathing the air, suspicion was a living act in the Fourth Reich. She had not seen him in years. Yet when he entered her circle of life her first thoughts were defensive. Why was he here, was he dangerous?

Valley Forge had said hit her hard, knock her off balance mentally. Blackshirt bureaucrats like Mary will always accept the most convoluted paranoid reason for events happening to them. So give them what they want.

"I don't work for Red Harter," he began, then pointed to his green arm band.

He volunteered, "He who has a way to live can bear any blow."

It was a twist on a saying by Fredrick Nietzsche and a basic canon of the Gestapo.

Her face which had grown progressively paler suddenly started to flush with a rush of energy. She waved her arm.

"Gestapo."

He had given her a paranoid reason.

The Gestapo, the dreaded secret police under Adolph Hitler, was pushed to the side when Hitler died and the new Reich chancellor brought in his Blackshirts. The Reich chancellor joined with the army to destroy the Gestapo. In the last few years the Blackshirts had pursued the Gestapo with greater energy than the American Underground.

Allen said, "The Gestapo will be strong again because they know in your heart you are with us. They sent me to you."

She felt invigorated; the Gestapo, not soft like the Blackshirts, with the Iron Fist only the Aryan race would rule.

"With the Blackshirts it was a mixed bag; criminals like Red Harter would protect inferior races for profit."

"What can I do?" It was not William her relative she was speaking to but a long cherished dream to help the enemy of her enemies.

"We know that an important message came to the Complex and shortly after that the Complex closed." He decided to impress with the knowledge of his fictitious Gestapo contacts.

"The Iron Fist knows the jet wing in Canada flew to Europe after a message from Berlin. We want to know the other part of the message."

She sat down. This was serious—to reveal a top secret message was a capital crime, a death penalty.

He saw her concern. "The Gestapo needs you," he assured her.

"Will the Iron Fist make sure not to reveal the source?" Her loyalty to them was greater than her fear of being caught.

"Yes, I guarantee."

"It was a strange message. After I decoded it I took it to the Reich protector and gave it to him personally. He was very upset by the short message, only ten words."

Allen nodded, a serious look to assure her how important this moment was and how important he considered her contribution.

"The wagner is gone and the nest is in flames."

She repeated the ten words and shrugged her shoulders; the lines around her mouth showed she was puzzled. She answered his unspoken question. "I don't know what it means."

They sat in silence. What did all this have to do with the world they lived in?

She asked, "Are you in touch with many of the Iron Fists?" Mary had crossed the rubicon with him but her question was another test of his credentials. Valley Forge had warned him the Gestapo was so pressured that they knew only one or two contacts to each agent.

"It is dangerous to know many of the Iron Fists. I only know my contact. He knows you are with us."

Allen allayed her fear once again. The Blackshirts had killed or jailed so many Gestapo in the last few years, but Mary didn't care they had sent a relative to her. The Gestapo would rule again, she knew it.

There was a knock on the door. Allen was surprised that Red was back so soon. It was only ten minutes since he left. Mary looked at him with imploring eyes that said don't give me away.

He raised his hand and told her the truth. "I will never tell the Blackshirts what you told me."

Mary whispered. "Thank you." Judy opened the door. "Red Harter wants you."

Allen grasped Mary's hand and squeezed it to reaffirm he cared for her even if he did not approve of her beliefs.

He went into the hall with Judy and immediately was aware something was wrong. She put her finger to her lips warning him to be silent. Judy guided him to a door leading to a stairwell and closed it behind him.

She turned.

"Something's amiss."

His eyes showed fear.

"Red Harter and his men have left the building and I think the guards are looking for you." She held his arm as if to reassure him he was not alone.

Allen said, "Red wouldn't leave me; if I'm caught he's implicated."

She reasoned, "I think Red might have told Reich Protector Kroft. He brought you into the building thinking this was just another normal shutdown and Kroft told him no, it was more serious. I doubt if Harter knew what was happening in the code room. Now if they can kill you no one will realize what breach of security has happened."

Allen immediately knew she was right.

Judy continued, "I've got to get you out of the building. There is only one way. I'll make a distraction and you must leave by one of the side doors. They are not on full alert yet. We have got to move fast."

She drew a small pistol from her pants pocket. It looked like a .38.

Allen shook his head. "Too dangerous; we go together or not at all. The message is gibberish; it's not that important. We can both try and get out."

She was startled, she was not used to anyone like this from the Underground. Valley Forge must have made a mistake to send Allen to her. Judy looked at him more disappointed than anything else.

Like Valley Forge, the cause was so powerful that human emotions of fear and lack of confidence did not affect her. Faced with a problem that conflicted with the revolution, only the solution mattered. She would assume control. It was Valley Forge dictum that when in crisis, make something happen.

Allen was confused. Everything had happened so quickly. He had come to the Complex, gotten the message so easily, and then found the message to be a joke.

His initial spirit of nervous energy was over; he was weak in the knees.

Judy held his hand and began to pull him along. "Look, William, Valley Forge and the Underground think the message is important. Certainly the Blackshirts think it is important, look at how they reacted. You have done a wonderful job—just a bit more and the Underground will be forever in your debt."

Her voice was confident, and when they came to turn in the corridor she held him by the waist and turned her beautiful face to him and kissed him. She was twenty years younger, but she spoke to him like her younger brother. He would do what she wanted, escape.

She respected him. He was a fine gentleman. If only he could understand.

"If you get out the Blackshirts might not even know we got the message to the Underground. This is the best way. We can't gamble; believe me, this is too important. Besides, the Underground must be waiting for you; they won't know me. Trust me and be brave. When I signal you must go, promise me you will."

He agreed. She was right.

Judy immediately turned to the left and walked away from him.

As he listened to her footsteps he looked at the wall map across from him. He could see the huge relief map of the world. There were small replica swastika flags on each country at the seat of government. Allen turned to focus on the big map to block out the drama unfolding before him.

He heard a shot. He stepped to the middle of the hall. He saw Judy pointing to a door and waving him to leave. A guard was lying on the ground, blood coming from a chest wound.

He ran to the door and she ran the other way never looking back at him. He heard another shot from the pistol; she was leading them away from him. He bolted through the door and as it swung shut he heard a series of rifle shots in the distance.

Allen was running up the steps and running with all the speed he had away from Metro Complex. He stumbled in the dark empty street, but he kept going. He ran two blocks and his heart was pounding, the blood throbbing in his forehead and he was out of breath. He must get away from the painful memory of what he knew just happened.

Allen ran another block and found the entrance to the subway. He went downstairs, the heat of the summer stifling and oppressive. He was panting and exhausted, soaked with perspiration. The subway did not cool off during the summer, even at night. He rested his head against a steel pillar. His stomach was rebelling and he felt faint in the heat. Allen tried to swallow hard to keep from losing his senses. The wait seemed an eternity for at that hour the subways ran infrequently. Out of breath, exhausted, Allen got on the screeching noisy monster. Ten minutes later he was at Penn Station. It was crowded because so few trains ran during the night. Many people, especially reds could not get a train at any other hour.

At 4:00 A.M. he was packed into a crowded railroad car standing, numb, and on his way to Oceanview.

Red Harter hung up the phone; he had never heard Reich Protector Kroft so upset. Red hesitated, then opened the right hand desk drawer and took out the secure phone. For $1,000 a month the phone was impossible to tap. It would buzz if someone was listening.

He didn't dial but picked up the receiver. There was a click at the other end. The phone was monitored twenty-four hours a day.

"Mr. Schoenrienst, please," Harter said.

From the other end, a brewery in Albany, a voice answered, "Hold please."

Schoenrienst, his heavy guttural voice instantly recognizable, said, "Yes."

"New York calling. I have something for you."

"Yes."

"Kroft and I were running a scam on the American Underground. I brought an American agent into the Metro. We had done this before. Take the money and months after the event we kill the agent and nobody is the wiser.

"When I told Kroft I took the agent to the code room he went crazy. He yelled I didn't tell him about the code room and something about the Reich chancellor, his wife's cousin. Then he ordered me and my men out. I left and just now Kroft called me back. A girl from the code room and a guard were killed and the American agent escaped. He wanted to know if I knew the agent."

"Did you?"

"No, he was brought to me by a slippery character I've met infrequently. No way to trace either one. Now it really gets strange, Kroft told me they questioned the head of the code room and she said she works for you. She claimed she didn't know the agent."

Schoenrienst was silent, then said. "We have no one at the Metro Complex; could this be a trick by Kroft?"

Harter answered a question he knew would come. "I don't think so; this is not Kroft style."

"Could the woman be an American agent?"

Red answered. "It's possible, but why bring an agent into the Complex and I used the woman before. She had a drinking problem—even the Americans are not stupid enough to use someone like that. I would guess the girl who killed the guard could be one of theirs."

Harter was agitated. What the hell was going on? He was more afraid of Schoenrienst than Kroft, Kroft would forget all about this when the next deal came up, despite the fact Kroft had not even counted the money in the bag tonight, but Schoenrienst would never forgive a mistake.

"I just thought I should call!"

Schoenrienst responded, "You did well." That was code that he would send Harter money by the next courier.

They both hung up.

Schoenrienst rubbed his ring on the desk with the insignia "Iron Fist."

What was wrong with Blackshirts? They had completely destroyed his organization from the Atlantic states to Chicago. They controlled the world but yet let American agents walk in and out of the Metro Complex like it was a local bar. They ignore the American Underground, but pursue us to the death. Schoenrienst would never tell Harter how weak the Gestapo was; he did not trust the man. His one agent in New York said the Americans were planning a demonstration in Battery Park near Wall Street soon. What were the Americans up to; he knew the Blackshirts and the German army were at each other's throats. Could the Army be helping the Americans? He did not respect the Americans. They could not cause trouble by themselves. His judgment was wrong that day. A twenty-four-year-old girl had shown more courage and dedication to her cause then any agent he knew or ever would know. If there were more like her the issue would be in doubt. Finally Schoenrienst winced at the talk of the man Harter had killed. He was a Schoenrienst man, a double agent, pretending to be American.

Chapter III

The train pulled into Oceanview at 6:00 A.M. Several passengers got off, including Allen. Standing on the platform he shivered as the breeze from the ocean two miles away was cold and damp. He waited five minutes not knowing what to do.

The platform was high, three stories above the street. Few people were moving in the town at this early hour, but Allen knew that people would be coming to the station soon to go to work. Years ago Oceanview was a departure point down the causeway to the public park and beach. Now few would travel to the beach or go to the park. No buses ran to the beach anymore and few owned a car. Oceanview was nestled by the side of the causeway with some fishing docks and seafood restaurants, sleepy and quiet. On the other side of the tracks away from the causeway were rows of houses. People who, years ago, settled here because they commuted to New York City and loved living near the beach now did neither. The majority were unemployed and lived on the public dole. Oceanview suffered from the same ills and blight that encompassed the rest of the land. Not enough oil and gasoline, without justice little incentive to build or start or grow. There were many taxes and the police would confiscate what they could. Without representation, people were broken and bent until they gave up and went on the public dole.

Allen jammed his hands in his pockets as two young boys came up the stairs toward him. People were afraid of young boys, many ran wild, hungry, runaways, dangerous, stealing and mugging to live and eat. Homeless, they could not go on the public dole. So they ran wild and terrorized, rarely bothered by the police. Allen backed away from the boys. He was a stranger, even in daylight in the open, he had little protection. The taller boy was sixteen or seventeen, thin but powerful in the shoulders. The smaller one, maybe a year younger, was staring at him and looked dangerous. He didn't see any weapons; however, they could have knives or a chain. Now Allen was against the railing; he looked wildly about, could he jump on the tracks and escape? Where was the Underground?

The taller boy took out a newspaper and deliberately unfolded the paper and refolded it again. Allen breathed a sigh of relief.

"You're waiting for me?"

"Mr. Allen!"

"Yes, I'm sorry I didn't pick up the signal—I've had no sleep."

The taller boy spoke. "Good, we waited all night for you; we began to be afraid you wouldn't come." He pointed to the dock area. "Come with us; there is no time to waste. The Blackshirts like to roust strangers. We waited for the squad car downstairs to begin rounds away from the station."

The boys led him down the stairs. The small one paused, made a thumb down sign and left them. The older boy and Allen walked toward the dock area. The breeze was quickening now, blowing strongly from the west, a smell of rain.

Allen was emotionally and physically drained; however, the breeze was refreshing and cool. He relaxed; it was almost over after a period of great tension. Clouds were scudding across the horizon over the bay; the threat of rain was very strong. He could smell the salt air of the ocean beyond the bay. They walked past the empty docks for the fishing boats had left before sunup. Very few people were about; it was tranquil.

At the end of the dock a man was putting up sails on a boat that Allen judged to be about twenty feet long. He could see the insignia on the sail, a lightning, a popular class. The boat was facing the wind and the sails were fluttering violently. By heading the boat into the wind, the wind could not catch the sails and drive the boat against the dock. The man gracefully stepped off the sailboat. He was perhaps thirty-five, well over six feet tall. His outdoor appearance was heightened by the way he stepped off the boat. An athletic man, trim and tanned from the sun and sea. Allen judged him to be a local official. He was not a fisherman, perhaps the manager of the dock.

The stranger extended his hand, "I'm David Schultz. William, I think you have a message for me."

His smile was friendly.

This was the man Valley Forge had told him about, a natural leader. A man men would rally around especially in times of danger.

William hesitated. I've got to tell him about Judy. "I had to leave Judy. I think they shot her. She insisted I go." Allen wondered if Schultz knew who Judy was.

Schultz looked serious, "We pay a great price today, we must be sure that those who sacrifice will not be for a lost cause, to make it right somehow we have to win. Now you must tell me the message." He was so intense that Allen did not doubt he was the right person.

"The wagner is gone."

"That means the Reich chancellor is dead." The excitement in Schultz's voice was infectious.

Allen was shocked. So this was why it was all so important. The ultimate ruler of the Fourth Reich was dead. Hitler's successor was gone and now it was out.

"Is there any more?" Shultz asked.

"The nest is on fire."

"That means that civil war has started between the Blackshirts and the army." Schultz rubbed his hands. "And now it is our turn."

He turned to the boy and despite a set jaw, there was a hint of a smile. "Freddie, go tell our friends inland. I'll meet you at the fishing station."

The boy flashed the thumb-down sign. "No quarter," he said.

"William, you done us a great service; we had to have someone to confirm what we suspected. The Reich chancellor has been very sick for the past few weeks. We knew that and we knew the army and the Blackshirts would fight for control at his death. When they closed the Complex we had to check if that was the reason. They have also disrupted phone service, so it was important you come here. Now we've got to let our friends know. I think it best you go with me and we'll get you back later."

Allen did not protest.

Schultz waved Allen onto the lightning.

Allen said to him, "So it was not the message that was important. It was the confirmation of the message that was important."

"Exactly, thousands of Americans will be moving now, but we had to wait to be sure."

"Judy was right." Allen mumbled, but Schultz did not hear him. He was thinking he said thousands would be moving, but it was more like hundreds of thousands. The first attack had to be timed to destroy the jet wing in Houston before tomorrow morning New York time.

"We've got to get across the bay quickly. Have you ever sailed before? It will be bumpy in the wind."

"Just once, but tell me what to do," replied William.

"You go up front and work the jib sheet."

The jib sheet, the smaller of the two sails, was held to a steel wire that ran from the mast to the bow of the boat. Two ropes attached to the back of the sheet, one ran left and the other right, ran through metal cleats and allowed the jib sheet to be pulled either to the port or starboard side by a man sitting in the middle of the boat. Schultz cast off and positioned Allen in the middle of the boat; he showed him how to work the jib sheet.

With a twenty-knot breeze the lightning sped away from the dock and moved smartly into the canal.

Schultz trimmed the main sheet and pulled the line with his left hand to hold the sail tight against the wind. With his right hand he set the tiller to point across the bay, four miles away. Schultz would follow the shoreline to his right and make the fishing station in less than an hour. The wind gave the sails lift and the waters of the bay seemed to race by the lightning as it cut through the chop. Now black clouds were pushing over the bay and scattered raindrops formed on the sails. Halfway to their destination the wind shifted and blew stronger and the rain began to fall. As the gloom descended from the west behind them to the east, daylight showed over the ocean. To the east a Nazi E boat manned by a crew of seven was entering the bay through the inlet. The E boat was coming into the bay after an all-night patrol. A lookout spotted the sailboat and the captain ordered the helmsmen to pursue.

Schultz saw the E boat come through the inlet and instantly knew it was a problem. E boats usually stopped boats and searched for smugglers, especially on a sailboat out in the rain. Then a more chilling idea struck him. Could Judy have talked? They might be looking for Allen.

The E boat swung directly behind them, three miles away. He had five minutes. Allen saw Schultz looking over his shoulder. It was a Nazi patrol boat silhouetted against the lighted sky and heading directly for them. He looked at Schultz.

Schultz answered his silent question.

"Yes, they'll stop us."

Schultz decided to swing the lightning toward the shoreline to the right. If they could get into one of the creeks that ran through the marsh, perhaps there was safety. The tide was in, but it was pretty shallow in the marsh for an E boat. He spoke to Allen. "We're going to come about, at my command duck under the boom that will swing over your head—drop the line you are holding and pull the other jib sheet line taunt." Allen nodded.

"Ready—hard a lee." Schultz pushed the tiller to the left. Allen ducked under the boom, dropped his line and, struggling, barely caught the other line. Before he could pull it taut, the lightning was pivoting, turning and as the wind lifted the sail making towards the near marsh.

Schultz steered toward the nearest creek, no time for selection. The captain of the E boat ordered a warning shot from one of the crewmen with a rifle. He decided not to uncover his cannon. The wind and rain was blowing in their faces and drenching Schultz and Allen. For a moment the rain let up a little and Schultz could see the creek was a large one, big enough for the E boat to follow. He cursed.

Just as the lightning entered the mouth of the creek, the E boat fired a shot.

The Nazis were less than three hundred yards behind. Schultz desperately scanned the shore. Should they beach the boat and run for it? If the E boat could cut them off they would be hunted down. No, he had to stay with the boat. Allen had taken off his glasses. He could barely see. "Look for a channel," commanded Schultz. Allen, in the gloom and rain, mistook a sandbar for a channel.

"To the left," he yelled.

As Schultz turned to look a squall of solid blinding rain hit. Blind, with no alternatives, he pulled the tiller to him. Schultz felt for the pistol under his seat. If it came to that they would not surrender. Freddie would be passing the information on to the others. Schultz was not an emotional man. He did not regret the long wait, the great news, and now his probable death. The wind let up; and Schultz saw that Allen made a mistake; they were heading into marsh grass. It was too shallow; the boat could not pass. He pulled the gun out as the E boat rounded the point and headed down the creek. Schultz expected the center board and the rudder to touch and give warning that they had run out of water. He did not realize the wind and high tide lifted the height of the water in the bay and the marsh. They passed into the marsh grass with water still under them.

Instantly Schultz reacted. "Pull up the centerboard," he yelled at Allen.

Allen obeyed, his hands raw from the wet rope, but not noticing the pain. Schultz tilted the rudder as high as he could and still maintained control.

They had a chance; the marsh grass was about fifty yards across into another channel. The lightning scraped bottom, but in the wind did not stop. The Nazis were shooting wildly, uneasy about the threat of running on a sandbar. No smuggler was worth having to pull an E boat off the sandbar. The lightning crossed the marsh grass and entered a channel moving away.

The Nazi captain hesitated; he could still uncover the cannon and perhaps hit them. No, let the crew pop away with small arms fire, probably unimportant contraband anyway. In the rain the E boat stopped, more than two hundred yards away. The crew, firing rifles, did not come close.

Schultz leaned forward, not daring to turn and look as he steered in the narrow channel.

Schultz yelled above the wind, "Are they still behind?"

Allen could see them halted and shooting as bullets whizzed overhead.

"I think they've stopped."

He craned his neck; the E boat was stopped against the lighted sky.

"They've stopped."

The tension broken, Schultz laughed. "Too shallow in here, the Blackshirts don't want to have to walk. Put down the centerboard; we're okay."

Schultz and Allen pulled away sailing steadily to the north and disappeared in the gloom and rain.

Schultz knew they were safe; he would steer to keep the lightning in the marsh and abandon the boat as soon as they could not travel further by water. It would be a tough walk, but they could reach the fishing station and the transmitter. An hour later, Schultz pulled the lightning on the shore and hauled down the sails. "We have to walk now my friend, are you alright?"

Allen, exhausted, said, "Yes." Schultz looked up at him. "They almost had us. You're lucky, historian. We were lucky today and I suspect fate was on your side at the Metro Complex."

"We need all the help we can get."

Schultz, with natural good spirits and relief that the long wait was over, caused him to joke with Allen about fortune.

He helped Allen as he slipped in the mud. The marsh would be tough to walk in. However, they were safe. Now the rain stopped and the sky was beginning to brighten ahead of them. He pointed the direction to Allen and thought of their escape. Maybe the historian was lucky, not a bad omen.

Chapter IV

They reached the fishing station just before noon with Schultz half carrying Allen. The walk in the marsh, no sleep for twenty-four hours, the tension, and he was out on his feet. He did not protest when Schultz dropped him on a cot to sleep.

The men at the station were silent men who had lived with danger for many years. They made no outward sign of joy at the news of the Reich chancellor's death or fighting in Germany, but there were handshakes and tight grins.

They uncovered the transmitter and erected the signal tower. Schultz wrote a cryptic message in code and at 12:45 the first signal of the news was flashed to the northeast relay.

In Florida, they heard the message at 1:30 E. D. T. Within two hours California knew the Reich chancellor was dead. The northeast relay sent back word that yesterday the Nazi jet wing based in Canada had taken off for an unknown destination. Moments later an operator in New Jersey reported that jet tanker planes based outside of Baltimore had departed from their base. Schultz told the group huddled around the transmitter that the tankers would be fueling the fighter wing for their ocean flight.

"Probably fuel them halfway over and they'll all land on the continent," he said.

All afternoon radio reports crisscrossed America from one section of the Underground to another. If the Nazi had a national security network, more attention would have been paid to the traffic. Because they were required to report such information to Berlin, there was no communication between the Nazi regions. Those that did report to Berlin received nothing more than a cursory look. The order was to send back acknowledgements, but only traffic on the continent was to be acted on. The Nazis had more important things to do than think of their satellites.

Only a few senior officials of the Blackshirts in America guessed that the Americans were aware of the events affecting the world over in Europe. It was very dangerous for regional officials to have communications without approval from Berlin. By keeping such regions separate, the Reich chancellor's cabinet believed that no foreign conspirators could be a threat. The policy of separation of regions within a nation was worldwide. Thus, no one or two Reich protectors could ever be powerful enough to challenge Berlin. The separation policy became more restrictive in the past three years, leading some Reich protectors to suspect a coup might have been unearthed.

A discrete communication from New England did reach the Reich protector in the Southwest who had control of the only jet wing left in America. However, without orders from Berlin, he did not bring the wing to full alert. He guessed that Berlin was occupied domestically, but he would not dare to move without their command. So the day continued ostensibly quiet and very hot, with little activity by the masters of America, very few aware that events away from them would affect their lives so dramatically.

At the fishing station on Long Island, the vortex of the mid-

Atlantic Underground, the radio continued to send directions throughout the tri-state area of New York, New Jersey, and Connecticut. Most days David Schultz was seated behind his desk directing the business of a four-boat fishing fleet; today he was calmly getting in motion thousands of men and women. He dictated orders without a change of expression.

"Tell Art to bring his people to Trenton; they can be a reserve for either New York or Philadelphia."

The aide, a twenty-year-old schoolteacher, dashed out of the room and gave the message to the radio room. It was translated into code and sent. The aide returned to Schultz with incoming messages.

Mel Underwood, perspiring in a wet T-shirt, still in high rubber boots, out of breath from leaping off the fishing boat, came into the room. He asked Schultz for orders.

"Mel, your boys will tie up all the local Blackshirts; I want them attacked the minute we start. It's more important that the timing be right than anything else. If you go too soon it'll spoil what we planned."

Mel heard Schultz say that many times. It was timing, timing. Mel's heart was pounding, excitement or fear? If only he didn't foul up; he wanted to stay and talk to Dave, it gave him confidence, but Schultz was busy.

"You'll do fine, Mel. Go along and remember when it starts, no one holds back and give them breathing room, they can link up—so attack, always attack."

He looked down at the message dropped on his desk by a young girl from the radio room. It was his signal for Mel to leave. It was important to keep them calm, but on the edge of aggressiveness. He believed they would do fine. He had known Mel Underwood since the first time as boys they swam the bay together. They were both afraid that day; the current was wicked as the tide changed. However, Mel didn't realize Schultz was afraid and Dave led them across and calmed Underwood when he got tired a mile from the beach. Since then Schultz was the leader and Mel was confident when Dave gave directions.

Schultz looked out the side window. It was bright and clear, the rain all gone. A breeze was coming up, an ocean breeze always came up in the afternoon. A gull wheeled gracefully over the end of the dock. The gulls were waiting for the boats to come inland and pick up remnants. Today they would be disappointed. Schultz loved this scene, its beauty never failed to move him.

"Working on the water is getting paid for something you wanted to do anyway," he would say.

He stood up, it was time to get moving. They were after sharks now.

Schultz pointed to another young man. "Tell our people upstate to cover the Syracuse arsenal. I don't think they'll have much trouble. Be sure and tell our people to wait for the signal. It's timing we want—good timing. When he comes tell Freddie to stay here, I depend on him to coordinate communications, and then drive the car to New York."

* * *

When Allen awoke, Schultz was gone. He was groggy and asked if David had left any word. The people he asked reported no messages for him. They knew of Allen, but he was a stranger to them and they were too busy to spend any time on him

They gave him lobster, clam, and shrimp soup. It was the best thing he had ever tasted. The men sitting at the table with him were friendly.

They teased, "A man of letters; we need some education around here."

Allen smiled and had a second bowl of soup with black bread and butter. "Sure eats like a fisherman. He eats like he likes your soup, Terry." The woman, Terry, was ladling out soup and was delighted when Allen took a second helping. The men were men of the sea. They all wore heavy black boots and their strong backs showed they were used to hauling large nets, and they all had guns. Each man had at least one gun and some had two. They had .45s strapped to their waist. There were shotguns and rifles leaning against the wall. Allen asked, "Those guns loaded?"

The man answered. "Loaded for Blackshirts—especially today. The transmitter is up. Any Blackshirts show today will not be welcome." He patted his pistol.

There was great activity in the fishing station, with boats pulling in and immediately departing. He watched the great effort and sat on the end of the dock trying to figure out what to do next. Finally the young man, Freddie, spoke to him. "I'm going to New York. Dave told me to drive you there if you want to go." Allen agreed and they set off.

They rode in silence along the badly paved roads of Long Island and New York.

Allen could see the Blackshirt decal on the windshield that would ensure them they would not be stopped. I wonder how much that cost. I think the Blackshirts would sell us the bullets from their guns if we paid enough. He would not have felt so comfortable if he knew the trunk of the car was full of explosives.

"My father calls you the Historian," said Freddie Schultz.

"Yes, my name in the Underground. I keep the records."

"In school they don't teach us how we lost the war. What did happen?"

Allen began to explain. "You must understand that the Nazis

rearmed when the rest of Europe wanted peace so badly they would give Hitler any concession. This was because of the great causalities of the democratic countries in World War I. England and France could not get their people to understand that another war would break out and they would have to defend themselves. Hitler lead a country with no such melancholy and his adventure met great initial success. The Nazis took almost all of Europe in lightning speed, and in 1941, after Japan struck at Pearl Harbor the democratic countries of the world and Russia were all that stood in the way of an Axis victory. Three great leaders on the Allied side could have changed the war: President Franklin D. Roosevelt, Winston Churchill of England, and Joseph Stalin of Russia. From what I read the plan was to mass American production and military might to defeat the Nazis first. FDR believed their technology would be dangerous if not defeated quickly. The first great tragedy occurred in 1942. FDR was not a well man and he died suddenly.

His successor accepted the advice of the Joint Chiefs of Staff to avenge the Japanese sneak attack with the major war effort in the South Pacific. This meant we could only give the English and the Russians token help. The Nazi tide in Europe continued to run very strong without our opposition. Even the war against Japan was a choice that went against us. We lost important carriers trying to relieve the Philippines. Later we would tie up whole armies in China and Korea when perhaps a policy of destroying Japanese shipping and island hopping would have been just as effective."

He continued his narrative.

"The die was cast. England tried to take back North Africa, but without our help the Nazi held them to a standoff. The Russians fighting bravely made impressive gains against the Germans, but insisted a second front must be opened. We launched an invasion with the English in 1944 against France. The weather turned bad and we did not support the invasion with enough materiel because we were so committed to a war in Asia. The invasion failed and the Anglo-American casualties were terrible. We lost most of our land force during the invasion and so we had to withdraw from France.

"Now the war began to turn against us. Germany produced a new plane, the jet. FDR was right; German technology was producing new weapons. With the jet, they gained complete control of the skies and then they developed a rocket that hailed death at England. Winston Churchill was dismissed from office as the English, burdened with war for many years, began to lose heart. They blamed Churchill for the failure of the invasion and the terrible losses. Nazi jets and rockets destroyed most of the English cities and in 1946 the English accepted a truce from Germany. In 1947 Stalin was assassinated. The Russians began a civil war and shortly after the whole country fell to the Nazis. So we were alone, the Germans masters of Europe. We were battling Japan and almost victorious in Asia; however, we were afraid of linkup between Japan and Germany through Russia, so all our troops were tied up along the rim of the Pacific.

"As terms of the truce with England, the Nazis took their fleet and also interned all our men in Europe. We were working on a superweapon, an atomic bomb, but so were the Nazis and they developed it first. Germany used the combined fleets of England and France to land a large invasion force in Mexico in 1948. Not only did the Nazi invasion have us outnumbered in terms of men, but their jets began to raid our cities and swept the skies of our planes. In 1949, they dropped two atomic bombs, one in San Francisco and one in Chicago. The American president sued for peace in 1949. Because Hitler was dead we believed the Reich chancellor would give us the same truce they gave England. We surrendered expecting that only a small Nazi force would be kept in America. The occupation began in earnest in 1950, all our cities occupied, and local Nazi sympathizers given control over the country. We were stunned, but in 1953 the Underground struck back. The people of Houston revolted and the Nazis used an atomic bomb against them. After Houston, real American opposition seemed to die, except for outbreaks."

Allen stopped talking, he choked, the thought of a free America and now the chronology of its defeat. He remembered many of the little things that made life so sweet before the occupation. Going to church for the Christmas service, driving a car, the World Series, Fourth of July, elections, reading a free newspaper, and living without fear.

The culture of America was being eradicated and forgotten. There would be no more Mark Twain, George Gershwin, Longfellow, Oliver Wendell Holmes, and many universities such as Yale were closed. The American heroes were being written out of the textbooks. Allen knew better than most how difficult it was to hold on to the past. Without Thomas Jefferson, Abraham Lincoln, George Washington, Betsy Ross, and Thomas Edison there was no American heritage. Allen knew that the Nazi plan was to destroy the culture and history of the captive people. If they could do this, it would destroy the will of the people to resist. Instead of a heritage of freedom and dignity the Fourth Reich would substitute armbands and hate.

They rode in silence. Allen asked, "So David Schultz is your father."

"Yeah, we go sailing and fishing together when he's not too busy with the Underground. He's tops."

Freddie was a good driver, he was happy. "My father said you did a great job for us. That's why the guys were so friendly with you at the station. They don't always welcome strangers. You work for Valley Forge. Now there is a serious man." Freddie laughed. He told his father that Valley Forge was too serious. He never smiled.

Allen asked, "Are you in the Underground?"

"Yeah, I work with dynamite." He said it as casually as if he was talking about model planes. "Got to be careful with the stuff, but its okay."

Allen was concerned that the excitement of the last two days were over. Now he thought about Judy and David Schultz. He would not return to his job. The men of the Underground treated him as an equal. He would work with them. Going to the Metro Complex had changed his life, that brave girl. He knew that he might be afraid again but it didn't matter. He had proved he could do it. Proved it to himself. He must see Valley Forge.

They reached his building late at night. He turned to Freddie.

"Look, I've got to talk to Valley Forge, my contact. I can't wait until next week."

Freddie looked surprised, he did not hesitate to answer. "Valley Forge will be at Battery Park tomorrow. And, Mr. Allen, if you have a gun bring it along."

"All right—thanks, I'll do that."

Allen walked up the stairs and dropped his mud-splattered clothes on the floor. He turned on the radio to the all-night news. There was no announcement about the death of the Reich chancellor. All the news was the usual propaganda. He didn't expect them to say anything about the Reich chancellor; still, it was disappointing that there was no change of life in the Fourth Reich.

Chapter V

Allen dozed fitfully, awaking well before dawn. Had it all really mattered, what was the purpose? After two days of tension and life meaning something, somehow the oppression of the Fourth Reich weighed on him again. He would abandon his job and reach Valley Forge; surely the Underground could use him. He knew he had proved himself. He could not be less active; his life must be the Underground.

Sitting by his window, he waited for the sun to come up. He looked over New York Bay, once a great port, now seldom visited by large ships. It was so early they hadn't put up the flag on the Statue of Liberty. As the first rays of sun burned off the morning haze he looked again at the statue. He pondered that they won't put up the flag in honor of the death of the Reich chancellor.

As the sun rose over New York, thousands of Americans looked to the Statue of Liberty as they did every morning and saw the absence of the hated flag. To many it was the happiest they'd felt in a long time.

Others listening to a New York City radio station heard a strange weather report; it included talk of an eagle flying. The traffic in the borough of Manhattan was heavier than usual at this hour.

Allen surveyed his room. Would he ever return to it? He decided to take his notes with him and the handgun hidden in the top of the closet. He unwrapped the packet and put it in a briefcase along with the .45 handgun he'd never fired.

Now it was time to leave. Already he could hear people on the stairs going to work. When he reached the bottom of the stairs it seemed there were fewer people on the street today.

He followed the crowd headed to the subway. As he reached the block where the entrance was he noticed the mailman of the neighborhood standing at the head of the stairs. Somehow he looked different today. Then Allen realized the man did not have a green armband on. All state workers were required to wear a green armband. He was talking to other men and they did not have armbands. Puzzled, Allen descended the stairs. Because the crowd was much lighter than usual, there was no wait for the subway. Allen got a seat and carefully examined his fellow passengers. They looked different; many were not wearing armbands. People were tense. Usually they were quiet, but the train had an eerie silence. When the subway pulled into a station, men and women would silently file off. As they became aware that most were not wearing armbands, they pulled off the identification. Some did it with trepidation, others obvious relish. The man sitting next to Allen leaned over and spoke. "It's gonna be a protest. I was in one two years ago, we protested the dole was too small. Don't stay too long, the Blackshirts will put up with it for a while, but if you stay too long you can get hurt."

When the subway reached Battery Park at the tip of Manhattan, a large crowd got off instead of the usual few. There were no subway attendants or police to be seen. The crowd filed noisily up the stairs as if about to emerge at some great athletic event. At the top of the stairs a woman with a bullhorn was making announcements.

"Form up alphabetically; form up by the letter of your group."

Behind the woman with the bullhorn others were pointing people in the right direction. Large standards with letters in large block print were placed in the park. The guides wore lapel buttons of red and white and blue. Allen stopped and stared at the grandeur of the sight. A wave of exhilaration gripped him. Hundreds and thousands were in the park already. He recognized people from his apartment house and from his office.

Strangers who had seen each other on the subway found themselves in the same Underground group, Beta chapter or other groups. It was noisy; people were talking and shouting orders. As each group emerged from the subway there was a moment of confusion and then directed by the guides they moved smoothly to their appointed areas. The guides were firm with questions and kept people moving. Most people had weapons; those that didn't were armed when they reached their standard. This was no protest.

Allen went to his group, the Alpha chapter. Next to the holder of the standard was the man known as Valley Forge. Valley Forge was directing the unit under his command, forming lines and getting into formation. Valley Forge saw Allen and directed him to stand close.

He put his arm around Allen. "Well done, my friend, well done. I saw David last night and he told me that the historian had done as much as any man."

Allen was pleased by his friendliness. "Thank you. Can I know your name and what you do? I don't want to call you Valley Forge today."

"My name is Michael Ford and I am a draftsman."

Allen shook his hand. "It looks like today we are all soldiers."

Michael Ford cautioned him, "You've done your job, historian. Stay in the park today. I cannot talk to you any longer, but stay here."

He directed Allen to stand just to the right of the standard bearer. The files were deepening, now twenty across, the guides were dressing ranks as quickly as they could. Under the Alpha standard the ranks extended forty deep. At nine o'clock the people were still coming into the park. The trumpet blast signaled attention. Suddenly everyone stopped as the first strains of the nation anthem were heard.

The national anthem had not been heard in ten years in New York City. By the second line people began to sing.

"By the dawn's early light." Tears streamed from the eyes of many. When the anthem was finished a thundering cheer went up.

Schultz, standing at the front of the park turned to his aide, Saul Irwin, who dabbed at his eyes.

Irwin said, "Men won't fight for an anthem, but they surely won't fight without one."

David Schultz turned to a man by the large flagpole in the center of Battery Park. "Run the flag up!"

For the first time in ten years the American flag rose majestically to the top of the flagpole. As the flag fluttered in the stiff breeze, Schultz snapped to attention and saluted the symbol of America. His staff responded in similar fashion. To the thousands in the park first a cheer that turned to a roar. Old Glory never looked better.

Saul Irwin asked, "They sound like they're ready, but will they fight?" The ultimate question before every battle.

Schultz replied, "They'll fight. They're high on emotion and hate."

He thought to himself, but for how long, we outnumber them but they have the firepower. It will depend on the squad leaders; if they lead the rest will follow. Schultz's plan was simple. The large group moving up Broadway will draw the fire of the Nazi tanks. His veterans were on the wings, one thousand on the left, twice that many on the right.

The veterans had fought in World War II and Asia; they were good. Armed with bazookas and machine guns they would attack from the sides. Schultz, who had not studied military history, did not realize this was the classic double envelopment. Hannibal had defeated the Roman army at Cannes in ancient times with this strategy. Hold your enemies attention in the center and destroy him on the wings. Nor did he think of the casualties the battle would bring. It was timing, his mind was going over details, the timing must be right. Don't commit too soon but strike with a hammer when the Blackshirts are off balance.

The crowd grew silent.

The assemblage stood at attention as the Stars and Stripes rose above the park. Who could tell what any man or woman felt at the moment? Was it friends who were not there, the church that was closed, the school that did not have an American flag, a relative in prison without a trial.

Schultz signaled Ford to begin. Michael Ford gave orders to his group.

"We shall move directly up Broadway, stay in ranks, follow the orders of the guides. You shall have further orders in a few minutes. Stay in line."

The Alpha group moved with dedication and purpose. They were not trained soldiers; still it was an awesome sight.

"Stay in line. Keep in step." The guides on either side of the group were active.

Allen laid his case down and opened it up. He took the .45 out and checked to see if the safety was on. He quickly joined the rear rank of the Alpha group moving at a fast walk and tried to stay in step.

Schultz saw Valley Forge lead his group out of the park and up Broadway. He raised his hand in salute and Valley Forge saluted him back. Schultz turned to watch the last of them leave the park, he saw Allen in the rear ranks. He thought, that damn historian, somehow he was always in the middle. He would need a lot of luck today.

There was no time to dwell on Allen. Schultz signaled for other groups to begin the move. By hand signal his aides directed leaders on the left and right to get under way. Three columns were leaving the park. In the middle, up Broadway led by Valley Forge, the first group, a thousand men and women, moved at a quick walk. On the left, parallel with the Hudson River, another thousand moved uptown. On the right, twice that number moved at a quick trot, for they would have further to go along the east side.

As soon as the first three groups left the park, signals were given and other groups formed up a reserve.

Valley Forge led his people to within eight blocks of the Metro Complex. At the corner of Wall Street and Broadway, they halted. He could see a tank rumble onto Broadway next to the Complex. Behind the first tank, another one rumbled onto Broadway. Black helmeted infantry formed behind the tanks.

Valley Forge raised his hand for quiet.

"We must attack; others are attacking from each side, but we must attack Metro Complex straight up Broadway. There will be sappers with dynamite and magnetic mines to attack the tanks."

They could see men and boys carrying charges, slipping in and out of doorways a block ahead.

"We must distract the tanks from the sappers until they can do their work."

He pointed at the forward group still moving ahead. The people in the front row felt a chill as they looked at the giant Nazi tanks. In the rear, the people could not hear him; however, the guides rehearsed all night and were repeating the orders.

"We must attack, keep moving ahead. Others will be attacking from the sides."

It was quiet, only the orders being passed back and forth broke the silence.

Chapter VI

The two Nazi tanks in the street next to the Metro Complex were Tiger IVs. This was the prototype the German army had used since 1944. There was no need to update such a weapon for Germany controlled the world and its energy was in building great architectural structures. The Nazi homage to themselves existed throughout the world. The inferior peoples could be kept in their natural place with Tiger IV.

The Metro Complex had seven tanks, but five were in the repair shop. The Tiger's main weapon was its 75-mm cannon. The crew of five did not load the cannon, expecting the Americans to protest and disperse after a few shots from the infantry. They dispersed an American protest last year with a few warning shots. The crew was slow to answer the alert and they watched lethargically as a machine gun was set up on the sidewalk. The street was relatively narrow and one tank was placed behind the other in support.

The first tank commander could see the crowd moving in good order toward them. There were more people than he expected and he ordered the machine gun to fire a burst. Suddenly a series of rifle shots rang out of the windows of the surrounding building. The shots that killed the Nazi machine gun crew came from the window of a building one hundred and fifty yards away. The first shots of the Battle of New York were fired by Amos Terry and Henry Windum. Henry Windum was forty-six, a veteran of the South Pacific and wounded on Guam. His great-grandfather fought at Gettysburg and was decorated with a Medal of Honor. His grandfather fought in the Spanish-American war and his father was killed in France in 1918. He came from a tradition of soldiers and now he was a handyman.

Amos Terry was twenty, black, and a resident of Harlem. He rode down to lower Manhattan at 4:00 A.M., his rifle disassembled and strapped to his leg under his pants. Terry and Windum fired almost simultaneously and later when people asked who fired the first shot, each agreed they had fired together. Besides being excellent marksmen, both shared the distinction of membership in the Underground since 1955.

Together they formed the most effective fire team the Americans had that day. If the Americans fired the first shots, the targets were relatively easy at a hundred and fifty yards. Windum and Terry were deadly at that range. They and others posted in the building on Broadway scattered the Nazi infantry attempting to form up behind the tanks.

George Ford, Michael's brother, heard the first shots. He was sixty yards ahead of his brother urging his sappers to keep moving. George waved to Michael to come on. He remembered his brother's final words, "If I don't make it, someday blow up the Domed Hall in Berlin." Then he gave the thumbs down, no quarter sign.

Some members of the Alpha group started to fire up Broadway at the Blackshirt infantry.

"All right, let's go." Michael Ford turned and began to run forward. The first tank fired. The shot was high, but many in the rear ranks were hit. A woman next to Allen slipped to her knees, covered with blood.

Valley Forge waved them forward running toward the tank, which was now firing a machine gun. People in the front rows began to drop. Many hesitated, they wanted to stop, to hide, to live, but Valley Forge urged them forward. The sappers were moving fast, not hiding or looking for cover. The tank fired again and the front ranks, only three blocks away, went down. The Nazi infantry pinned down by snipers saw Americans attack on the east and west side of the Complex. The second tank was firing at the buildings trying to stop the snipers. The gun from the first was raking Broadway.

Valley Forge could hear the cries of the other groups up ahead. They were calling, "No quarter," and attacking fiercely. He looked at the sappers getting close to the tanks now. If they could keep the tanks' attention for another few seconds the sappers could attack.

He called to the few that were close to him. "One more rush, just one more rush!"

They arose and, screaming, ran directly ahead.

The Tiger 75-mm cannon killed them all a block away from the tank. Twelve died at the intersection of Broadway and Garden. A sapper darted from a doorway and hurled his dynamite at the Tiger IV. It did not hit the tank, but a great cloud of dust and stones engulfed the street. Another man ran through the dust and hurled a flaming bottle of gasoline. The oil on the tanks ignited, more sappers were moving in, Freddie Schultz's group from Oceanview, hurling dynamite and flaming gasoline bottles. Suddenly behind the fire, a mine exploded on the second tank and it caught on fire.

The Alpha group sacrifice had occupied the tanks and the terrible price of their mission extended behind for six blocks. There was no time to stop, more Americans were racing past the burning tanks.

The groups from the sides coordinated perfectly. A burst of machine gun fire, then a rush to the formed up Nazi infantry. They broke over the Nazi infantry like a wave.

Ten years of garrison duty had softened the fiber of the Blackshirts and the mixed ranks of Nazi veterans and turncoat Americans melted when engulfed. The group on the Nazi right firing at people coming up the west side was overrun and cut to pieces.

The American cry, "No quarter, no quarter" rang out louder.

The group on the left firing at their attackers coming up on the east side broke and ran for the Metro Complex. Most Blackshirts did not make the Complex. The Nazis attempted to barricade the door, but the Americans broke it open. "No quarter, no quarter," their shouts echoed in the halls. They charged through the halls, destroying all in their way. A knot of Blackshirts attempted to stand on the second floor at the top of the stairs and were brushed aside and killed. Even as the last shots were fired, people were still coming out of the subways and were forming up to attack. A group pulled down the statue of the Reich chancellor in the administration building. Suddenly the yelling and the shooting stopped. It was done, revenge was for the weak, the Americans immediately stopped their rampage. They did not regret their theme, for "no quarter" would be repeated again and again that day.

Allen was breathing so hard, he had to stop when he got to the Complex. Allen never fired a shot and he was panting, blood on his pants from some unknown person and the smell of burning gasoline choked him. He sat on the curb and tried to catch his breath.

Hundreds of people were lying on the sidewalk and the street, injured and dead lay side by side. The Americans not in the battle began to care for the wounded. David Schultz knelt by Michael Ford with his brother George. They picked him up and carried his lifeless body inside a building, out of the sun. Schultz put his hand on George's shoulder and left him with his brother. Never would he ask Michael Ford to lead an attack again. Michael Ford would never challenge his judgments, or recruit members of the Underground better than anyone else. He asked Michael Ford to lead the attack because he knew Ford would press home and not stop. As Schultz walked past the burning tanks and saw all the dead and injured, he knew if he had seen this sight two hours ago he could not have given the order to advance. Even the American flag flying above the Metro Complex did not lift his spirits.

He could not think in terms of price; he tried to drive it out of his mind and make his senses go numb. This was the beginning and he was responsible. Oh, he would miss Michael Ford, and the thought of Michael darkened his spirit. Who was he to tell people how to die, and what mattered the flag?

An old man was laughing and waving a rifle. He was wearing a T-shirt that said 82nd Airborne.

"These bastards kept me in prison five years. They beat the crap out of me once a week. Today I kicked their ass. I kicked their ass."

He pumped David Schutz's hand. "We did it. We did it."

The old man was thirty-seven years old. Schultz felt better.

He stopped. Sitting on the curb was William Allen covered with blood. Schultz went down on one knee.

"William, are you hurt?"

Allen gasped for breath. "No, I'm not hurt. I'm just out of breath."

It was incredible; the man led a charmed life. Schultz knew the casualties Alpha group suffered and yet Allen survived again. The shock of seeing Allen woke him from his depression. They had asked him to be the leader and he'd accepted. There was work to be done and no time to waste.

Allen was our lucky charm. He was going to keep him close. What had Michael Ford said about him, "He's the historian, he going to write the final chapter of this war."

His epilogue will be our history.

The winners get to write the history! But Allen seemed to be more than a writer. Ford had said Allen is not much to look at, but I think he has something inside him. Ford was right. Freddie had told David about the car ride, "Mr. Allen knew all about the war, he's really one of us. He won't flinch when it comes to the time." The sappers were always talking about "the Time," the moment to use explosives. Schultz had seen the young men attack with great bravery today and he knew his son was safe. He said a silent prayer. "Thank you, my God, for keeping my son safe."

Schultz pulled Allen to his feet.

"No time for small hurts. We've got to take over and reorganize, help the others. My aide was killed, so you've got a promotion. All right, William, let's see what the Blackshirts left us."

He turned and walked through the broken door of the Metro Complex and Allen, still wheezing for breath, followed him.

Chapter VII

The Americans established headquarters in the administration building. The first act was to establish communications with other American forces. The radio operators were unhurt for Schultz kept them away from the battle.

Quickly, contact was made with the transmitter at Oceanview. Oceanview reported that police barracks and stations all over Long Island were being attacked. Mel Underwood was wounded leading an attack, but would be all right. Resistance was fierce in some of the areas until noon. Then many Blackshirts tried to surrender or deserted, most heading east to the North Shore and escape to New England. Word of the Metro Complex falling reached the surrounding area immediately. Schultz counted on that and the reaction of the Blackshirts in the metropolitan area. Without leadership and confronted with the tireless American attackers, the Blackshirts melted away.

The news from New Jersey and Connecticut was good. The American surprise was complete and they were gaining rapidly as packets of Nazis were forced to retreat because of the populous uprising. The nearest area reporting heavy fighting was Boston. The

Underground radio said that the Americans encountered heavy tank fire and then did not report again.

They tried to reach the rest of the Underground along the national network, but only in the Southeast was the news conclusive. Blackshirts headquarters in Atlanta and Miami fell quickly to the surging American tide. Everywhere fighting was heavy with the Americans attacking with numerical strength, without heavy arms. Shortly after talking to Long Island, word came to Schultz that the main radio room was in contact with Mark Collins, the leader of the Underground. Collins was the regional commander of the Southwest. Communications patched the call through to Schultz. David Schultz and Mark Collins were friends from the battle of Houston in 1953 and both carried the burn scars of the atomic blast. Mark Collins built the Underground, region by region, starting after the American surrender. He was the glue that held the regions together. It was natural for Collins to call Schultz at this moment. Collins knew that Schultz would do well in New York, but in time of confusion he needed as much reassurance as the next that their venture was going well.

"Dave, how are we doing?"

"Good. We've taken the Metro Complex. However, the price was high. Local resistance has faded with the word the Complex was taken. We've told our people not to let them form up, but to keep attacking. How is it going with you?"

"Good in Houston, very tough fighting in Dallas and Fort Worth. We caught them by surprise. Still, the issue is in doubt. I've heard from most of the others and it started everywhere. In the Southwest we attacked at 1:00 A.M., and destroyed all their jets and yet when others attacked at Dallas and Fort Worth at 7:00 A.M., it was still a surprise. They didn't coordinate their defenses at all." The biggest surprise to the Americans all day was how ill prepared the Blackshirts were for their attacks.

Collins continued, "There's no doubt that the various Reich protectors have not talked or helped each other. I captured the local guy Fredericke, and he told me Berlin would not answer his request for orders. He could not bring the base to alert without his superiors' approval. He knows there is a battle going on between the army and the Blackshirts, but he has no idea who's winning."

Schultz asked, "Are they using atomic weapons?"

"David, he didn't want to answer that question. But I kept after him and he said he thought they were. Also, I'm convinced that our information was correct; they had no atomic weapons in America and only one jet wing, which we destroyed."

A big question for the American Underground was the status of Mexico and Central and South America. While North America was controlled by the Blackshirts this area had divided control, Army and Blackshirts.

Schultz asked Collins, "Have you heard anything south of you?"

"Yes, we picked up radio reports the German army in Mexico City was heading south into Central America. They have units in Brazil too. I expect a pincer movement. Also, our intelligence reports a big air battle over Venezuela; the Blackshirts have big oil refineries, a natural target." The intelligence group in Miami, the strongest the Americans had, had predicted a real slugging match between the army and the Blackshirts south of the border with inconclusive results. They told Collins the battle in South America would mean America would not be attacked from that direction for months and probably years.

Schultz reported another issue. "Our people refused to take prisoners. We suffered a lot of casualties, and while I would have preferred to take prisoners, for ten years the Blackshirts have been building to what they got today. I think in our battles it may be better to continue this No Quarter, let both sides know this is a fight to the death unless you surrender before the fight starts."

Collins answered, "We took prisoners, but since 1953, the Blackshirts have a low profile down here." This dual response was consistent all over America; where the people had suffered greatly they gave no quarter.

Now they concentrated on the areas they had not heard from and they knew some of the news would be bad. Schultz mentioned a problem that both of them were worried about.

"We can't get anything from Ira Sawyers in Boston. I think they had too much for him. "The Nazis were particularly strong in Boston and both men feared the Americans could not win there.

Ira Sawyer was a Harvard law professor. He lectured on the Magna Carta and its meaning to Western men. He had been jailed four times for teaching laws that didn't exist anymore. Even the Underground begged him to stop. He was considered the bravest and most respected man in Boston.

His wit and intellect would have made him a great judge. Today he lay dead on Boston Common. When the early morning attacks started, the Americans gained quick advantages. Then considerable numbers of Nazi tanks and infantry halted their progress. It was evident that the day was lost and several asked Ira to retreat. No, he was adamant; they must keep attacking.

Not only must they buy time, but other Americans would succeed if they kept the Nazis occupied. He rallied them and on Boston Common they made their last stand. After the battle was finished the Nazi captain who rolled his body over to see what the American leader was like was surprised. He was small and thin, his face calm, the face of a poet not a warrior. The captain was an educated man, but they shared little in common. One a victor, the other vanquished.

One respected man believed he could live by laws he developed himself; one believed only in power and force. The captain would have scoffed at the little man if he knew his philosophy and beliefs.

Ira Sawyer told his followers, "We want to live by the laws of the courts; they want to live by the laws of the jungle. They give man no dreams, no hope, no respect and that is why they must lose. There will be hard fighting ahead but they can only win if we do nothing."

Today he was puzzled at the Americans' courage and especially their leader. If the rest of the Americans fought as bravely as the men who lay on the Common, it would be a difficult period ahead.

Schultz and Collins did not know of these events; still they made their plans, preparing for the worst. Schultz deferred to Collins, respecting his judgment.

"Dave, if we don't hear from Boston, we have to assume we've lost there. Now the key to New England is Massachusetts and we can't let the Nazis have a base in Boston. So go up there, secure the armory at Leominster, that's the key tactical spot. Rally as many people as you can and attack Boston. Boston is as important to us as New York is."

"Okay, Mark, we'll take care of it." His confidence was decisive and infectious. Collins hung up the phone and he knew the Northeast would be all right. Now to call California. He would call back to New York later. Now to check the progress of the rest of the rebellion.

Schultz called a meeting of his lieutenants. Three were missing and would never attend another meeting.

He began. "We have done well; the Metro Complex was the key to New York. Throughout the area our people report wholesale desertions of the police and Blackshirt sympathizers. I have a casualty report and it is heavy. It includes one of our girl agents who worked at the Complex and was killed."

Allen looked down at the floor. The price of liberty was not cheap.

"As you know, my aide, Saul, was killed, so William Allen will be my assistant and I know will receive your support. We will have to go to New England the day after tomorrow at 4:00 A.M.

The key to New England is the Leominster armory. They have one hundred tanks there, not in operational order. We need their tanks and the artillery and just as importantly to deny them to the enemy."

One of the men asked, "Will we go directly to Leominster?"

"No, we'll stop the Blackshirts on the road from Boston and the small group that holds Leominster will probably surrender.

"I want you to form up in regiments. We are not Underground anymore, but the American Militia. Report to William how many people you have available. We will probably be limited to how much transportation we have. So pick your best people to travel and leave the rest for garrison duty under George Ford."

Schultz picked Ford because he was a good leader and also the Ford family sacrificed enough today.

George would develop backup support if they needed it. The room was hushed; they did not expect to be moving so quickly after today's triumph.

"Now for transportation. Is Harold Kilyus here?" Kilyus, a master mechanic and World War II veteran, stood up. He was a quiet man and in charge of ordinance and transportation.

"Yes, sir."

"Harold, we need as much transportation as you can get ready."

"We will work all night, sir."

"Good. Now I understand the Nazis had five tanks at the Metro Complex. How soon can they be ready?"

Harold felt a pressure at the pit of his stomach. He'd already looked at the tanks and even if they found the parts it would take a great deal of work.

"Well, with us working all night to get the trucks ready, we probably can't get the tanks in shape in less than a week."

Schultz shook his head.

"A week. Harold, you have two days."

"Two days, sir. That's impossible."

In a very soft gentle voice Schultz said, "Harold our people charged tanks today with only their courage. We may have hard fighting ahead. Without those tanks, I will have to ask our militia to fight at great disadvantages again. You must get us those tanks; we all depend on you."

Harold gulped, "Yes, sir."

Harold would have the tanks ready after forty-eight straight hours of work and then suffer a heart attack.

"Now, do we have any questions."

George Ford spoke. "If you are going to take my sappers, we only have seven not hurt. I suggest you put Jose Aguire in charge. He was the man who destroyed the second tank today."

Schultz agreed and the meeting ended. Allen followed the lieutenants out of the room and compiled a list of regiments and estimate of the fighting strength of the New York militia. Then he quickly checked with Harold to see how many could travel with the trucks that would be available.

Finally, Allen took the report in to Schultz. David tilted back in his chair and rubbed his eyes.

"We've got a long night ahead."

They were brought coffee. Allen savored the coffee. It was hot and good. Schultz read a report; people were constantly coming in and out of the office with information. David looked up. It was late and he was tired.

"Well, they weren't ready for us today. They had five tanks that were not operational. There was no real preparation or defense against our attack. The Nazis are not supermen. The Reich protector has been gone and reported drunk for two days. Probably on the news of the civil war in Germany."

A report was dropped on Schultz's desk. He was a quick reader. He finished it and placed it in his folder.

"We are sure that nowhere outside of Germany were there atomic weapons. Here is the general order and documents the order. The Reich chancellor did not trust anyone outside of Germany with atomic weapons."

Allen looked serious, "The battle in Europe must be devastating. If the Blackshirts and the army destroy each other, that would be the best for us."

Schultz crushed his coffee cup.

"We can't count on that. Besides, we have to win here. Our strategy is to keep attacking. They still have the advantage in arms. We've got to take that advantage away. Americans have always been great light infantry—Rogers' Rangers, the Green Mountain Boys, Robert E. Lee and the Thin Gray Line, the finest sharpshooters in the world. We will use our aggressiveness and our initiative." Schultz received another message, read it, and crumpled the paper and threw it on the floor.

"Those bastards, they had a death camp in New Jersey where they were killing people—killing people with systematic murder. Those dirty bastards—we're fighting for our lives, William. Maybe someday it will be for liberty and freedom. Today it's for our lives and we will give no quarter."

Allan and Schultz worked through the night. At one o'clock they got word that the attack in Boston failed, the Nazi still controlled parts of New England. Shortly after that Schultz wrote out the order to form a convoy and leave the following day. They would go to Eastchester, recruit more troops, and take the armory in Leominster. Once there, Schultz planned to arm as many as he could and attack Boston.

Chapter VIII

General Togo, military ruler of Japan, called the meeting for 10:00 a.m. Admiral Tanaka and Air Force General Yanoki were in their places at 9:50 at the long conference table. They would never consider arriving late or even at the exact hour the meeting was to be convened. The general had a fetish for punctuality and discipline and as he got older his standards grew more strict.

They stationed themselves with one empty chair between their chairs and the end of the table where he sat. Behind his chair, a huge window gave a panoramic view of Tokyo Harbor from the twenty-eighth floor of the army-navy headquarters building. Two of the new super battleships rode at anchor and if Admiral Tanaka would have looked he could have seen them. Instead the admiral stared straight ahead waiting for the general to begin.

The general began exactly at 10:00 A.M.

"We are here to discuss the current world situation and Japan's military posture. General Yanoki has graciously consented to record our minutes on these matters and all discussion will be considered secret. General Yanoki will keep the minutes in his safe."

The general, with graceful strokes, recorded the date on a plain white tablet. They were not surprised at the security, for when he ordered the meeting and confined it to the three most powerful men in Japan they knew it was on momentous matters. Still among the most powerful, the divisions were great. General Togo would make all military and political decisions for the empire. They were there to assess the strength of the army, navy, and air force. General Yanoki was an appointee of General Togo and supported the general in his views without question. Admiral Tanaka, a distant relative to the famous Admiral Tojo, was not a rival, but any naval officer felt the intense rivalry between the services. The navy and army feuded in Japan for many years and only the fact that Tanaka owed his career to General Togo kept the friction in a manageable state. Traditionally, the army wanted an aggressive foreign policy with expansion into other parts of Asia while the navy, which would have to maintain the supply lines, wanted a more conservative policy. Despite a distant relationship to the famous victor of the Russian-Japanese war of 1905 Admiral Tanaka had little power as World War II began. With the destruction of the Japanese fleet by the Americans, he was one of the few not to be blamed for naval defeats. Then he was General Togo's compromise candidate for chief of naval operations.

General Togo continued, "The empire has a treaty with Germany, signed with the deceased Reich chancellor. Because of the civil war in Germany and the death of the Reich chancellor, we may consider such treaties null and void."

Both men agreed, despite silence from Germany and knowing the Nazis would never consider the treaty affected by their current problems.

"Thus if Japan has no allies, we must determine our military power in terms of all nations." Neither man moved as he tactically asked them to measure their strength against the Nazis.

"First, we have no word from Europe since the day the war began. Our intelligence cannot determine who is winning the war. However, our intelligence is agreed that the Blackshirts will win."

General Togo would have been frantic if he had known that his chief agent in Germany was in the pay of the Blackshirts. The agent was paid to report to Japan that the Blackshirts would win the war. However, even he was confused by what was happening.

General Togo adjusted his glasses, a sure sign there would be no discussion of the eventual Blackshirt victory. "We know that much of the wealth of our sphere of influence is shared with the Nazis and yet we must bear the military burden of India, China, Korea, and Indochina. This is an intolerable situation. We must exclude the Nazis from their unfair exploitation of our area. Thus I will begin with a comparison of our army and the Nazis. Because he fought the Americans and suffered the weight of their great industrial power, our army is only now beginning to regain the strength we had before the war. Still we are tied down in India, China, and Indochina. The rebels in these areas continue to obtain arms from unknown sources and offer great resistance. The Nazi army has been the most powerful force in the world, but if the Blackshirts win it will mean their destruction, so I assess we are stronger."

Admiral Tanaka spoke, "Are we stronger then the lackeys of the Blackshirts?"

General Togo was glad that Tanaka challenged him. This was the free discussion he wanted; they would accept his decision in the end.

"Yes, even the captive nations cannot influence the course of battles with our army. General Yanoki, what about the air force? Can you measure its power?"

General Yanoki cleared his throat.

"We are superior in number of conventional aircraft, the Nazis have the advantage in jets. They have taken both of their jet wings out of Asia." The wings had left the Philippines and Okinawa in the past few days. "If we take their bases, I am sure with carrier and land-based planes we have the advantage.

"If we attack first in the Pearl Harbor style you suggest we can deny them their bases and we will control all of Asia?" asked General Togo.

"Yes, I'm sure without carriers penetrating our waters we will control the air."

Admiral Tanaka spoke for the first time. "Our carrier strength is far superior to the Nazis. Because they have the combined French and English fleets as well as their own, they have more ships. If we take their air bases we can control the Pacific against them."

General Togo said, "I believe once the civil war is decided, the Blackshirts will be weaker. We shall begin to negotiate the Nazi withdrawal from Asia. If they refuse, once our atomic weapons are ready, we shall attack them. Dr. Aki has told me they will be ready in a year and a half. His life is committed to the time table."

Admiral Tanaka asked, "What shall we do in China and India? The slave drains the strength of the master. Even if we starve millions they are a drain on our food supply?"

"Admiral, I agree, we cannot forget our control of India is hurting us economically as much as Indochina and China tie us up militarily. We must withdraw from India despite the Nazi insistence we garrison the country. We must sign a treaty with the Communists in China. They can have parts of the interior; we shall control the coast. Then we can turn all our attention to Indochina. Indochina and those areas that benefit us economically shall be in our sphere of influence and we shall not share with anyone."

There was a pause. "Do we agree on this cause of action and are there any questions?"

Admiral Tanaka looked at the general. "The industrial might of America troubles me. They have not produced at an impressive level in years, but we must remember they built giant navies and armies in their war with us."

General Togo did not change expression, but inwardly he winced. Time would not erase the memory of how destructive was the war with the Americans. Japan was almost beaten, but the American prisoners had paid for their transgressions against the empire.

"The Nazis have not been able to develop American industrial might. If for some reason the Americans were to be free of the Blackshirts I don't think they can challenge us, their spirit is broken. America will never be a world power again. Someday we may consider them part of our sphere of influence."

Air General Yanoki adjusted the papers in front of him. He had been in the Philippines when they had first broken the American power at the beginning of the war. An army general at the time, he had ordered the Bataan Death March. When the Philippines resisted he had them killed with their American friends. Then he instructed his officers to institute a small thing but an important one in the campaign. Each day as thousands of Americans were marched into captivity, without food and water, when they halted at noon they were forced to sit in the tropical sun.

Yanoki had ordered his officers to make sure they sat in the sun without their caps. No coolie would be without a hat in the noonday sun, but this would show Asians that the whites were a beaten race. When some villages had tried to give the Americans food and water Yanoki had ordered the mayors of the village to be hanged in the village square.

* * *

Heinz leaned his head back on the pillow. Trudie was walking back and forth combing her long blonde hair that hung to her waist.

Without clothes he never tired of looking at her body. No matter how many times he had seen her, she reminded him of a Ruben painting-so round, so firm. He wanted her to come to bed; she was in an exotic mood. It was always best when she was this way.

Heinz was cooing his love for her, which he considered ridiculous. He was fifty-two and fat, she was twenty-three and not pretty, but a body that turned heads. The car, the apartment, the fur coat, what else did she want, why the silly talk. At least his wife didn't bother with such nonsense anymore.

The ringing of the phone on the table next to the bed made him jump. Who the hell could that be? It must be a wrong number. Only Fluor, his secretary, had this number and Fluor was not to call unless an emergency occurred. Even then, Fluor was not to call today. He picked up the phone.

"Hello."

"Herr Heinz, it is Fluor."

"Fluor, why do you bother me?" he yelled.

"Herr Heinz, I'm sorry, but I have the new Reich chancellor on the phone. He insists on talking to you."

Heinz sat upright and swung his feet on the floor. He moved for a bath robe. No wonder Fluor sounded so nervous—even Swiss bankers snapped to attention when the ruler of the world called.

"Heinz," the voice was soft, but he frightened him when he talked.

"Yes, Herr Reich Chancellor."

"Heinz, a plane will land in Zurich tomorrow at 2:00 P.M. It will carry gold bullion. Meet the plane with a heavy truck. The previous chancellor's account is now my account."

He quoted the weight and Heinz knew it was worth millions of Swiss francs.

"My men will provide protection so you will accompany them to the vault."

Heinz added the value of the gold to the painting, jewelry, and other valuables in the vault, now over thirty million in gold alone. A total well over one hundred million marks.

The only account even close to that size was Nazi general at twenty million marks.

"Heinz, I expect the usual security. Do you understand?

"Yes, Herr Reich Chancellor."

The Reich chancellor hung up without saying good bye. Heinz hung up and stared into space. Trudie turned and left the room when he was like this; she could do nothing with him. It depressed her, for her control over such a wealthy man gratified her ego.

Heinz was lost in thought, his mind calculating various scenarios. This was the second deposit in the vault in a very short time by the Reich chancellor. The first was the standard hedge the day the civil war broke out. But this would be a much larger deposit. An army general gave him a deposit when the war opened, but none since.

It was a sign that the Blackshirts were losing, the Reich chancellor was preparing a treasure reserve. In thirty years as a Swiss banker, he had seen this happen before. Always initially a small deposit, then larger deposits by the loser as he prepared to escape the oncoming disaster.

He thought for a moment, if the Blackshirts lose, it will disturb the world order. Always a dangerous portion for certain investments. Heinz dialed the phone number of a trading desk at a friendly bank, whose discretion could be trusted. He gave them all orders on various security and commodities he owned. He decided to continue to sell securities and thus put his account into a short position. If a disaster came, he would benefit by being short. He would invest in gold. Gold was too high and he hated gold because it didn't pay interest. Protection was more important now. Heinz hung up the phone. He was confident of one thing, his bank would survive. Perhaps he should borrow money and short more securities.

What Heinz did not know was that the deposit in his bank was one of four accounts that the previous Reich chancellor owned. Over one hundred million pounds in gold, more than that in jewels and securities.

This was the reason the jets were not ready in Houston or the tanks in the Metro Complex. For years the military budget was pillaged to go into the bank account of the leader of the known world. The best thing the people of the world had going for them in their quest for freedom was the greed of the unchallenged leader of the Fourth Reich.

Arlie West signaled the charge was in place. Chips leaned back, nothing to do but wait for the train now. Chips rolled a cigarette with a cupped hand, so that the fierce wind did not blow the tobacco away. The wind didn't bother Chips, his weather beaten sun tanned face was use to it. Years of sheep herding on the outback gave a man a natural indifference to weather.

The train from Sydney would go over the trestle in twenty

minutes. At least it would try to go over the trestle, until Chips would push the plunger and Arlie and the rest of the dingos would pick up the arms that were not damaged. Chips and Arlie had dynamited so many trains that Chips considered this an easy day's work. As easy as dispatching the Italian troops the Nazis brought to Australia and sent into the outback after them. Poor fellows who didn't want to hurt anyone and provided the Australian resistance with most of their arms. In the early years of the Nazi occupation the Blackshirts accompanied the native police and Italians in chasing the resistance. Then the distance and the terrain wore them down. Now there were only token raids by the police and rarely were the Blackshirts seen. In the last two years several towns were taken back by the dingos.

Chips would laugh. "Those shits want to sit in their big houses on the coast and drink. They don't want to chase dingos like me in the outback."

Chips did not think in terms of driving the Nazis from Australia; their presence did not affect him much. He knew their atomic weapons and jets could not alter the wide spread influence of the resistance in the desolate western range. His private war would continue with them until they went away, for it was his range and they were interlopers and would have to pay the price for bothering him. He could soldier weekends for a long time; it broke up the monotony of sheep herding.

Drinking beer, blowing up trains, sheep herding—that was the life. He heard the whistle in the distance and knelt down to get into position.

Dr. Kurkov sat on his horse dripping wet as the rain showed no sign of letting up. Huddling under a set of trees the partisan band did not complain. You did not complain when you were with Dr. Kurkov. He was the leader of the Russian partisans in the Ural Mountains. Dr.

The Last Reich

Kurkov had been fighting the Nazis for almost twenty years, ever since an SS unit captured his small village. The Germans had brought many wounded with them. The children of the village had been forced to go to the hospital to give blood to the German wounded. Originally Dr. Kurkov had helped with the transfusion because of threats to his daughter. But he protested when he saw children being dangerously drained of blood. A Nazi guard hit him with a rifle butt. He awoke hands and feet tied. The Germans had shot all the people in the village and buried the children dead and living in a large pit and covered the pit with dirt to hide their crimes. This included the doctor's daughter. The German doctors needed his help and told him he would live as long as he worked for them.

The night he had escaped he killed four German wounded before he left.

As he built his partisan units the first pledge a recruit took was that he or she would take no prisoners.

Five years ago they captured an Englishman working for the Nazis and one of the captains asked if he should be spared. The doctor had taken his pistol and smashed the captain across the face. The question never came up again. So the Nazis and the partisans fought one of the most brutal wars in all of Europe. The only time anyone had heard the doctor say anything good about Germans was when he asked how a people who wrote such beautiful music could produce such murderers and criminals.

Last night a short wave radio transmission from a station on the Bering Sea said they had picked up a radio transmission from America. The Americans were rebelling and their battle cry was no quarter, no prisoners. The doctor said, "The Nazis are great teachers; they teach us all to hate them!"

Chapter IX

After two days Allen and Schultz at 4:00 A.M. watched the first district American Militia form up and get ready to leave the Metro Complex. They were loaded on trucks, and armed with rifles and machine guns from the Metro Complex. Men and women had worked for two days and nights to prepare the weapons including four bazookas but little ammunition for the bazooka. Harold Kilyus said he would have three tanks ready in a few hours and they would follow on flatbed trucks. Schultz said he could wait no longer. In the lead jeep, Schultz and Allen pointed the convoy up Broadway. They left New York City through the Queens Mid-town Tunnel and onto the Long Island Expressway. At the Bronx Whitestone Bridge a contingent from Long Island met them and fell in behind the last trucks. They traveled up the New England Thruway, deserted and quiet. Some people along the road waved and cheered. The New Yorkers waved back, but most slept as they jostled and bounced along. It was going to be hot, the sun cutting through the early morning haze.

At 9:00 A.M. in Boston, Colonel Michael Lorentz pushed a map case across the table to his attentive panzer commanders.

"Gentlemen, the situation is this. A general uprising of the populous has taken place all over America. In Boston we crushed the uprising on the Common. I must tell you I am an American and it was a sad sight for me to kill so many of my countrymen." Lorentz believed his candid confession would impress the commanders. He was wrong; since he was the only American, they mistrusted him. In keeping with the Nazi policy the commanders were mixed nationalities.

Rarely would an American hold such an important position in the country of his origin. Lorentz led them well yesterday; still he was an American and if the Americans attacked again would he hesitate to kill his own countrymen. They never expected to see such fierce attacks from the Americans. There was no warning.

The commanders included two Koreans, two Germans, one Canadian, two Russians, and one Brazilian.

The American Lorentz was the son of a Iowa minister. His father ran off and left the family when he was small and until Michael joined the Blackshirts he had never known the world to listen to him. He believed the Fourth Reich would last a thousand years and it was foolish not to be in the forefront of such a movement. His ambition and ability to lead tank units in the steppes of Russia against guerillas made his star rise quickly in the Blackshirts.

Until the uprising, he had never fired on Americans. He said he was sad to shoot at the rebels, but in truth he considered them fools and not representatives of the population, who he believed accepted their place in the Nazi constellation. His place was secure; he had money, power, position, and above all, women. He liked women and they liked him. He was dashing and confident.

Lorentz spread the map out on the table. "We have thirty panzers in Boston and five thousand infantry. I intend to lead ten of the panzers later today to guard the armory past Concord near

Leominster. We have heard that the rebels have been striking at such places. I will take up defensive position at the armory and secure it until we are sure there is no such threat. I will take five hundred of the infantry with me to clear the road of mines and enemy infantry. The balance of the tanks will stay in Boston under the control of Major Kim." Major Kim of Korea was the second in command. His tanks blunted the major American attack and their aggressive pursuit of the rebels caused more American casualties than less zealous commanders would have.

Major Kim disliked Lorentz, considering him a pompous egotist, not to be trusted to recognize Kim and his position in the Blackshirts. It was no secret that in the Blackshirts a great deal of racism existed. Major Kim hated the Americans and he truly loved the killing. He desired the rebellion to continue, but he resented the glory that Lorentz would receive because of their victory. As Lorentz's second in command he would probably be given the job of selecting the tank crews to go to Leominster and he would make sure the best, his Koreans and the Germans, would not be going. Kim considered Lorentz lazy and stupid to delegate such staff work to his next in command. Major Kim never allowed such latitude to his subordinates. Captain Adu, the Brazilian, raised his hand.

"Colonel Lorentz, we did not see our jets over the city today. The men were questioning why we did not have air support."

In truth none of Captain Adu's men asked the question, none would have in a unit where Major Kim was second in command. Captain Adu was new and he did not know the full wrath of Major Kim. Captain Adu was terrified at the battle the previous day. He never expected to see the power of the Fourth Reich challenged as it had been and Captain Adu wanted to know where the jets were.

Colonel Lorentz scowled because he himself wondered what happened to the jets from Canada. After the battle the Reich protector told him that the jets were sent somewhere else where there was a more urgent need. He flattered Lorentz by telling him that with the tank unit led by Colonel Lorentz, the city was safe from the rebels. Lorentz accepted the explanation, yet aware that the attack was serious and the jets might have been needed. Lorentz felt an obligation to answer the question of his men.

"Captain Adu, we don't need jets to take care of this rabble. The jets were sent to an area where we are less secure. They are available if we need support in Boston."

Colonel Lorentz would have been less confident if he knew that most of the jet wings had been destroyed today over Munich, and that the balance, battered and smoking, would be needed to fly cover over a retreating Blackshirt convoy of tanks and trucks.

Colonel Lorentz pointed his swagger stick at Major Kim.

"Major, we leave at two o'clock for Leominster, please assign ten tanks to assist me." Colonel Lorentz promptly left for a breakfast party he had planned all week.

There was a delightful lady who would listen breathlessly to his description of the battle. She was an actress, striking and charming. Lorentz would not spare any details in his heroic defense of the city.

He knew that Major Kim could have the tank force ready before noon, but Lorentz would not change his plans. She might not be here by the time he came back from Leominster.

Chapter X

The first district American Militia moved well until they left the New England Thruway and turned north to Eastchester. Once an excellent road, lack of repair caused innumerable tie-ups and delays. They reached Eastchester at noon tired from the struggle to push the trucks through a gully where a bridge was washed out. On entering Eastchester, Schultz and Allen in the lead jeep were halted by scouts from the local Eastchester militia.

Schultz was delighted when Alex Liva, their leader, introduced himself. Liva and Schultz were strangers to each other except by reputation. Liva was a former policeman, who had been dropped from the force by the Blackshirts. He described the battle of Eastchester.

"We fought all day, house to house, they had no tanks, but it was tough. My boys beat them, beat them in the alleys and the cellars where it was dirty and mean—they won't try Eastchester again. What news of the rest of the East?"

Schultz replied, "New Jersey is good, New York City good, upstate we don't know. Philadelphia didn't have many Blackshirts so that should have been easy. The problem looks to be Boston. They were strong in Boston and I hear it was bad, too many tanks. We believe Ira Sawyer is dead. Besides losing Ira, we can't let Boston remain in their hands. If we do well elsewhere, and Boston remains an open port, they can bring supplies in, then we've got problems."

Schultz knew it was important to get Liva's support. He must be diplomatic, because he judged Liva to be suspicious of their intentions. "We've come to capture the Leominster armory. I think it's the key to New England and Boston."

Liva was silent.

"Alex we need your help; will you bring your people with us?"

"I haven't heard from Ira; he's in charge in New England."

Schultz tried to be gracious.

"Well, of course, you'll lead the column, but I don't think we are going to hear from Ira and time is important."

Liva was upset. The New Yorker was pushing too hard and fast. Liva knew Ira Sawyer, and liked him. He may have been a Harvard professor, but Sawyer was a good guy whom he trusted. Liva wasn't going to be pushed by David Schultz.

"My place is in Eastchester. What if the Nazis attack here, who is going to defend my people?" Allen struggled to hold his temper.

"Mark Collins called us and asked us to make sure Leominster is not lost to the Nazis. Now, you've got to realize the importance of the arms there."

Liva thought, if we leave Eastchester unguarded and then we will probably meet the Nazi panzers on the road. No, he'd stay in Eastchester with his people.

"I won't leave Eastchester undefended until I get orders from Ira or Mark Collins."

Allen pleaded with him.

"You can leave a group to defend the town. Without Ira Sawyer,

Dave would be in charge and responsible to Mark and the revolutionary committee."

Liva remained adamant. He would not leave Eastchester or let his people go with the New Yorkers.

Schultz was impatient, they probably didn't have a lot of time to reach their objective. He decided to challenge Liva directly; they were getting nowhere trying to reason with him.

"If you don't want to meet the panzers on the road, you stay here and let your people come with me."

He touched a nerve. Liva exploded in a string of invectives. Schultz cursed at Liva under his breath; that was the end of it. He outranked Liva in the revolutionary movement, but he couldn't force him to follow orders.

The American Militia was not a regular army. It did not have the discipline that was so important. Sectionalism would plague the Second Revolution as it did the thirteen colonies two hundred years before.

Schultz and Allen left the Eastchester leader disgusted and mad.

"If we can't work together, winning this war is going to be a lot more difficult," Schultz said.

Allen assured him that this must be an isolated incident. A man followed them to the jeep.

"Alex is stubborn and wrong, the Eastchester men will stay with him, but I can help get some men north of here."

The radio operator in the second jeep waved to them. "A ham radio operator in Boston is sending a signal that he spotted ten Nazi tanks leaving Boston on the road to Concord."

Schultz turned to the stranger.

"What's the best place to intercept them, before they link up with the armory and form a defensive position?"

"Meet them outside of Lexington. Some of the road goes between small hills. It will be harder for them to maneuver their tanks." He pulled out a map and showed Allen and Schultz the position.

Schultz pointed to the spot on the map.

"Get all the people you can to meet us here. We'll hold them as long as we can, but we'll need reinforcements."

The man agreed and told two friends the plan.

The three men fanned out heading north on different roads to warn the populace. Word was passed down the column they were moving and that the Nazi tank force would be met on the road.

* * *

In Boston there was a delay and the Nazi tank force left after two o'clock on the road to Concord. They moved leisurely to allow the infantry to keep up. The front five tanks were commanded by Colonel Lorentz, followed by infantry, and the last five lead by Captain Adu. The Nazi tank column was spotted by a second ham radio operator as they lumbered down the highway. He began to broadcast a warning to all he could pick up.

"Ten Nazi tanks and infantry leaving Boston. Ten Nazi tanks and infantry leaving Boston. Do you read me?"

The first American Militia heard the second warning just as they got under way. They radioed back if other operators could follow the progress of the Nazi tank force.

Immediately a third operator checked in.

"They should be in sight within fifteen minutes. I'll go down to the highway and check and radio back shortly."

In this way the progress of the Nazis was plotted and Schultz knew where they were at all times. By hard driving the first American Militia reached the spot on the map an hour before the Nazis were expected to arrive.

Schultz halted the column. "They should be here soon. We've got to pick some ground to fight." He and Allen raced their jeep down the road. Several hundred yards ahead, he halted the jeep.

"Here, we'll attack them here."

The trucks were brought up and unloaded. Sixteen hundred Americans with small arms and machine guns and four bazookas. They had no rockets, artillery, or mortars. The majority were men, yet many were women, all veterans of the Underground. Despite the requirement of Underground experience a number were teenagers.

They deployed quietly on either side of the road. There were no illusions about the upcoming fight. The stretch of road between two hills was parallel by two deep culverts.

Gullies and small brush crisscrossed the valley between the hills. A line of trees on each summit added to the natural amphitheater effect.

Allen sent a jeep with scouts ahead to set up an advanced listening post. Another jeep raced west to speed up any reinforcements on the way. He and Schultz looked at the position. Schultz ruled out an ambush. "Not enough cover anywhere on the road to surprise them; it's a good defensive position. We need more help. If we get support we can win."

David Schultz called a meeting of his lieutenants. They included Freddie, his son, the young man from Oceanview who led the Long Island sappers, Jose Aguire, his counterpart in New York, Mildridge, who commanded the machine guns, and Amos Terry and Henry Windum, leaders of the snipers. William Allen was in charge of the rest of the infantry. Schultz explained his strategy.

"When they get here, William and I will talk with them to stall for time. The longer we can delay, the more help we should get. Now where do we want to place the machine guns?"

He and Mildridge quickly agreed where to set up the machine

guns. All the machine gunners were veterans of Southeast Asia; they were good. Schultz explained the rest of his plan.

"We have to keep the tanks on the road. If they leave the road or flank us, we have trouble. So Freddie, I want you and Jose to dig up some of the road and pretend it's mined. Put your mines in the culvert, maybe we can slow them up and keep them on the road that way."

Schultz turned to Mildridge, "They'll probably send the infantry forward to clear the road, then, and only then, work on the tanks. It won't stop them; however, you'll get their attention."

He turned to Windum and Terry. "Where do you think it's best to put the snipers, up on the tree line?"

Amos Terry spoke up, "We think the trees are too obvious and we want to dig in among the bushes in foxholes."

Schultz agreed. "Okay, and if possible, try to pick off a tank commander before they cover up."

Amos Terry smiled and looked at his partner Henry Windum. "We will give it a try. More people have joined us; they say they're from a shooting club. I'll post them with us."

Schultz said okay, absorb any help into the defensive position as quickly as they could. Now he turned to Mildridge and the snipers.

"Once we halt the tanks, keep the infantry back." He put his hand on Freddie's knee. "Freddie, if the infantry leaves the tanks or gets pinned down, you and Jose have got to attack. You may not be able to see so watch me and I'll raise my arm for the signal. Remember it's a three-step action. One, halt the tanks by faking mines. Two, drive the infantry back. Three, Freddie and Jose attack the tanks."

In a better time he might have been a coach, teaching, patient, calm, pulling them together. But this was not a game.

Freddie turned a thumb down.

"Remember, no quarter."

Several said in unison, "No quarter."

The Americans knew there was no going back; they would stand until there was a decision and if spirit was the test, they would win. As they moved to their positions, Schultz cursed their lack of heavy weapons.

"I never want to ask men to attack tanks again without support. Damn it all."

* * *

Ten miles north, one of the men from Eastchester pulled his motorcycle into a small village. This was his tenth stop and he wondered how many people would heed the call. He got off the bike in front of the village store and yelled out.

"Nazis en route one twenty, Nazi coming up route 120. Anyone with a weapon is needed. The militia is west of Lexington."

People immediately gathered around him.

"Nazis from where?

"Boston, the bastards are heading for the Leominster armory."

"We don't know, but the militia needs all the help it can get."

Louis Gurzano, who owned the store, questioned the rider.

"You're from Eastchester. It is Alex Liva and the boys from Eastchester who are going to stop the Nazis."

The rider looked upset.

"No, it's the New York militia. The Eastchester boys are not going to help. That's not important, we can't let the Nazis get to Leominster."

Louis questioned again, "What are the New Yorkers doing here? Our boys run this part of the country. I know Alex Liva and he's a good man."

The rider cranked his motor into action. "The important thing is to stop the Nazis. He pointed the bike north and roared off.

They looked at Louis.

"I'm not going to get into this if the boys from Eastchester aren't along. The New York people ain't our concern. I don't know what the hell they want."

Others from the village came running over and he told them the news. His wife Lilly stood on the sidewalk. She hung back from the crowd, quiet as usual. He was loud and boisterous and the unofficial spokesman of the village. Lilly turned and walked into the store. Her hand shook and she bit her lip, she would do it. In all their years of marriage she had never disobeyed him. Lilly began to take bandages and gauze from the shelves, as much as she could carry. She took down a knapsack and began to pack it.

Louis came in. "What are you doing?"

"I'm going to help the militia."

"You're what?" He looked at her in disbelief. "You can't, what about me and the boys?"

"I'm going for the boys; it's about time we did this for them."

He was shocked; she had lost her senses.

"What do you mean it's time we did something for them? I didn't bring the Nazis. It's not my fault; what the hell is wrong with you?"

She tightened the belt on her knapsack. "I'll take the bike, there's food in the icebox."

He watched her ride away and couldn't believe it. She was forty years old and did not weigh one hundred pounds. What could she do? Damn this war, it broke up families, one of the few times she had even disobeyed him. He supposed a few fools would join the militia.

He clenched his teeth. Maybe he should follow. No, he would stay here.

Lilly and many others were moving toward route 120. Size, age, and sex did not matter, only that they were moving to the pike.

Chapter XI

Allen sat in the culvert with his arms across his chest, his head rested back against the steel. It was hot and the sweat poured off him. His shirt showed two stains under his arms and a fly buzzed, breaking the silence. Schultz sat across from him, trying to judge how many men and women it would take to stop ten tanks. More people were coming now, sliding in among the already entrenched New Yorkers. Perhaps the Americans had two thousand; not enough, Schultz thought. If we hold them for two or three hours maybe enough will come.

Schultz was changing his tactics. At the Metro it was attack, all full-out attack. In Massachusetts a holding action, try and hold until more people would come and even the battle. They had received a message three hours ago that the tanks had left New York. If only the bazooka team had more ammunition.

Allen looked at him. "David where do you want me?"

"When they arrive you and I will take the jeep and parley with them. We will stall as long as possible. When it begins, you go back up the road and direct people into the battle. If the Nazis break off the road, try and send more men to that side. If they break through us, have everyone attack the lead tank to keep them on the road. Don't let them out."

Allen was exhausted mentally and physically.

Schultz did not like to see one of his officers so despondent.

"Historian, I understand you're an expert on Lincoln?"

Allen barely looked up. "I've studied Lincoln."

Schultz persisted. "I heard Lincoln was very mentally tough. Do you remember any Lincoln stories where he inspired his men? Maybe they will help us today."

Allen hesitated. "There is one story I'm fond of." His voice trailed off.

In a strong voice Schultz said, "I want to hear it!"

Allen began, "Lincoln couldn't find a general to defeat Robert E. Lee, and he kept trying. One of his generals reluctantly let Lincoln review the troops at his headquarters. To show up Lincoln, he gave him a mule to sit on. Here was this tall man in a stovepipe hat, his feet almost touched the ground. He looked foolish.

"The soldiers were country boys but they were not stupid. They recognized that this great man was willing to humble himself and try to inspire his troops and support a general to beat Robert E. Lee.

"And the soldiers loved Lincoln, he always reviewed soldiers coming from the North heading for the South. He wanted the men to see their president. The Civil War was so bloody and long and difficult, there were lots of deserters on the Union side and many would come to the White House to talk to Lincoln, and frequently they would return to their units."

Schultz asked. "And the lesson Lincoln gave us!"

"Never give up, no matter how many defeats, never give up. The man had immense courage."

It was Schultz's turn to talk about his favorite subject. "If FDR hadn't died we would never have lost World War II."

The Germans were lucky but President Wallace, FDR's successor, made some big mistakes. He halted work on the atomic bomb, forced General Marshall to resign and appointed General Clark to command the invasion. Clark launched the invasion in bad weather and half the invasion force never made it ashore. I know a member of Clark's staff and he said General Eisenhower begged Clark not to land the paratroopers so far from the coast. The paratroopers without heavy weapons were slaughtered by the Germans."

Schultz kicked at the dirt with his boot.

"You gents want a sip of cold beer?"

Henry Windum, head of the snipers, handed Schultz a can of beer, the foam sitting on the top of the can. "I found a cold spring down there." He pointed to the divide between the hills. "Boy is that water cold! Made the beer good and cold."

Schultz took a drink. "God, that is good."

Allen took a sip. His head cleared. He didn't feel tired anymore.

Windum was in a happy mood. "The boys feel we're in a good place; we've won here before."

Allen was puzzled. "What are you talking about?"

"The colonials and the British two hundred years ago. They chased the British down that pike at Lexington." He pointed down the road. Yes, Lexington was less than three miles away.

"The British were destroying rebel stores, the American militia fought behind fences and trees that day and drove them back to Boston."

Schultz asked Windum, "Do you think they were as good a shot as you, Henry?"

"Better, with the kind of guns they were using."

Schultz stood up.

"Yes, we are in a good spot." He clapped his hands together. Now he was genuinely pleased.

"The American farmers beat the last foreign army here; can we do less." He was shaking hands and patting men on the back. They had never seen him so ebullient.

The men were standing and smiling.

"The British didn't have tanks, general." More and more men were calling Schultz general.

He answered. "And the Americans did not have bazookas."

He did not add that his four bazooka teams each had only five rounds of ammunition—not enough to practice. Their shots must be sure; it was one of the reasons to keep the German tanks on the road.

A large group of men gathered around him straining to hear what he was saying.

"Why, after we beat this bunch we'll go right to Canada and clean out that crowd."

"Right on, general!"

The men were cheering his every word. He used a line he had heard General Patton use.

"By God, I almost feel sorry for the Germans."

For the first time in days Allen was not afraid. If there was going to be a fight let it come. He knew it was David Schultz who was energizing the Americans.

They could not replace this man.

Other Americans were too far away to hear Schultz. They crouched behind bushes and stretched out on the grass. Hot, hungry, dog tired, many were afraid. A few understood what he was saying, many could not hear him. But all, even the two or three arriving every minute knew who the leader was. From the walls of Jericho to the hot, muggy road in Massachusetts at this moment, people looked for a leader before battle. Someone who seemed in control, more confident and less afraid than they were.

Schultz may not have been a recognized captain of war, but he had picked the ground well. The son of a Long Island fisherman, he had quit high school to fly gliders before the war. Drafted in the infantry he transferred to glider school and was with the first wave that flew into Normandy during the invasion. Despite being shot up, he flew his glider to a safe landing. Fighting his way with the airborne to the coast, he escaped to England in a small boat. The failure of the invasion paralyzed the English and American forces until England signed the truce. Schultz and two others stole a sailboat and he sailed the Atlantic to return to America never believing in the truce an American president signed. He was an early leader in the Underground.

Burned in the atomic explosion in Houston in 1953, he returned home to build local Underground units. At thirty-seven, he had been fighting Nazis for sixteen years. He believed they were bullies and liars, never respecting their power. As he became older, his patience and courage gave him the leadership on Long Island, then New York, and finally the region. Mark Collins always referred to him as the American Eagle. He did not know the other Underground leaders as Mark did. Several knew him by reputation as he knew them. His good humor helped him endure the ten years his country was a defeated nation. Never did he doubt they would be free, for his confidence gave him strength to overcome his mistakes. He regretted he couldn't convince Alex Liva to come with them today, but he believed his countrymen would respond to the militia's call for support today. Now he would face the Nazi commander, the men from Eastchester told him that the Nazi was an American.

How could an American turn against his own people? He believed the man must feel some guilt.

Schultz looked up the road. So an American would lead tanks down this road against his fellow Americans. Unless he had no conscience he must feel dishonor. Perhaps guilt and dishonor were a weapon.

He was standing on the road looking east. Many Americans could see him standing there.

One of the veterans of Vietnam turned to Mildridge.

"I'm glad we got that son of a bitch."

Mildridge agreed. "He's the best I ever fought with. I just hope he remembers the English didn't have machine guns here two hundred years ago." Amos Terry and Henry Windum dug foxholes behind low bushes about halfway up the hill. They gauged the distance to be two hundred yards. The two were fast friends because of their mutual interest in shooting.

"We got to take those turkeys."

Amos sighted down his scope. The crosshairs were sighted on an imaginary target. "It's going to be tough. We got to get a tank commander."

Henry said, "There's a way."

Amos questioned, "What do we do?"

We both sight in on anybody we can see. The minute the parley breaks up we burn him.

Amos chuckled. "Yeah, we started it two days ago. We'll do it again today."

The waiting Americans grew alert as the advanced scout party came back in the lead jeep.

Freddie Schultz shook hands with Jose Aguire from the Bronx. "It's time."

Frennie Schultz told his group, "Did you see that Aguire on Broadway? He has guts, we can't let the boys from the Bronx outdo us today. He checked the equipment and shook hands with his team.

This was the young men's way of encouraging each other to be brave and aggressive to do the time.

Then they saw a Tiger top the low rise and they could hear other tank motors. Almost 2,400 Americans flanked the road. The Nazis spotted the Americans on the road obviously putting in mines and many on the hillside. For a moment Lorentz thought of leaving the road, but before he could decide a jeep carrying a white flag appeared and moved toward them. The jeep halted one hundred yards away. Lorentz signaled for his touring car and directed the driver to meet the jeep. Schultz hoped the Nazis would not disperse and attack for tank tactics clearly showed they should not limit their maneuverability and firepower by staying on the road.

When Lorentz's car reached the jeep he was confident that the Americans had intended to fight, but lost heart when they saw his tanks. This would be easy. He chose to be friendly.

"My compliments, I am Colonel Lorentz," he smiled.

Schultz did not smile. "I am David Schultz, leader of the First Militia."

Lorentz smiled again. "Schultz, that is a German name. Were your parents German?

"No, my parents were American."

Lorentz said, "I am an American too."

Schultz reacted calmly.

"No, you're not. All the Americans are at this end of the road." He pointed behind him. "I see only traitors and Nazis where you stand."

The minute Schultz saw Lorentz step out of the staff car he

changed his strategy. He would not delay but try and bait this pompous man to a rash attack. The polished boots, the red scarf, the way the man moved. Schultz gauged him to be arrogant and overconfident. If the tanks would stay on the road, they had a chance.

Lorentz winced at the insult from the big man. The American was dressed in khaki, no insignia or medals, yet the man moved with confidence. No one had talked to him like this in many years. His anger mounted as he was insulted after trying to be friendly.

"Leader of the militia, you have five minutes to lay down your arms and surrender."

"Leader of traitors, you have five minutes to leave; we take no prisoners or give no quarter."

The hate between the two men was visible.

Lorentz ordered his driver to return to the column. He was furious and ordered the infantry captain to report.

"Clear the mines off the road and quickly. We shall sweep this rabble out of here. And, captain, we take no prisoners.

The captain could see he was red faced and mad.

"Sir, I think we should get off the road."

Lorentz interrupted him. "I'm in a hurry, captain, that rabble has nothing that can stop us."

Amos and Henry sighted in on the third tank. The commander was standing up looking over the American positions. He was several hundred yards away—the longest shot they had ever attempted. They fired simultaneously. Lorentz heard the whine of the bullets and looked up to see his commander slump over dead.

"Attack," he screamed. "I order an attack, now sweep them out of here; we will kill them all."

The captain of the infantry was uneasy. Lorentz was out of control. The Americans had upset him. His face was red and he was screaming. The captain blew his whistle and waved his men forward. They streamed past the first tank and the battle began. The second man to die on the road was a Nazi corporal who dropped from a sniper's bullet at three hundred yards. The fire from the machine guns raked the road and the Nazi infantry fanned into the culverts. The first mine in the culvert went off. With the machine-gun fire overhead, the Nazi infantry was pinned down. Colonel Lorentz impatiently rapped his driver on the shoulder. "Move up the road fifty yards."

The tanks were firing now not picking targets, blasting at the hillsides. Lorentz's tank was just behind the infantry that was halted in the culverts. A second tank pulled up behind him.

Lorentz opened the hatch to give an order. "Captain, get your men forward, we shall cover you."

Three of the five American machine guns were not firing. One was jammed and two destroyed from tank fire. With only two machine guns firing, the Nazi infantry began to advance again.

The American Militia, perhaps not the marksmen their forefathers were, but using superior weapons, began to inflict casualties among the Nazi infantry.

Americans were dying from shrapnel and tank fire, but this was no consolation to the Blackshirts. Many of the Blackshirts were down, wounded or dead.

The Nazi captain rallied his men, they arose amid a hail of bullets. For the Americans to rise up and shoot invited death from the tanks. Henry Windum sighted down his scope, waited until the captain rose again, ignored the death around him, led the captain, and squeezed gently. The captain fell dead. Other Nazis were dropping and now the infantry melted away—moving backward, they beginning to run hunched over and finally bolting for cover. The two Nazi tanks on the road dealing death were immune to the fire from both sides of the road. They were ahead of the main force, the stellar destructors of the Blackshirt force. The Tigers weighed 56 tons, had a speed of twenty five miles per hour and fired a 75-mm cannon. All the American bazooka fire was ineffective.

Crouched on either side of the road were the American destructors. Two groups of young men, all less than twenty years old. The only impressive attribute was their courage. On the right, Fredrick Schultz, Freddie, the son of the American leader. He and several others carried satchels of dynamite. They would attack the monsters on the road on the signal from David Schultz. On the left was Jose Aguire with the sappers from New York. The New Yorkers carried Molotov cocktails. They would be ignited and thrown to shatter against the tank. The blaze usually fed on the oil film covering the surface, turning the tank into an inferno. These young men were the spearhead of the American militia, its cannons, mortars, tanks.

David Schultz saw the Nazi infantry had left the tanks alone and raised his arms—the signal to attack. Freddie broke from cover and ran twenty yards to a clump of small shrubs. It was open with fifty yards to the second tank. Four other young men followed. He arose and was running at top speed toward the road. He ducked, twisted, and with a bound was over the culvert on the road. An amazing leap only an athlete could make. He ducked under the fire of the tank and slapped the satchel against the side. Freddie dove and rolled over the side into the culvert. The explosion rocked the road and the second tank was totally destroyed. Freddie was stunned, bruised, bleeding from his left hand, but he dashed back to the tree line. The machine gun from the Nazis on the other side of the road killed Jose Aguire.

From the right, two other young men raced ahead; they were cut down before they reached the culvert.

Freddie, panting and out of breath, sent the last two forward; they died from the machine-gun fire of the third and fourth tanks.

On the left, the New Yorker sappers were all dead or wounded. For long minutes the Nazi tank fire was unopposed. Half the American force was dead or wounded. Under the murderous fire, Schultz saw a man to his left turn and run. Many Americans were not firing now and some were beginning to edge away.

Schultz could see Freddie crouched by the tree line. He could not—he would not—ask him to attack again. The odds were too great. It was eighty yards away—their eyes met and Schultz did not look away. Freddie nodded at the unspoken order. He arose and ran to pick up a satchel of dynamite. Again the dash to the culvert, ducking and twisting with the grace and power of a halfback. He cleared the culvert. This time the Nazi bullets found him. He twisted and fell back into the culvert. He lay spread eagle, staring at the sky. Death came quick and without pain. He was sixteen years old, the son of a Long Island fisherman.

David Schultz stood paralyzed; he couldn't breathe. It was a greater pain than at Houston. Schultz couldn't move and the American cause was dim. Despite reinforcements the battle was going badly for the Americans. Only one German tank was disabled and the rest were pouring a devastating fire from the road. Then a chance of fate, perhaps luck, the dividend of continuous American pressure. A man, an older man, sixty-two, who came alone that day. Aaron Cade was not there for love of country, for he did not love anyone or anything. Aaron Cade was hard as the rock fence that surrounded his farm, ten miles from Concord. Maybe he hated the Nazis more than he hated the rest of the world, because he moved from the left and picked up two Molotov cocktails from the dead Jose Aguire. Cade slipped into the culvert unseen. He found a break in the culvert and slid through onto the road. Slowly, with patience, he edged to the first tank and smashed the flaming Molotov cocktail against the back of the tank and ignited it. The lead tank went up in a fiery furnace and Aaron Cade slipped back off the road, never seeking or gaining recognition for what he had done. Cade had killed the Nazi leader, an American. Three men heartened by the destruction of the lead tank tried to attack the third tank. Two failed, but the third man succeeded. The Americans would not quit, they were hurt badly, but they would not quit. It was their country and they were willing to fight and die for it.

Lilly from Eastchester was curled up in a ball. She was shivering from fear. When a shell would burst close by she would shake and bite her lip. When the first shots were fired she had dropped to the ground. Her bandages and medical supplies lay in the mud next to her.

A young boy lay dead a few feet away. He lay on top of an American flag he had carried. Perhaps a hundred men were hugging the ground behind her. None was firing his weapon. Some were crawling away too afraid to stand up to run.

Suddenly Lilly heard a roar of a cannon behind her. Had the Blackshirts gotten behind them? No, she saw an American tank. Help had arrived from New York. Schultz, the American leader, waved two more tanks into position. Still outnumbered, but the fight was not as one-sided.

Lilly saw men running toward her, men from her village. She saw her cousin leading several others still too far away to fire at the enemy. Lilly got to her knees and tried to yell at the men behind to join the fight but the noise was too great.

She staggered to her feet and pulled the American flag from underneath the dead boy. She faced the Americans near her and waved the flag back and forth. Several tightened the grasp on their weapons. But none fired.

Now Lilly faced the enemy. She held the pole with two hands extended above her head and began to wave the flag defiantly at the Nazis. Men moved forward, some on one knee, and fired their weapons. But none stood straight up as the five-foot-tall, ninety-eight-pound woman. She was the rallying point.

The smoke began to billow on the road—three tanks were on fire. Allen was directing more volunteers to either side and now people were firing again at the Nazi tanks. Captain Adu was frozen with fear. He knew Colonel Lorentz was dead and the smoke was blinding. He could see more Americans arriving every minute, streaming down the hills. Captain Adu panicked; he ordered his tank off the road and two others followed him.

They turned and churning dust and dirt went around the end of the column and rumbled east back to Boston. This was a dividend of Major Kim's selection of the poorest tank crews for the battle.

Four tanks were left on the road, leaderless. The smoke and noise deafening and blinding. A machine gun opened fire on the left and the small arm fire was heavier than at any time. The numerical superiority was beginning to be felt. Men and women were pouring fire at the tanks. A tank pulled off the road and hit a mine. The crew was not hurt, though the vehicle was disabled.

Schultz, kneeling on one knee, knew he could not help his son. He was responsible for the people fighting fiercely at his side. The test of wills was over; it was time to finish the battle. David stood up; he was two hundred yards from the closest Nazi. A hail of bullets and machine-gun fire crisscrossed the road. Smoke billowed from the two tanks directly in front of him and now over five thousand Americans were firing from the perimeter. Some were carrying battle flags from past wars. The American leader began to walk directly toward the Nazis. Allen, waving on ever-increasing numbers of people into the battle, saw Schultz stand up. He was afraid David would be hit; Schultz was walking toward the enemy. Allen began to wave for people to move forward. Slowly men and women began to move, some crawling, some hunching over.

Hundreds were close enough to throw grenades and Molotov cocktails, people leaped on the tanks and fired into the open slots.

Finally, with a rush, they charged and minutes later the battle was over.

Chapter XII

The shouts and shooting stopped and the burning tanks signaled an American victory. The battle was over and the silence was broken by the cries of the wounded. After such a great effort, many stood in shock not able to hear or speak. Allen saw Schultz carry his son away from the road and up the hill under the trees.

Schultz's eyes filled with tears as he carried the lifeless young man away from the smoke and pain of the scene. He ached for the loss of his son.

Allen waited. Did David want to be alone? No, this was a time for a friend to share the grief of a father's sorrow. Schultz turned away when Allen sat beside him. They did not speak. Finally Schultz pointed to a tall oak.

"There's good shade there, I think we will put him there."

Allen went down the hill, got a shovel, and dug a grave. The surrounding hills cast shadows in some parts of the valley. They sat under a tree watching the clouds pass in front of the sun and create sections of dark green on the hillsides.

People were bringing food and medicine to help the wounded

and exhausted soldiers. The second great battle of Lexington was over.

After they buried Freddie they were lost in their own thoughts. For a long time Allen thought that at the end of the battle when Schultz had walked ahead of the American tanks toward the Nazi tanks that he wanted to die. He would never ask him that question.

Schultz sat against a tree. He was numb. He could not win another battle like this. His son, Freddie, was gone, part of his heart was dead. Tomorrow he must give orders and strategy to thousands who waited and bled and fought and deserved his best, but that was tomorrow.

Schultz had a favorite picture of Freddie. They had been out sailing and as they came into the inlet Freddie at ten years old hung from one of the wires. His leg far over the side and laughed. Schultz snapped the picture and it was in his wallet. He vowed to look at that picture every day for the rest of his life. Schultz would begin many traditions at that time. He would come once a month to the grave and the day after he took the oath as president of the United States he would visit this site. Occasionally his best friend, William Allen, would join him. They would sit on one of the small benches under the trees by the grave. By then this place had become a national shrine. Many graves were in this hallowed ground bought and paid for with American blood. Whenever he came, Schultz was deeply touched because there was always fresh cut flowers at Freddie's grave even in winter. If the grave of Freddie Schultz was the most honored grave in this place, second was the grave of a woman. It was said she died waving an American flag at the end of the battle and she was a local woman it was said.

Schultz was trying to remember the poem by Alfred Tennyson, "Crossing the Bar." He could only remember a few lines.

When I put out to sea for though from out our Bourne
of time and place
The flood may bear me far
I hope to see my pilot face to face
When I have crossed the Bar.

Yes, to go to sea and meet God.

It was dark when they descended to the road and Henry Windum was waiting for them. Windum spoke to Allen.

"I know this is a bad time, but someone should speak to Winfred Ho." Windum pointed to a small Chinese boy sitting on the running board of a truck, an old army jacket around his shoulders. By the light of other trucks one could see his face was a mass of cuts and bruises.

"We left him and two other men at the junction. But when the big trucks came through carrying the tanks they were going so fast and with all the dust they turned the wrong way. Ho chased after them, fell down several times. Finally caught them after two miles when they were going up a hill. He got them turned around. I know it's a bad time," Windum repeated.

Allen shook his head.

"No, it's a good time."

Allen walked over to Schultz and explained what had happened. Schultz sat down next to Ho, put his arm around his shoulder, and spoke softly to the boy.

It was the right time.

If Lexington was a small battle, great battles were fought in Europe. After the army and the Blackshirts heard of the demise of the Reich chancellor, both moved quickly on the news of his death. The navy remained neutral, waiting to side with the victors. It was expected that the Blackshirts, who controlled the air force, municipal government, large secret police force, and all troops in foreign countries, would win quickly.

However, they suffered a number of embarrassing defeats. Two developments changed the balance of power and upset their plans. The civilian population unexpectedly sided with the army and gave them support. Also, many air force units deserted the Blackshirts and fought with the army. Both sides used atomic weapons the first day and two days later, with the country devastated, declared a truce. At the truce both sides agreed not to use atomic weapons and the fighting started again the following day with conventional weapons.

Fighting for control of the Fourth Reich was a life-and-death struggle and neither side reacted to the news of the uprisings in the captured territories. Only victory in Germany mattered.

Berlin knew that America, Canada, Greece, and Norway were in active revolt and that serious fighting in Vietnam and the Philippines tied up their troops. The last areas were shared with the Japanese.

The Blackshirts, confident in the beginning, were on the verge of panic. The civilian population, who lived in fear of them, continued to support the army with acts of sabotage. Without the iron discipline of the chancellor, the Blackshirts stumbled and there were stories of high officials attempting to flee to Switzerland. The army resented the Blackshirts' power, for they fought the battles and suffered the casualties in Russia, France, and around the world.

The army was uneasy about the death camps and excesses of the Blackshirts in the captive countries. When many air force units came over to the army side this took away the advantage the Blackshirts expected would lead them to victory. The air units pulled away from the occupied countries, were neutralized and destroyed as they arrived in Germany. With the skies neutralized, the army was confident they could destroy the Blackshirts in a matter of days.

The army's plan was to mass two great forces, one east of Berlin and the other west of the city and roll through the Blackshirts. Their jets would assemble just outside the city and fly close support. The final victory would present the great problem of how the rest of the world would be treated. The general staff was in agreement that a more liberal policy of treating the German people must be immediately implemented. Foreign countries could not be totally dominated and in some cases like North America, perhaps a lasting treaty should be signed and no attempt made to occupy such areas. The general staff was in agreement that France and Russia must remain under Nazi control.

These were historic enemies and would be a threat to the new Germany if allowed to rule themselves. Indeed, they were considered inferior people and not worthy of self rule. The French were a decadent people and the Russians an uncivilized race. The English were respected and would not be occupied as long as a friendly government remained in power. Spain was an ally and would dominate southern Europe and North Africa with Italy as a partner. The northern countries of Norway, Sweden, and Denmark would continue to be controlled by political parties that accepted the German supremacy in the world. The army considered its policy liberal and by Blackshirts' standards it was. They did not understand the hatred of all things Nazi.

Ten years of occupation would not be forgotten by the English or the Dutch. The captive peoples did not differentiate between the Blackshirts and the army. They were German and represented the greatest tyranny mankind had ever known. It would be difficult to control the world's people by treaty as the democratic peoples were not able to convince the Germans after World War I to exist in peace.

There German people did differentiate between the Blackshirts and the army. The Blackshirts terrified them, and every man was subject to arrest and internment in their death camps.

The great wealth that was stolen from the captive nations was not shared with the population, but kept for the Blackshirts and their supporters. The people considered the army part of the heritage of Germany. The Wehrmacht had defeated armies all over the world, even successfully invaded North America. It was a subject of pride, with a glorious record. The Army sponsored the Olympic Games at the 250,000-seat Nurenberg Stadium. This was a public-relations triumph and was deeply resented by the Blackshirts, who had originally allowed the army to control the Games. The Games were testimony to the greatness of the German nation.

The country greeted directions from the Reich chancellor in the Great Hall with less enthusiasm that called for greater sacrifices from the people. The battle in Germany affected all the world's peoples.

A minority would have sided with the Blackshirts. In most of the world's nations, this minority controlled the governments. Outside of Germany, the world leader waited for news of the civil war, his fortune tied to the victory of the Blackshirts.

Major Kim in Boston would have been more concerned if he had known the true situation of the Blackshirts. He was told by the Reich protector he could not expect any reinforcements at this time from Germany. The Reich protector downplayed the civil war. He said that a small uprising had taken place in Europe and this was the reason for the absence of the jets. The Reich protector also discounted the seriousness of the American uprising. The major was not fooled. The situation in America was serious. If the Blackshirts limited their support, they had troubles elsewhere. The return of Captain Adu and news of the defeat at Lexington gave him mixed feelings.

He executed Captain Adu for cowardice and this gave him pleasure. Sooner or later he would have taken his wrath out on the captain. His retreat from Lexington was a flagrant act of cowardice. The major was shocked that the Americans, without heavy weapons, could defeat the tank column. He knew from the battle of Boston Common they could be brave soldiers, but for civilians to defeat tanks was almost inconceivable. The major never saw them fight so fiercely in Southeast Asia. Like many other nations, the Americans would fight harder in defense of their own country than as a conscript overseas. Kim was puzzled that Lorentz acted so foolishly in handling the battle. For the tanks not to flank the Americans was insane. He hated Lorentz and was pleased at his death, yet he wondered how such a veteran tank commander could make such a mistake. The Americans would probably attack Boston, and the major would meet them with new tactics. They would not beat him with suicide infantry attacks.

Major Kim called a meeting of the tank commanders. He was seated at Lorentz's desk, while the rest stood at attention before him.

"Gentlemen, if we wait in Boston the Americans will gather strength and attack us. I propose to take the initiative, leave Boston, and destroy their main force. I have instructed Captain Beckenhauss to study their tactics and drill our troops accordingly. Captain Beckenhauss, how do you suggest I lead our tanks?"

Beckenhauss, a German, stepped forward and snapped to attention.

"The Americans attack under covering fire with suicide squads after they have driven the infantry back. We must support our tanks with infantry. The tanks must go first, with the infantry in close support, some riding on the tanks. We must not allow our units to be in a static position where the Americans can attack with infantry."

Major Kim signaled his approval. "Good, remember some of our Tigers do not have machine guns."

Captain Beckenhauss, second in command, asked, "Do the Americans have any tanks or heavy guns?"

"No, they have little armor and certainly they have not had time to prepare such equipment. They are a civilian army and as such, we are under no obligation to treat any of them as prisoners of war. They do not take prisoners."

His last statement sent a chill through the Blackshirts tank commanders. Most of them had killed Americans without concern. The recognition that they in turn would face an armed, fierce enemy without sympathy made them uncomfortable. They had no illusions of their fate if they lost the battle.

The day after the battle David Schultz slept all day in his tent. Next morning Allen tried to bring coffee to Schultz, but David waved him away.

"I'm tired William, come back later."

Henry Windum spoke to Allen. "The men at Leominster Armory surrendered and this morning we began to assemble some of the guns. There are twenty 88-mm guns at Leominster and plenty of ammunition. In fact we have five of the guns working and the men are practicing firing them. Not only are they a powerful weapon, but very easy to work with. We will be experts in two days."

Allen checked. "So this won't be like the bazooka that failed us?"

Windum answered, "These make the bazookas look like popguns, with armor-piercing shells they'll knock out a tank easy. What are Schultz's orders?"

Allen answered, despite the fact that Schultz had not given any orders, "Just get everything ready; we'll fight in three or four days."

Windum had one more item. "A man named Chamberlain wants to see Schultz."

"I don't think Schultz should see anyone now."

"Well I think he should see him; he is the grandson of Joshua Chamberlain of Maine and his two brothers were killed yesterday."

Allen remembered his history. Chamberlain, the hero of Gettysburg, was the most decorated soldier in the Union Army during the Civil War.

"What does he want?" asked Allen.

"He wants to talk to Schultz. He said he's a fisherman like Schultz and he has something to give to Schultz from his grandfather."

Allen thought this may help Schultz. "Okay, bring him in."

A small man in his fifties, barely five feet tall, came into the tent, dragging his foot. At first Allen thought he was wounded. Then he realized the man was crippled. He was dragging a deformed foot.

"I'm Abraham Chamberlain." When the man shook hands, he had the most powerful grip Allen ever felt; his hand hurt when the man released it.

He brought Abraham into Schultz's tent and shook Schultz awake. He explained to Schultz who Chamberlain's grandfather was.

Abraham shook Schultz's hand, and David recognized the grip of a clammer. Pushing two clam rakes together hours at a time would give someone an iron grip. Abraham was a man on a mission. He did not wait for Schultz to speak.

"My brothers and I came down two days ago when we heard the militia was at Lexington. You have to understand coming from a famous family is not easy. They expect so much from you, so we had to come. I didn't want to be here; I was afraid. I was the runt of the family. My brothers always protected me, so I came along.

He looked down. "My brothers Ted and Eddie were killed by machine-gun fire, but I couldn't fire my gun. I hadn't fired all day, but when at the end you stood up and walked toward the Germans I started to fire at them." He was out of breath; this clearly was very hard for him.

"You being a fisherman like us, I want you to have my grandfather's watch. He carried it at Gettysburg. My father gave it to me when I was little, but I want you to have it."

Schultz realized he must accept this precious gift from Abraham. This was a supreme moment for this man.

Abraham continued, "I'm not a religious man but please join hands with me."

The three men joined hands in a circle. Abraham spoke, "Dear God I have not come to you often so forgive me. I am with brave friends. Protect them O Lord and give them strength for our cause and Lord we pray for my two brothers and David Schultz's son. We know they are with you."

Abraham stopped and all three men said, "Amen." The emotion was so deep that no one could respond and Abraham left the tent.

Schultz sat down and looked at the watch. He was deeply touched.

Allen had to say something.

"We found 88-mm guns at Leominster."

Schultz, now alert, looked up. "88s? I didn't know they had 88s up there."

Allen said, "In fact, twenty guns—and the boys are firing some of them now. Henry said our experienced gunners will be experts in two days; the guns are easy to work with."

Schultz stood up. "I faced those guns in Normandy. They are tank killers; we won't have to use sappers to attack tanks anymore. I saw one gun knock out eight English tanks. We should make plans for Boston." Now Schultz was himself again. He handed William the watch. "This was generous of Abraham. What did his grandfather do at Gettysburg?"

William answered, "Chamberlain's men were attacked all day at Little Round Top. Finally they ran out of ammunition. It looked like the only option was to retreat, but he ordered a bayonet charge and won the day. They gave him the Congressional Medal of Honor."

Schultz again looked at the watch. The day he took the oath of office as president of the United States, he placed one hand on the Bible and in his upraised hand he held Joshua Chamberlain's watch.

Four days after the battle of Lexington, Major Kim's patrols located the main American force. Major Kim led his tanks out of Boston supported by five thousand infantry. They met the Americans twenty miles outside of the city on a grassy meadow. It appeared the Americans would deploy their now-familiar infantry tactics of rushing the tanks with small squads of sappers, while larger groups would attract the enemy fire.

Kim radioed Captain Beckenhauss. "Captain, attack on the left with your tanks and I will attack on the right. Drive through them and display no charity for women and children with them; they are all soldiers."

So the Blackshirt line of twenty tanks advanced with close support, confident they would sweep the field.

Suddenly, from the flanks artillery from the Leominster Armory opened fire. Their fire was accurate, for the guns were manned by veterans of the Asian wars and World War II. Captain Beckenhauss's tank was hit and went on fire. Major Kim was stunned; he had not expected such fire. The Nazi infantry began to experience heavy casualties and three tanks were disabled. Major Kim ordered the tanks to advance faster and reach the American lines. They picked up speed and soon left the infantry behind. Now the Americans opened up with rocket fire and more tanks were disabled. Kim was completely confused; he hesitated and then signaled a retreat. Only half the force heard his orders and several tanks continued forward to be destroyed by concentrated fire.

David Schultz, seeing the Nazi confusion and beginning to retreat, ordered his own tanks to attack. Five Tigers, repainted with blue stars on the side and driven from New York after being refitted by crews that worked two days and nights, rumbled from undergrowth on the right. From the left, three tanks from the armory opened fire and advanced. The Nazis were not prepared for such opposition and the surprise of the ambush destroyed their discipline. Two Tigers collided as they wheeled away from the Americans. Major Kim's tank was hit and the crew scrambled to safety. As the enemy broke, Schultz and Allen ordered the American line to advance and keep control with the pursuit. The rout was on; all Nazi resistance ceased. In a few short rounds of fire the Reich's forces were transformed from the invincible to a featureless mob that strove to escape. The battle was over; only the killing remained. On the flanks, the American tanks burst on the fleeing Nazi infantry. Only two Nazi tanks escaped the battle and both headed north to run out of gas on the road. Major Kim was killed by a bullet from the First American Militia.

The battle for New England was over and that night the American Militia rode into Boston to cheering crowds. The last battle produced the fewest American casualties of the week despite the numbers involved. These were still small actions compared to some of the other battles fought in America. In Texas thousands were engaged outside of Dallas as the Nazis brought reinforcements from Mexico. The constant was the American aggressive attack against their former captors.

At twenty-six years old, Mitch Iberson was the youngest American Underground leader and yet he was in command of the largest area—California, Oregon, and Washington. He looked at his watch. Ten minutes until the glider he was riding in would touch down on the Golden Gate Bridge. He thought of coach Happy Feller, the man who brought him and his twin brother, Richie, into the Underground just after high school. Coach Feller had tried to get the twins into college on a baseball scholarship, but when all sports in America were suspended, they had devoted their energy to revolution instead of sports. The three were naturals at the dangerous business of recruiting and within two years Coach Feller was the leader of all of northern California. He directed the twins to Oregon and Washington, where again they were successful at developing Underground cells, their sports contacts a big part of the success. This all changed when Reich Protector Essner was put in charge of California and he began to pursue the Underground. Coach Feller was captured, along with many innocent people, and shot at Essner's direction. Essner established the evil distinction of killing more Americans than all the other Reich protectors combined. A time of chaos and fear and the Americans turned to the most mature and confident leader available, Mitch Iberson, at twenty-three years of age. Iberson had learned organization from Coach Feller and added his unique style of leadership—very calm, always with a plan—adding the fire from his brother, Richie.

When Richie, at five, had jumped off the two-story garage roof, his mother had said, "Richie, the younger, had jumped first and Mitch had judged when he jumped the softest place to land and jumped next."

Mitch shifted uncomfortably in his seat as the loud sound of the DC 2 motors, pulling the glider, drowned out all sound. He looked at his brother in the cockpit, ready to pilot the glider to land on the long entrance to the bridge from the San Francisco side.

His brother, Richie, turned to the group inside and yelled above the noise, "Five minutes to the bridge." He held up five fingers.

Mitch looked out the window and saw the first faint rays of the sun coming up, not much wind. Thank God, this was bumpy enough. He looked at Richie and knew his brother was loving this. A chance to land a glider on the Golden Gate Bridge—what a thrill.

When they discussed the plan to barricade the bridge to stop all Blackshirt reinforcements from Marin County reaching San Francisco it was Richie who said, "Let's attack the block house by propping a glider just where the bridge starts and skip the toll booths two hundred yards below. When Mitch questioned the sanity of such a plan Richie had won the argument with the simple answer that there would be fewer casualties if the block house was taken first. At the same time as the glider was heading for the bridge several hundred Americans were preparing to attack the police station in San Francisco.

On the other side of the bridge a Blackshirt garrison of two thousand men and ten armored cars would be expected to attempt to relieve the pressure on the police station. If Mitch and his men could hold them three hours he expected the police station would fall and all the arms distributed and the Blackshirts would never control San Francisco. Suddenly the glider uncoupled the signal three minutes to the bridge.

It was quiet and the fifteen men in the glider locked arms for the upcoming crash. Several of the men had helped to build the glider and now prayed they had built it strong enough.

Mitch looked in the cockpit at Richie hunched over the controls-only his third time to try and land the craft because they were afraid too many practices would damage the glider.

Mitch said silently under his breath, "Do it, Richie, do it."

He could see the twin spans were lined up; they were coming in correctly."

"Do it, Richie, do it."

Twenty feet off the ground Richie hit the chute to reduce speed and the glider bounced once on the ground and skidded to a perfect landing, the right wing touching the block house as it stopped. The impact of the sudden stop threw the copilot out of the front windshield, unconscious.

Richie turned to the crew and yelled, "We're here." But men were out the side door already. The first smoke grenade was thrown and was followed quickly by the explosion of grenades thrown through the opening in the block house.

Now Mitch was reacting. He turned to the radio operator sitting next to him. "Send it," but the man was stunned; his head had hit the roof on the landing. Mitch grabbed the radio. He was the backup operator. The radio frequency was tuned to two stations, an outlaw station in the valley and Mitch's men waiting outside San Francisco's radio station. Mitch flipped the switch and spoke. "Americans on the bridge, Americans on the bridge. Gold Rush, Gold Rush." The signal to attack the police station, capture the radio station, and call for volunteers to help the Underground in the coming fight.

From the outlaw station he heard the welcome answer. "I've got you, Mitch, loud and clear, Gold Rush."

From across the street from the radio station he heard, "We're taking the radio station and we're signaling the attack on the police station, Gold Rush."

Richie was at his side. "We got the block house; is the copilot okay?"

Mitch held up his hand for quiet; the outlaw station was broadcasting. "Americans have taken the Golden Gate Bridge. Gold Rush,

Gold Rush. If you are close to the Golden Gate Bridge or police headquarters in San Francisco the Americans are attacking. We need your help. If you have weapons, join us. If not go to the police station. We will supply you with weapons. The time to strike is now. Strike for yourselves. Strike for your family. Strike for your country."

The big radio station would begin repeating this message five minutes later.

Matty Plummer leaned inside the glider and yelled, "We got the block house and I can see the headlights of our men heading to the toll booths." The sky was beginning to brighten but it was dark at the bottom of the bridge.

Mitch looked at his brother. "Good landing, Richie."

Richie was euphoric. "The wing hit the block house; didn't mean to come that close."

Richie's sense of humor didn't desert him. "How about we do it again tomorrow Mitch? I'm sure I can do it better."

The radio operator groaned. He was okay but groggy. Mitch handed him the radio. "The outlaw is on the air. Check to make sure the big station comes on the air."

Mitch exited the glider and flexed his knees. He was a bit wobbly. He looked at Matty. "Report!"

"No casualties, Mitch, except the copilot. Has some broken bones."

Mitch did not waste time. Lots to do. "Okay. Matty, take five men and move down the bridge and report back what's going on at the toll booth."

Now they could hear shots at the toll booth area.

Mitch turned to Richie. "You want to do it again tomorrow? Try and find some volunteers, because once is enough for me. Now take three men one hundred yards up the bridge and if anything moves report back quick. Once the buses are here you come back on the double."

The plan was once the toll booths were secured, large school buses would drive to the block house area and be set up as a barricade. The radio operator called out, "The big station is on the air."

Mitch signaled he heard. The operator signaled again. "The boys have the toll booth. They'll be here in a minute."

Mitch looked down the bridge. He could see cars coming toward them, then men in trucks, and finally one hundred yards back several yellow school buses slowly were beginning to climb the upgrade.

Matty was back. "They're coming." He thought he had never seen Mitch so calm. Mitch was going through a checklist in his head—so far, so good.

"All right, Matty, the school buses will be here. You take charge. Line them up and turn two of them over to build the barricade. No gasoline until I say." If the Blackshirts could break the barricade, Mitch planned to set the buses on fire.

One of Richie's men, breathless from running, was at Mitch's side.

"A German scout car came to the middle of the bridge. Took a look and turned around and went back."

"Go back and tell Richie to bring everybody here and the buses will be here soon."

The man asked, "Don't you want us to be a forward lookout?"

Mitch's answer was why the men had so much respect for him. "No, I think we will be putting a lot of fire on the bridge and I don't want anybody out in front of us. Also, we'll put men up on the bridge wires; they'll be good lookouts for us. He put his hand on the man's shoulder.

"Tell Richie to come back."

Now the cars were there with the bazookas. Mitch took his three squad leaders aside, who reported only one casualty at the toll booths.

"The two outside buses will be turned over. The middle one is upright; place your bazooka and machine guns so you have a good field of fire."

"Ned, place your snipers and lookouts on the girders of the bridge and tell your men to hold their fire. We have a forward reconnaissance coming back."

Ned's men were climbing the bridge. He yelled, "Hold your fire; we have guys coming in."

Ned turned to Mitch. "How many do we have at the barricade?"

"We should have five hundred."

And Ned asked the big question. "How many volunteers do you expect?"

Mitch answered, "I hope at least one thousand; the trucks have guns for that many. Now Ned you go back to the toll booth and coordinate and arm any volunteers. Send them up here with one of your men, one hundred at a time.

Mitch believed that if the militia could hold the Blackshirt reinforcements at the bridge long enough, all resistance to the militia in San Francisco would fail.

The radio operator called, "The attack on the police station has started. Our guys say volunteers are coming in already. Mitch was surprised the radio call had only been broadcasting for ten minutes and already people were joining the Americans.

Now Richie was back and the truck loaded with armed militia and the buses were at the barricade point.

Ned turned to Mitch. "My guys are ready and I've just spoken to the toll booths. They've got fifty volunteers already and most of them have guns."

Mitch was astonished. They had been on the bridge only fifteen minutes. Where were these people coming from?

"Ned, you better get down to the toll booths and remember, only one hundred at a time."

"Richie." Now Mitch spoke as the American leader, not as his brother. "When Ned's people bring the volunteers up, you take charge; don't let them mix with our people. Hold them as a reserve—if we have enough we may use them as a counterattack."

Mitch signaled Matty. "Matty we may have more volunteers than we thought. Position the middle bus so we can move it quickly and leave a gap that we can attack if we see an opportunity."

Matty was surprised; it was supposed to be all defense.

"I can hold the bus back a few feet behind the other two and it will still be a barricade. If we move, it will create a big opening.

"Good!"

The sun was up now. It was going to be a beautiful day.

A lookout perhaps one hundred feet up called down. "The German armored cars are on the bridge, no infantry, moving very slowly. Will take ten minutes to get here. The first bus was overturned and the men were positioning their weapons.

Mitch yelled to his squad leader, "Hold your fire until they get here; they can't know what's happening." He signaled the snipers to wait.

The German armored cars slowly came halfway across the bridge and waited for two hundred infantry to join them. By the time they started again it was twenty-five minutes since they first had been spotted. The Blackshirts had tried to call the block house and the toll booths. When they got no answer, they were puzzled.

The barricade was complete with all Mitch Iberson's firepower ready. Six bazookas and seven machine guns.

Richie crouched with two hundred volunteers about fifty yards behind the barricade. Mitch moved to the volunteers, who sat silently waiting orders. He was glad he had held them back. There would be no premature firing; his men would wait. Mitch could see many of the men were military veterans by their hats and jackets. He could also see another one hundred were coming up the bridge.

He held up his hand. "I'm Mitch Iberson; I want to thank you men for joining us. Now here is what we are going to do. The enemy has a reconnaissance in force, three cars and perhaps two hundred infantry. We're going to let them get close and then blast them. Then we'll pull the yellow bus away and we want you men to attack through that gap.

Several men called out "Let's go, this is what we're here for. Just tell us what to do."

Mitch signaled for attention. "This is my brother, Richie; just follow him."

Mitch turned to Richie, "Move the group up a little; you have another one hundred in a couple of minutes. Tell them what we're doing. When I signal, go like hell. I think the Blackshirts won't know what hit them."

Now Mitch could hear machine-gun fire from the front two cars; they were firing from two hundred yards away and doing little damage. No American had fired his gun.

Mitch hunched over and ran to the barricade. He would wait.

At less than one hundred yards Mitch cried "Fire!" A wall of fire exploded from the Americans. One armored car blew up as two bazooka shells hit it. Simultaneously, a second car on fire was out of action. The third car hid behind the one on fire close to the rail of the bridge. Half the German infantry was dead or wounded. The rest hugged the roadway, stunned at the unexpected overwhelming firepower that greeted them. Mitch was on his feet. The bus moved and in less than a minute Richie and the volunteers were racing forward, with no Germans firing at them. Instantly Germans rose with hands up to surrender. The volunteers with shouts and whoops, began to round up the enemy nearest them.

The third armored car hoisted a white flag but one of the gunners, not hearing the order to surrender, fired at the Americans, wounding four men.

The Americans covered the car with fire. Now Richie was in front of his men. "Push it over the side." The group mobbed the car, tilted it on the railing, and sent it spinning over two hundred and fifty feet into the bay. A huge cheer rose from the American side. The Nazi car thrown into the bay was sweet after ten years of occupation. The moment was electric and even Mitch grinned.

"I don't know how Richie is going to top today."

One of the snipers with field glasses called down.

"The Blackshirts are gathering on the other side of the bridge—cars, infantry, and two tanks."

Mitch ordered Matty to get the men back behind the barricades, and get the gas ready if they couldn't hold the tanks.

If Mitch was exploring his options, the Nazi commander was really confused. In less than an hour he had been roused from his bed to find all his communications with San Francisco cut off. He had sent a patrol to the other side of the bridge and seen it destroyed. Twenty minutes ago firing from hills above had started, now hundreds of Americans were firing down on his men. He had two hundred casualties. One of his tanks was firing on the hill with little effect. The Americans had thrown one of the armored cars into the bay and it had frightened his men. With his tanks he could probably break the barricade, but spotters told him there were hundreds, perhaps thousands, of Americans at the base of the bridge on the other side. He did not want to retreat and leave his base of supplies, but could he stay here?

Mitch looked down near the toll booths. There were over three or four thousand men and more coming. He could see cars and trucks with men and women coming from miles down the highway. The radio told him that the same thing had happened at the police station. They had expected hundreds of volunteers; instead there were thousands. For the first time that morning he knew he could hold the barricade and probably defeat the forces opposed to him.

Ned was at his side. "This is unbelievable; we've run out of arms but most have guns anyway. A new supply will be here from the police station."

Mitch replied, "The Nazi commander is seeing the same thing we see. In another couple of hours, we'll outnumber them ten to one. He must be taking casualties from all that firing from the hill. Take a car with someone who speaks German under a flag of truce and go over there. Tell him San Francisco is lost. If he surrenders immediately we'll accept it, but if he wants to fight, we can't control our people and I think they won't take prisoners. Tell him he has ten minutes."

Mitch knew this was not a bluff. He would not be able to protect the Germans if they did not surrender.

Ned drove over the bridge and delivered the ultimatum. The German commander accepted the terms. His only question, "Who are you?"

Two hours later Mitch had everything organized. They had transportation for two thousand men. The German cars and tanks would be driven by prisoners until the Americans became more familiar with the vehicles. Los Angeles called, like San Francisco, the response for volunteers was overwhelming. Reich Protector Essner had escaped from Los Angeles, but San Diego revolted and Essner was trapped on the coast highway.

Mitch spoke to Richie. "We leave in an hour unless you have something to do later today."

Richie pulled an old beaten baseball cap from his pocket. Mitch had not seen that hat in years; it was Coach Feller's old hat. Richie pulled it on tightly. "Still looks good. He always said this hat would lead when we finally beat the bastards. What do you think the coach would have said about today?"

Mitch laughed. "He would have said that your approach to the bridge was a bit too high. But with practice you'll get it right."

Chapter XIII

Reich Protector Essner stood on a hill overlooking Avalon, a sleepy beach community on the island of Catalina, twenty-two miles off the California coast.

He was instructing his adjutant where to place the guns.

"Place a gun in that crest." His hand swept across the magnificent view of blue sea lapping on a white sand beach. A pier extended from the beach out into this harbor. Small boats were tied to one side of the pier and similar fishing and pleasure boats rode at anchor on the calm crystal blue water. The surrounding green rugged mountains embraced the white buildings of the town of Avalon, a picture of incredible beauty. The Reich protector looked at the scene, but he did not see the beauty—only a defensive position to prepare against the Americans he expected to attack later in the day.

"Make sure all the guns can sweep the piers. They will land there. They must—they have only the big steamers to carry their men."

"Reich Protector, after we destroy their landing party shall we receive reinforcements and return to the mainland?"

"Yes. Yes, Albert. We shall be receiving reinforcements shortly. We must hold them for two or three days," he lied. There were no reinforcements coming; there was a submarine coming for him tomorrow if they could hold. He must lie, so they would fight hard. He would leave his men to the Americans. However, he would come back and avenge them. He was not naïve, to believe this would satisfy the Blackshirts who were preparing the defense. Yet he must leave to get reinforcements and return to punish the Americans. He would punish them, so they would curse the day they turned on Reich Protector Essner. There would be death camps, not just for Jews, but for all.

Now the Americans had too many, they were not equal to the Blackshirts, but now there were too many. They had driven the Blackshirts out of Los Angeles with both sides suffering heavy casualties. He heard the fighting in San Francisco on the Bay Bridge was hand to hand with the Americans driving the defenders back and hurling the Nazis from the bridge into the bay.

"Albert, has the radio picked up any other Reich protector or Blackshirt signal?"

"No, Reich Protector, we had contact with Dallas until this morning, then it went dead. We have attempted to call all the Reich protectors, but we get no answer."

"Berlin was foolish not to let us have communication among the other Reich protectors in America. They did not even answer our calls after the Americans started attacking. Berlin abandoned us while we remained loyal to them."

He stopped talking, lapsing into private thoughts. All week long during the uprising he repeated the theme that nagged in his mind. He repeated it again. "The Americans caught us by surprise because we did not warn each other."

He assumed the rest of the Reich protectors were dead, and when he returned he would be the leader of all America. He would insist that Berlin not regionalize the occupation. If they thought he was severe before, when he returned there would be a gallows in every American town.

Albert made a suggestion, "Reich Protector, should we try and ask the Americans for a truce until our help arrives?"

"No, Albert, they would not give us a truce. The Americans have vowed to kill me. They are not an army, but a mob. You cannot talk to a mob."

"That is the trouble, Reich Protector, they have no discipline. They have never understood we did not hate all Americans, but only wanted to cleanse their race. Some of them are not inferior. For in the uprising all sectors of the populous rose against us. They do not understand the world order."

Their foolishness reminded Essner of some of his own countrymen. Before the war they had to put many Germans into camps, because they misunderstood the role of government and its citizens. The government was to establish the rules men live by, and each section of society must adhere to these rules. The Nazis has established a perfect world order. The Blackshirts, the most powerful and aggressive people were at the top. Even the army must defer to their wishes. Next would be the greens, people whose value to the government gave them a certain respect in the hierarchy of the order. The reds and the oranges common people; their lives were better for they lived without the confusion of a shifting society. Finally the yellows, a dangerous strain to be eradicated from the world.

For all these people were members of the white race and if this order did not survive, the lower orders, the blacks, the yellows, would destroy them. The Americans were too stupid to accept this.

Albert said, "When we first came here, I thought they would accept us."

The Reich protector inwardly snarled. Albert was foolish, he was not worth taking tomorrow.

"They never liked us, even when we rebuilt San Francisco. The Americans pretended to accept their lot after Houston, but they must have planned this for years."

Albert would never forget the attack on the Reich protector's home last Tuesday. They had attacked like madmen. He and the Reich protector almost did not escape. Then they were driven from Los Angeles and down the coast road with the tanks fighting a rear guard action. With news that another American column was headed north from San Diego, they had taken seven heavy guns and two remaining tanks over to Catalina.

At dawn a patrol boat spotted the Americans preparing the steamer that regularly ran to the island with a vast landing party. The patrol had not returned and they knew the Americans destroyed it.

The Reich protector scanned the defenses. He was uneasy. The Americans should have been here already.

Albert peered through his glasses. Suddenly he focused on a spot on the horizon. "They're here!"

He pointed off to the left, the sun dancing on the water made it difficult to see. It was so bright, without any clouds to shield the sun.

Essner focused his glasses. Yes, the big white steamer. He believed they could only land on the pier and the guns should cover them. There were smaller boats with the steamer.

Slowly, maddeningly slow, the steamer came closer. The Blackshirt troops found the progress agonizingly slow. For almost an hour after they spotted the white steamer Essner waited for it to come into range. It was as if the Americans were teasing them.

Essner felt his stomach turning. He wanted it to begin.

Essner felt for his pack of cigarettes. Only one left. He looked down at his feet. He had smoked a pack in the last two hours;, the stubs lay on the ground. He felt uneasy. Why didn't they attack?

The submarine was scheduled to arrive at dawn tomorrow. Could they hold out that long?

"Reich Protector, Reich Protector!" He and Albert turned to see a man running up the path to them. "The Americans, the Americans. They landed on the other side of the island; they are behind us—thousands of them—they will be here in a minute!"

Essner looked wildly about. A trick! The steamer was a decoy! Now the white steamer was heading for shore. They were trapped between two American forces. They heard small arms fire on the flanks. The Americans who had used hundreds of small boats during the night to land on the island were filtering behind the Blackshirt defensive positions facing the harbor.

Albert cried out in fear, "What do we do?"

Essner pointed to the harbor. "A small boat—we've got to get a small boat." It was a mile from where they stood down the winding path and streets of Avalon to the pier. He could see figures moving toward them from the ridge above.

"We've got to hurry." He threw away the field glasses and began to sprint down the path. Halfway down, the shooting was very heavy. As they reached a paved street, he could see Blackshirts in front of them a half mile away crouching on the beach, driven from their position on the right. Some men were attempting to launch a small boat from the pier. "Cowards," he cursed them. The white steamer and other American small boats were coming at full speed into the harbor. No Blackshirts were firing the heavy guns; they had abandoned their guns and were running for safety. Albert tripped in front of him and rolled down the steep grade of the street. Essner decided to keep going. He swerved to avoid Albert, then he saw the crimson spot on Albert's chest. He had been shot. Essner came to a stumbling halt. Americans at the bottom of the hill coming up after him and firing. Bullets ricocheted off the pavement. Out of breath, his heart pounding, he turned, sweat and fear drenching his shirt. He took two steps when a man emerged from the street on his left. The man swung a rifle butt hitting him in the shoulder and knocking Essner to the ground. He struggled on all fours, pain coursing through his arm, staring at the man who stood in front of him.

"Don't shoot me," he gasped. "Don't shoot me."

The man, relaxed, he recognized the Reich protector immediately. It would be a rare Californian who did not recognize that hated face.

"We are not going to shoot you, Essner."

Essner did not answer.

A young athletic man roughly jerked Essner to his feet. He pointed to his cap. "See this cap? A great man wore this cap, and you had him shot. I'm going to wear this cap to the court house when they condemn you to death."

Down on the beach, hemmed in on all sides, a dwindling group of Blackshirts were firing at the advancing Americans. The battle for Catalina was finished. The last remnants of the Nazis were destroyed. Nowhere in America did they have control. Many of their sympathizers were free, but they were being hunted. The country grew still as the sounds of battle grew dim.

Chapter XIV

And so the Second American Revolution was completed. Fittingly enough it started at the tip of Manhattan in New York and ended at the westernmost part of California. Millions of Americans participated without reference to age, sex, color, religion. Not even the Underground leaders expected such support, for they had no way of knowing the undercurrent of resolve that existed. A wave of patriotism swept the land more powerful in uniting the country than any political party that existed before. Sunday, exactly five days after the revolution started, America was free after ten years of occupation. A national day of Thanksgiving was observed.

It was not a time of loud joy, for the price of freedom came too high for merriment. It was a rare American home that was not touched by the tragedy of those who gave their lives for the revolution.

Many churches were opened and filled that Sunday. People gathered with friends and relatives. No one considered medals or recognition for the events of the five days. It was impossible, for so many proved so heroic during this period. Political prisoners were released from Blackshirt prisons and the death camps torn down. This was a grim reminder of the evil that was cleansed from the land. Fugitives of the Blackshirts returned from hiding in rural places and were greeted as heroes. A solemn flag raising in Manhattan commemorated the sacrifice of the Americans who gave their lives against the Metro Complex. To ask if the sacrifices were worth the price was sacrilegious, for all gave freely in the effort to defeat the Nazis.

Essential services were quickly restored. Fire service, a volunteer group in most of America, had been a hotbed of the Underground and was quickly on duty. The police department was completely turned over with many former Americans who had been dismissed regaining control. Civil government was purged of all Blackshirts and their sympathizers, though it turned out many had been members of the Underground. The Underground, now the American Militia, was in most cases, the civil government. However, because of the need to reestablish the country a mood of American town meeting prevailed. National leaders were elected with shared responsibility. For it was not a time of the leadership carrying all the burden of government. Americans had been shut out of how their destiny was decided for too long. They wanted to participate and work together, for they realized that the time of peril was not over.

Despite the destruction and damage of the battle, some aspects of life quickly improved. Under the Nazis, the telephone service had been disorganized for each region only supported local service and the local work was very poor.

With a national effort, strong areas helped the weaker and service immediately improved. This was a great benefit to civil and business leaders. With improved communications, insurmountable problems became solvable. The metropolitan area of Cleveland and Detroit, which had suffered food shortages, began to receive grain from the excess in Iowa that had been held back from the region because another Reich protector had controlled it.

The national government headed by the Underground leaders announced national elections in one year. If the victory had been sudden, the leaders headed by Mark Collins agreed that the national government must act as caretakers to coordinate the defense and safety of the country.

Collins did not waste any time forming a cabinet of the Underground leaders representing the geographic areas of the country. The cabinet voted Mark Collins of Texas chairman. The leader of the American Revolution would have won a popular election by a wide margin, much as George Washington was the obvious choice for president after the First Revolution. The cabinet convened in Washington, D.C., the last week of June with prior agreement that some agencies already functioning would give reports.

The eight major geographical regions of the Underground were represented. David Schultz of the Northeast sat at the left of the oak table facing the audience of Americans who were able to witness the first open cabinet meetings. Behind Schultz was his deputy, William Allen. Next to Schultz was Carl Weldon of the Mid-Atlantic region, the tallest member of the cabinet at six foot six inches and the only black member of the cabinet. Third was Ted Tenensky of the Rocky Mountains, a substitute to the Underground leader who was killed during the uprising. Tenensky was the deputy to the fallen leader who died the first day of battle and an able replacement.

Mark Collins of the Southwest sat in the middle and was the only member of the cabinet to know all the others before meeting in Washington. Next to Collins was Kevin Carlson, whom Collins recruited into the Underground in a Miami bar in 1955. Carlson was such a great organizer that the South was the easiest victory for the

Americans. Next to him was Archie Quotoius, a decorated World War II bomber plane ace understood to be the leader of the new American air force. It was Quotoius who planned the attack on the Nazi training jet wing in the Midwest with trucks breaking down the outside fences. The attack spared four planes not operational. So the American air force had four jets and by best count two hundred conventional planes located all over the country. There was no civilian air force; all planes belonged to the militia movement. The seventh member of the cabinet was its youngest, Mitch Iberson, twenty-six. Iberson landed with his fellow Californians on the Pacific side of Catalina Island while his brother delayed outside the harbor and kept the Nazis' attention. Both brothers were in Washington as a team, working together since joining the Underground as teenagers. Last was Martha Lawrence, the widow of the underground leader in the plains states. She and her husband started the Underground organization after their youngest son was shot in 1952. Unfortunately her husband died in the last action of the region, the street-to-street fighting in Omaha. It was a group with a strong common interest, the success of the revolution, and all had paid a price. Only Mark Collins was over forty years old. None was wealthy or represented financial power. They would have been considered middle class except for Kevin Carlson, who came from a famous New England family. They had been tested in the most ferocious of arenas. The leadership of desperate brave men and women challenged by a cruel and powerful enemy. They faced their new challenge, the administration of a mighty country, with confidence, knowing that the enemy still waited on them. In the audience were many members of the new government and representatives of the new agencies

The first report to the cabinet was Adophus Kinder, head of the Department of Industrial Production. Kinder was seventy-two years old and regarded as one of America's greatest industrialists before his retirement in 1950. He worked closely with the Underground during the dark years and immediately took over the large industrial plants in the Midwest on the completion of the uprising. Meeting with the leaders of the auto unions, they agreed that the sabotage and poor work of the occupation would be replaced with top-flight production.

Kinder was tall, white haired, and his ramrod serious mein commanded the attention of the eight members of the cabinet.

He waited until the chairman signaled him to begin.

Kinder cleared his throat. "I will be brief because with the cabinet's permission I wish to return immediately to Detroit. Both labor and management have agreed in general to the following conditions for the next year. All people employed in national defense industries will work six-day weeks and twelve-hour days. This is beneficial because we expect our first tanks off the assembly line in three weeks. You know, of course, it took three months to produce tanks for the Nazis and they experienced great mechanical problems in Southeast Asia. I guarantee that the quality will be superior. Our jet plane production is subject to some bottle necks, but much design work on new improved models was done by designers and engineers during the occupation clandestinely and while it will take us two years to produce the number of planes that the Nazis can turn out, I believe we will make a superior plane. We plan to specialize in defensive fighters and I promise you an outstanding plane in a few months.

"I am especially happy to report that our communication and transportation networks are working far better than we expected. Coal is flowing to Pittsburgh and steel to Detroit. Our people recognize the need to forgo consumer goods under the present conditions.

"We cannot expect our people to work continuously and sacrifice at these levels forever, but for the next year or two they will. The productivity of the American people is a great weapon. Americans are a nation of engineers and mechanics; their love of the automobile proves that. We want our industry to be free and grow with the initiative that is one of our national resources. Thus we have attempted to dispense with large national bureaus instead. Corporations will be structured with stated defense goals and will subcontract to smaller companies; the unions will be major stockholders. I have picked a number of corporate leaders around the country to run these corporations. If they do not produce, we will replace them."

Kinder's list of leaders was called two days after the shooting stopped. Every man he reached jumped at the opportunity to work as a manager again. All accepted the condition that results would determine their tenure.

Kinder continued, "We want no bureaucratic disasters like the Nazi energy policy. It will take much work and much trust, for we will make mistakes, but our people have not forgotten how to work."

The cabinet stood up and applauded Adolphus Kinder and a great wave of confidence was realized among the leaders of the Second American Revolution. Archie Quotoius, who knew Kinder, turned to Kevin Carlson. "Adolphus is serious when he says everyone has to produce; he is one tough guy."

Carlson answered, "I'm really glad I heard this report. A number of the textile people in the South have called me and asked what they could do. Now I know who to direct them to."

Mark Collins called a two-minute recess and followed the old man from the room.

He grasped Kinder's hand. "Adolphus, you've done wonders. We owe you a debt of gratitude. The warmth of his handshake was comforting to Adolphus and the charm of Collins's manner would make many Americans give more than they knew they had. Adolphus Kinder did not require charm or gratitude; he was as happy as he had been in years. Kinder was working twenty hours a day—sleeping in his office and loving every minute of it. No one else could do the job he was doing and he knew it. They would have their tanks and planes before the scheduled time. Never had he seen people more willing to work together; it was the professional manager's dream and he was a professional manager.

The next report was from Wallington, the minister of defense. He said that there was no need for a draft; volunteers from both the militia and civilian population would bring the standing army to one million and the army would be ready by winter. They were overwhelmed by volunteers for the air force, by pilots from the past wars. The navy would be structured for defense with the submarine emphasized as the primary weapon. Three Nazi submarines were captured and would be the nucleus of the undersea fleet.

The final open report was the Justice Department. This report was not so optimistic. The country contained many lawless elements and the major question was would they accept the new civil codes. This was especially true of the many homeless young men who had turned into brigands. All members of the cabinet urged the Justice Department to try and establish a respected court system and it was mentioned that if the young homeless men would join the army they would be housed and fed.

Finally, Chairman Collins ordered the hearing closed and requested that only members of the cabinet and their aides remain. The audience got up and left and the guards closed the doors.

Mark Collins leaned forward. "Under the National Security Agency, I have two reports. First in Asia our friends tell us that Japan is completely tied up with new uprisings in the Philippines and

Indochina. Apparently when the Nazis pulled out in the areas they shared with the Japs, it set off great insurrections. The Japanese are overextended to begin with and it is doubtful we have anything to fear from them at this time. Now our major problem."

There was complete silence in the room, the members of the cabinet were waiting for his every word.

"We do not have any news from Germany about the civil war. We do not have any agents in Germany and no country in western Europe has responded to our radio signal.

"The Nazis have instituted a communications blackout over Europe and we know they're good at that. I suspect not even many of their satellites know who is winning. Gentlemen, we must know what is happening in Germany. Our national policy may depend on events over there.

"The best undercover work and security system was in New York, so I am going to ask David Schultz to take over national security with the major responsibility Germany. A small section under Mike Fumrando has already been set up in the old FBI headquarters and they will report to Dave."

Schultz agreed to take the post last night when Collins spoke to him. It was a tough job and he wished that Michael Ford was alive to help. David nodded his assent when Collins announced the position, but did not speak. Colllins reported that the Canadian revolution was successful and a delegation would arrive in Washington next day to work out mutual defense pacts.

Collins then brought up the second major report. Professor Keating, an expert on atomic energy, was ushered into the room. Once Keating was seated, Collins explained.

"Under national security I have included atomic energy. Because of the secrecy required, I have asked Professor Keating, who worked on an atomic bomb before the war and worked for us in hiding the last five years."

The professor spoke, "We do not have an atomic bomb and I cannot promise you gentlemen when we will have a bomb. As you know, only the Nazis have the atomic bombs and they have enforced a worldwide ban on the development of all materials necessary for the bomb. So no one has a bomb except them."

Now Collins asked Professor Keating what it would take and how long to produce an atomic bomb.

"If we had the money, less than a year. Even with all the willingness of many in industry and labor to work for nothing, it will cost one hundred million dollars for two bombs." The professor had worked on this project for five years in a lab in the Rocky Mountains, an area always controlled by the Americans.

Collins said, "We don't have anything near that kind of money." For five minutes the group talked of what kind of taxes could be levied to raise the money.

Collin's assistant, Mark Hingus, said, "If we develop the bomb what target would we use it against? What is our priority, an invasion by the Japanese? Some kind of attack by the Blackshirts?"

Pat Sandstrom, first in his class at Harvard, was number two to Kevin Carlson and considered to be among the finest minds among the American leaders.

"No, we've got to save the bomb if the Blackshirts establish jet bases in Central America again. Central and South America are still very friendly to the Nazis."

Hingus responded, "To do that we have to develop a bomber to deliver the weapon."

Professor Keating said, "If you plan to use a bomber it may influence the size of the weapon I will be building."

Kevin Carlson responded, "Can we use the two Nazi tanker planes we captured in Baltimore and convert them to bombers?"

Sandstrom replied, "Before we complete building our bombs, perhaps we should use propaganda to show our enemies we have atomic weapons. It may deter them and buy us time."

Kevin Carlson asked Professor Keating, "If we build only one bomb, will it cost less than fifty million dollars?"

By now the meeting had deteriorated to a series of side conversations, and members were jumping from topic to topic. Collins felt helpless. They were not accomplishing anything.

Patrick Sandstrom was particularly agitated. He argued with his boss Kevin Carlson about building one bomb or two. Then he and Hingus got into a heated discussion about the use of tax money, and if there were other national defense projects just as important.

Professor Keating asked Kevin Carlson if he really had a plan to steal materials from the Blackshirts.

The noise in the room had risen so high that Collins could not hear what others were saying.

Sandstrom thought of Aristole's remark about democracy. "A democracy is a government in the hands of men of low birth, no property, and unskilled labor."

Mark Collins tapped his pencil on the table to restore order.

"Gentlemen, one at a time; we are not getting anywhere."

Suddenly Hingus and Pat Sandstrom were standing and shouting at each other arguing whether Kinder should run the project.

Collins was shaken by the riotous behavior; these were important matters. There were so many questions and ideas. Where to start? Collins looked at Professor Keating, who had pushed his chair away from the table and had a look of consternation on his face.

Collins stood. "Stop shouting. Everyone keep quiet. Sit down, Patrick. Sit down, Mark Hingus."

They sat down with sullen looks. No one was satisfied.

Collins could see David Schultz had written several notes on a legal pad. Collins would ask him for his ideas.

"David, what do you think?"

David Schultz adjusted the pad and deliberately said, "Before we address all these very good ideas, we must establish a committee with clear responsibilities and a leader. At the head of the committee, let's call him a czar whom everyone reports to."

Schultz had drawn a box on the second page of the pad with lines moving to other boxes.

"The czar will be in charge and answer only to Mark Collins. Since Kinder is working eighteen hours a day, he cannot do this job, but he will pick the czar and it must be stressed this man does not have to know about atomic bombs, but must be the most talented manager Kinder can find."

Patrick Sandstrom was on his feet; he banged his fist on the table.

"Kinder is our most talented man; he must run the project." The group was speechless because of Sandstrom's outburst.

Sandstrom waited for Schultz's reply. But Schultz did not speak.

Sandstrom declared again, "I'm sorry to interrupt, David, but Kinder. . ." He again waited for Schultz to speak. David Schultz fixed Patrick with a stare. It was said this was the same expression that they saw at the end of the battle of Lexington when Schultz had walked toward the Nazi tanks.

Now Patrick was desperate for Schultz to accept his apology. "I'm really sorry, David." Schultz continued to stare at him. Patrick sat down and mumbled, "I'm sorry."

Schultz resumed as if nothing had happened.

"Once we have a czar in place we have five major areas of responsibility. One of our most critical, the technical side of the work, we are fortunate to have Professor Keating doing the work. Two—financial. This is all our problem. Since I'm head of security and probably will be dealing with the Blackshirts and Swiss bankers, I'll take it for now but anyone with ideas, let me know. Three—transportation and logistics. Let the czar find someone to be responsible for this area; it is very important. Four—security for the project. Let the czar pick the man. Five—strategy. How do we use the bomb? Again, the czar will have overall control of this, but I see two heads working together. Mark Collins should pick out a military man as one half of the strategy side."

Schultz turned to Patrick. "Patrick, you have the most contacts among the university people. Find a man with some atomic energy knowledge, but with vision. It is critical we make the right decisions on the use of the bomb. We won't have many to work with."

For a moment Patrick thought Schultz was extending an olive branch over the explosion, then he thought Schultz does not extend olive branches, he is giving me a job and he expects I will do it right.

Mark Collins asked to see David's notes, silently he scanned the notes and his head nodded affirmatively for the blueprint was accepted for the building of an atomic bomb.

Chapter XV

Mark Collins was in great pain when the meeting ended. Some of them wanted to talk, but he excused himself by saying his wife Sara was waiting. He went into one of the conference rooms in the building and doubled up in pain. The pain was so great he could barely breathe. He didn't want his wife to see him like this. He loved three things—Sara, his country, and Texas. Well, he would never see Texas again. The pain subsided; the thought of never seeing his ranch again saddened him. The doctor said he had a year. A year. There was too much to do with only twelve months left; he wouldn't be able to go back home. The cancer would cause him great pain—the legacy of the atomic blast in Houston. Operations wouldn't help; three doctors told him there was no hope. He had one of the doctors look at Schultz without Dave knowing the true reason. No problem, thank God.

They didn't know he had a year left. He smiled. They didn't realize he gave out all the jobs today, without one for himself. His job was to prepare them for the future when he was gone. He timed the elections so that he could not be a candidate, knowing the people would elect another member of the cabinet. He judged the next president to be Schultz or Carlson.

Carlson was good today. The man was bright and he came up with some excellent ideas in a short period of time. Schultz was brilliant.

Collins remembered the first time he saw Kevin, a bearded drunk in the bar in Miami. He and a few others were all that Mark had in the South. The miracle was not finding him, for Collins didn't think he was any good either, but in developing Carlson. Once Kevin took over he was a man possessed, his intellect overwhelming and drawing the diverse interests together. Carlson was the best leader the Underground had the last two years.

Schultz was different; he was always a great leader. Collins remembered the first time he saw Schultz. A wild man in the fighting in Houston, never losing control and yet a man people turned to in a battle. He remembered his smile and optimism, the way he kept their spirits up.

Schultz was quieter now, the loss of his boy had changed him a bit. He was not as smart as Carlson, yet he teamed up with a good man, Allen. What did they call him? The historian. And he had survived some tough spots. It was so like Schultz to pick someone to complement him.

The pain was gone. He stood up. Well, were any of them as good as the old Texas longhorn? That was his nickname, and he carried it with pride. Now, would the Nazis give them any breathing space? What the hell were they up to? The advantage of the closed society was its security. In his mind, he weighed the alternatives. If the army won, and if it was bloody enough, they might want a truce. The country would have to keep rearming, for in the long run, there could be no peace between them. If the Blackshirts won, it would start again quickly. There would never be a truce with those murderers.

He thought of Carlson. Kevin hated all Germans and he would not want to accept a truce even if it was to the American advantage.

Schultz didn't hate them. He said they were criminals and gangsters and that every country had its share of people who would become Nazis. Maybe because Dave saw them with less emotion he never lost faith in the eventual American victory. Even in the dark days of 1955 when Collins had dark moments, Schultz was confident. "The Nazis are criminals; they'll fold. In the long run, their power will ebb and we'll have our chance," he would say. Collins recollected it so well and thought back to the events that introduced Schultz to the Underground.

* * *

At the time England was signing its truce with Germany, Schultz and two others escaped England in a small sailboat. David was afraid the English would intern Americans who stayed there and he was right. The three men battled storms in the North Atlantic and it took many days to reach land. After reaching Nova Scotia they sailed south and on a snowy December day he maneuvered the sailboat into Oceanview harbor. He had pneumonia and it took a year for his family to nurse him back to health. His wife, Joan, stood by him and with all the sad news of the war, their son, Fredrick, was his great joy. David was assigned to a training group on Long Island until America surrendered.

The following year the occupation started in earnest and ironically he prospered for fishing was lucrative under the Nazi regime since there were food shortages. He expanded the family business from a single boat to a fleet of five. Local people were hungry and it was obvious his business venture could not fail. One night, two old friends came to see him. They asked David to be the leader of the local Underground. The Underground was springing up all over America.

The front for the Underground varied from fraternal organizations, fire departments, fishing clubs, and anywhere people could meet without suspicion. Veterans organizations were banned by the Blackshirts. Joan was against his participation. He had a family and a growing business, she said, he had done enough. His friends prevailed and slowly, carefully, he built a powerful organization on Long Island.

After three years, Nazi oppression reached impossible levels. Active guerrilla war was waged between the Blackshirts and the Underground. Schultz, as the New York regional leader, was invited to a secret meeting in Houston by the national Underground. He remembered the night he told Joan he was leaving for Texas. She broke down and cried.

"You can't neglect us like this."

"I'll be back soon."

"You might never come back; you didn't come back for five years after you went to Europe."

She was not hysterical. He felt a pang of guilt. She was not the person he married and a part of it was his fault.

Schultz tried to comfort her. "I know this is difficult for you; we owe it to our friends and family to turn back the Nazis."

"No, you can't beat the Nazis. They're too powerful. Why can't we live with them; they don't care about us.

"Don't believe that, Joan, if they kill people we don't know today, next they will come for us."

He would not compromise that they could live with the Blackshirts.

"If you go, I won't be here when you come back."

He did leave and in Houston he met Mark Collins, the head of the Southwest Underground and the best-known American leader. The weather was steamy and humid in Houston as the meetings began. Maybe it was the heat or a quirk of fate, but the Nazis attempted to arrest several local Underground leaders who were members of the fire department. Shooting broke out as the Underground resisted the Blackshirts and the incident spread. Within hours the city was in full revolt. Local leaders asked the national Underground leaders to assist and Mark Collins did not refuse, though they all knew the timing was wrong. The people of Houston united quickly and drove the Blackshirts from the city with heavy casualties on both sides. It was a time of jubilation and Collins was preparing to expand the uprising when the Nazis dropped an atomic bomb.

The dead and wounded totaled almost half a million. Both Schultz and Collins were injured, burned by the searing heat of the explosion.

It was over and Collins was forced to go into hiding in Texas while Schultz prepared to return to New York. Collins was depressed, ready to forget the Underground and Schultz tried to cheer him up.

"It could be worse, Mark. You might come to New York and forget you're a cowboy."

Collins forced a smile.

"I'm low, Dave. I don't know if we can start it again."

"Mark, you go home, stay in hiding, let the winter go by and in the spring start it slow and quiet. You and I can't quit, we're in it now."

"I don't know, Dave."

"Look, Mark, what are you going to do, pretend they don't exist? You can't quit as long as the Nazis are here, because you're the best we've got to beat them. We need you, Mark. It's what you do better than anyone else."

Collins managed a grin. "Damn you. A philosopher yet, well, get your ass home and I'll send you a letter in the spring."

When Schultz returned home Joan had left for good, leaving Freddie with Schultz's folks. It was a hard winter. In the spring Schultz and Collins started working again.

Schultz and Allen found Mike Fumrando sitting at a clustered desk piled with papers, looking slightly perplexed.

"Glad to see you guys, there is just so much work to be done and sometimes we don't know where to start. We've set up a staff to deal with national security domestically and we can work with the regional militia staffs. We have some contacts with agents in Asia and a liaison with the Chinese communists, so we can put together a pretty good scenario on the Japanese. They have troubles and if you put some pieces together I guess that might be thinking of the Nazis more than us."

Mike Fumrando was a veteran secret service agent and he could make some interesting guesses. His natural suspicions allowed him to put together bits and pieces, add a dash of the national character of the people he was analyzing and deduce answers.

Allen said, "Mark Collins directed us to find out what's going on in Germany. Do we have any information on Europe?"

Mike ran a hand through thick black hair, his dark complexion wrinkled in a frown. "Nothing, we have nothing coming from there, it's unreal the silence."

He blurted it out, as if to share the burden of the mystery.

Schultz asked, "Do we have any contacts or agents in Europe?"

"Two. Mike Cafferty is a retired American businessman who went back to live in Ireland before the war. He's a personal friend of mine and we've corresponded with him for years. Mike's old and in bad health. However, he can travel on the continent and he'll do whatever we ask."

"Okay, who is the second?"

"The ambassador in the Brazilian embassy in Switzerland is with us. We can reach him on the radio, yet he can't seem to find out what's going on in Germany."

"Does the ambassador have anyone who will go into Germany?" Allen questioned.

Mike responded, "I don't know; we can try. The most recent call mentioned that a prominent Swiss banker close to the Nazis appears to be desperate for money. It's all over Zurich that he's got a problem."

Allen looked at Schultz. "We've got gold from the holdings of the Reich protectors. Why don't we offer it to the man for information?"

Schultz redirected the question to Fumrando. "Will the Brazilian ambassador contact the banker and make him an offer—gold for information?"

"I'll radio and see."

Schultz and Allen waited in Mike's office reading the pile of reports, while Fumrando sent the message to the Brazilian. The ambassador radioed back he would make contact with Herr Heinz. Now there was nothing to do except wait.

The ambassador went to see Herr Heinz. He explained that he represented an overseas power that needed information on the status of the civil war in Germany. The overseas power was willing to deliver gold for such information. Herr Heinz was puzzled; the rumors of the civil war and the political and military positions of the world far outstripped the solid information that was available.

He could understand the Japanese, or perhaps even the Americans, wanting him to get reports on the civil war. He heard stories that the Americans had successfully revolted. It was maddening to try and make investments in a world of darkness. World order had to be restored and Germany was the key. Herr Heinz was tempted, very tempted. He needed money; the market had gone against him.

The only way was to travel to Germany. For an instant he considered it. No, it was too dangerous; he would borrow from the winner in Germany. He would not gamble on spying against the Nazis.

* * *

Mike Fumrando brought the disappointing news. Schultz said, "You better get word to Mike Cofferty. It will be slow; we got to get moving."

When they left the building, David and William walked in silence. The heat of the day was ebbing along the Potomac. They could see the great cemetery as they walked.

"David, do we have time to land agents and establish a network of spies?" Allen asked.

"William, we'll have to do that in time; however, we just can't depend on that now."

They walked further, pausing at the water's edge.

Schultz said, "Suppose we try to set up a system of transmitters to pick up any radio signal from Germany."

"Can we be sure they'll break their radio silence?" Allen asked.

"No, we can't count on that."

They started to walk again, oblivious to everything but the problem. They considered dropping a parachutist into Germany, but discarded the idea when the question of fuel for the plane and getting the man out made it impractical. Even the use of the captured submarine was considered. There were too many logistical questions. They continued to walk well after dark, posing and turning down idea after idea, beginning to believe it was foolish to try and solve a problem that was virtually unsolvable. Maybe luck would come their way—a decision would be reached in Germany and the Nazis would announce to the world the victor.

As they approached the hotel Allen said, "David, listen to this.

We run down a Nazi agent or sympathizer in this country and see who's giving him his orders. We'll find our answer right here in America."

Schultz stopped. "If an agent or one of their friends is in contact with the winner, it will tell us what and where. Maybe we can turn him around, make him work for us. William, I think you've got an idea."

Schultz appointed Henry Windum head of state security for the Northeast. Windum's agents purged the files of the Blackshirts at the Metro Complex and arrested several Blackshirt secret agents and Red Harter.

A meeting was convened at the American headquarters with David Schultz, William Allen, Henry Windum, and Red Harter. Harter recognized Allen as the American agent he had brought to the Metro Complex what seemed ages ago, but was only weeks.

Allen began the meeting. "Harter, we need information. The subject we want to know about is what is happening in Germany and what is the status of the civil war?"

Harter adjusted his red prison jacket. This was the bargaining chip he was looking for; they needed him.

"I would love to help," he said. Allen could tell a "but" was coming.

"But . . ."

Harter twisted in his seat, his smile a warning the price would be high.

"But I need to be out of prison to help you and it will take money!"

Red fiddled with the button on his jacket. He could stall this out; it might take months and perhaps he could escape.

Allen was impatient. "We don't have a lot of time."

Harter answered, "Look, I've got to run down contacts, make calls. You can't expect me to work miracles. I've been in jail. You fellows put me there. I may have to travel."

Harter was trying to blame them for any delay on his part to get information. It was the classic Red Harter "I didn't do it, and even if I did, it was not my fault" defense.

Allen and Harter haggled for twenty minutes about what support he would receive from the Americans, with occasional comments from Henry Windum. How much cash he would need, would he be watched, some of his contacts needed to be assured no one would arrest them, if he could get the information would he be paroled.

David Schultz was ominously silent.

Schultz cleared his throat, a signal for the group to listen. He produced an official-looking paper from his briefcase. Harter listened with concern.

Schultz began. "This is a writ issued in the sovereign power of the National Security Agency. A grand jury has investigated Red Harter for crimes against the American people. You have been charged and convicted with the death of the following Americans." He read off names of seven Americans including Judy Tyler, the code clerk from the Metro Complex. Schultz placed the paper on the table. "If I sign this writ you will be executed."

Harter protested, "That's illegal." Schultz brushed aside his protest. "Numerous other crimes are still pending—treason, extortion, etc. I will sign this in two weeks unless you show us real progress in what we want to know."

Schultz had given Harter the ultimate motivation to help them.

He stood up, put the paper in his briefcase, and walked out.

Harter did not have to ask if Schultz meant it. The man had made great sacrifices for his cause. Red Harter's life was of little consequence to him.

Harter turned to Allen now. He was serious. All that had gone before was a game.

"I have to work out of my office. I'll need two dedicated phone lines, phone operators twenty-four hours a day, perhaps an overseas transmission, and I probably will have to promise some big cash payments."

Allen agreed to the terms with a warning. "Don't try to escape."

David Schultz, William Allen, and Henry Windum sat at a large conference table at Schultz's new headquarters in the Empire State Building.

Windum fed a spool of tape into a tape recorder. He explained, "Red Harter made ten phone calls over the lines we provided before he made this one. This was made over a secure phone. If someone is listening, the line will buzz, but we found a way to tap the phone by recording the message. He couldn't tell we were taping. This was done this morning; the call was from Red Harter to a brewery in Albany, New York."

"Hello, I'm calling from New York."

"Yes."

"The Americans have come to me with a proposal. If I help them find out what is happening in Germany they will pay two hundred thousand dollars in gold for the information."

Long pause. "You want me to help?"

"I do Herr Schoenriest. Things have changed, I think we have got to change sides here. The Blackshirts are finished and we need to join the new powers in town."

"Mr. Harter, it may be easy for you to change, but I still have an organization to run." Schoendriest was still pretending.

Harter's voice betrayed anger.

"Organization, my ass! The Nazi movement in America is finished. They arrested every Blackshirt and Gestapo agent in New York. That fool Kroft had a list of names in his office and they have the names. You had one agent in all of the Atlantic region. One agent for the great Gestapo. Now I'm switching sides and if you can help, you better too. We can split the money, but if we don't produce something we're both finished."

"Is that a threat?" said Schoenriest.

"Herr Schoenriest, I don't threaten, but if we both want to live let's give them what they want."

Windum switched off the machine. "The call ended there," he said.

Allen spoke. "Glad to see Red's loyalty to his cause remains firm." He smiled.

Windum pressed a button on the machine and the tape moved forward.

"Here is a second call from Schoenriest back to Harter one hour later."

"Calling New York."

"Yes, Herr Schoenriest."

"I'm in touch with someone who recently came from Germany. He has talked to me about the situation and will strike a deal with the Americans. He wants asylum and I do too. For the right price we can tell them what they want to know.

"Does he know who won the civil war?"

"Yes, the Blackshirts won." Allen, Windum and Schultz all looked at each other in surprise. Rumor from all previous contacts they had made had the army winning, but they were only rumors.

Windum held up his hands and Red Harter spoke.

"Do you know who the new Reich chancellor is?"

"Yes, Herr Albert Lobert is the new Reich chancellor—a former colleague of mine."

"You know Lobert?"

"Yes, we met under very difficult circumstances. Difficult for him, not for me."

Harter chuckled. For the first time, he felt in control.

"I can bargain with the Americans; this is very valuable. We can get more than one hundred thousand in gold for each of us and what about the contact, will he meet with the Americans?"

"Yes, the key to him would be asylum. He barely escaped from Europe and he's not used to being hunted; he's not like us."

Harter asked, "What about money for him?"

"He has money. What he wants is peace. I think he believes he can strike a deal with the Americans about his money. But New York, I need money so bargain well with the Americans."

"All right, Herr Schoenriest. I'll arrange a meeting. You'll probably have to come to New York and bring your friend. I'll run the meeting."

"I want iron-clad assurances. Can we trust them?"

Harter was now in full control. He would run the meeting and strike the best deal for Red Harter.

"They're new at the game. I think the Americans can be trusted."

Both hung up.

Allen looked at Schultz. "Can we be trusted?"

Schultz placed his hands on the table. "Trusted to be loyal to our cause. There's a lot here. What did Schoenriest mean when he said his former colleague, and that the circumstances were difficult for this Lobert character?"

Allen had picked up on that too. "I think it's possible Schoenriest thought we might be listening and was sending us a message that he is a key guy. Don't bet on Red Harter."

Windum agreed. "These guys are all double dealers; they don't trust each other. I think William is right; Schoenriest doesn't want Harter to set his agenda."

Windum pulled out his list from the Metro Complex.

"Schoenriest's name is on the list we found at Kroft's office with a notation not to be arrested. That's why we left him alone." He shrugged his shoulders, "But safe from the Blackshirts, why?"

Windum had written on a pad a sentence with a question. A higher former Nazi official wants peace but doesn't need money. Does he have the money here and he wants to be free to get the money? Windum showed the pad to Schultz and Allen.

Allen spoke. "I'll bet the money is in a Swiss bank. He had to flee Europe as a hunted man; no chance to get to his vault. But if he can strike a deal with us he can get part of it.

Schultz said, "We need contacts with the Swiss Banks. Maybe this becomes more than learning about Germany." He turned to William.

"How do we play this?"

Allen answered, "First, we take Harter out of the equation. Strike a deal with him and then he gets to save his life but there are other crimes he has to pay for. The other two, let's see what they know."

Henry Windum received a phone call from a cocky and confident Red Harter. The next day the bargain included one hundred thousand dollars in gold for both Harter and Schoenriest. In addition Harter, Schoenriest, and the stranger were given immunity for a list of crimes against the United States of America in papers signed by David Schultz. Conspicuous by its absence was the crime of treason. Did Harter fail to notice this or did he think it didn't matter?

Harter said to Schoenriest, "Let me do most of the talking, you and the general answer the questions. These guys don't have any money. I can show them some deals we can all get rich on, just watch them come around."

Chapter XVI

Thus three men were driven to the Empire State Building. American headquarters exactly two months after the historic battle of Broadway. Henry Windum and six very large military policemen greeted the trio as they entered the lobby. Windum and two policemen ushered two men to the elevators, as a shocked Red Harter was taken into custody by the four other military police. As the group rode up eighty floors they were all silent.

Windum showed the two men to a large conference room with a panoramic view of the city. The two military police joined a pair of the others to form a guard outside.

Schoenrienst and Herr Mueller were introduced to David Schultz and William Allen. They did not shake hands.

Schoenrienst, his antennae sensitive after thirty years of undercover work, asked, "Mr. Harter will not be joining us?"

David Schultz replied, "Harter was needed for questioning about other matters. We will go forward with this meeting without him."

Schoenrienst and Mueller sat down at a long table. It was obvious that Schultz was in charge at the head of the table. Mueller, a short man, was dressed in an ill-fitted blue suit and was distinguished by a very close haircut and a monocle. He was every inch a former Prussian general.

Schoenrienst asked, "Do Herr Mueller and I have to be concerned about the deal we signed?"

Mueller and Schoenrienst sat on the right side of the table facing the large windows, Allen and Windum across from them. Schultz, at the head of the table, answered, "You do not have to be concerned about the deal we signed; we keep our word. You will be paid as we agreed and given asylum for the truthful answers to the questions we have."

Schultz continued, "However, since you are guests of our country, let me explain some of our laws. Foreign nationals who transact business within these shores must give full disclosure of all financial transactions and are subject to legal and transactional fees."

Schoenrienst sat back. Harter totally forgotten, the Americans were better at this than he had expected.

"In other words you are not going to prosecute us, but if we do not give you full disclosure of our other assets you will take them and if you know about our finances you will tax them."

"That is correct."

"What is your tax?"

"Half."

Schoenrienst was relieved. This matter was a better deal than he would have gotten in Germany. Schoenrienst believed this man, the Americans were going to use them but they must cooperate. The message was clear.

"What do you want of us?"

"First, information; then we will talk of other things. The more valuable you are, the quicker you resolve your finances. If the money is overseas we can work out solutions."

Mueller was quiet, the Americans were not as naïve as the man Harter said they were. He guessed that Harter was out of it. A small fry, better he was gone. Schultz was a military man. He could see it. Now it was Schoenrienst's turn to introduce Mueller as William Allen pushed a note to Schultz. The note read, "He's a big one. Number two on the general staff." William had compiled a dossier on almost all the military leaders from the files at the Metro Complex. He recognized the general from his picture as soon as he walked in the room.

"This is chief of staff Helmut Mueller of the German army." Mueller stood up, clicked his heels, and sat down. The American did not react. They recognized, in effect, he had saluted himself.

Mueller choked one month ago. He commanded an army of one million men. Today he had one suit of clothing. For the past twenty years a corporal had shined his boots every morning and he had changed to a new uniform after lunch. Today he dressed himself and his twenty million marks were in a Swiss back and without the help of these men he would never see the money. To escape Germany he had dressed as a peasant and shipped over on a tramp steamer from Spain. He shared his tiny cabin with a priest who spoke only Italian. He would now have to tell the Americans about his defeat by the Blackshirts. At sixty years old this was the low point of his life.

Mueller must explain the details of the defeat, for he could not let them think that he and his fellow general lost the war.

"We massed two great armies to envelop all the Blackshirts that stood against us in Germany. They were on the verge of surrendering. We had beaten them. Both sides agreed not to use atomic bombs because the devastation was so great. They broke the agreement, several atomic bombs dropped on both wings of the envelopment. They destroyed our armies and the air force wing we massed." Mueller hated the Blackshirts.

Allen asked, "Did you expect they would use atomic weapons against you?"

"No, in the beginning both sides used atomic weapons and the casualties were cataclysmic. We called a truce and agreed to fight with only conventional weapons. When we massed our armies we expected complete victory."

Schultz was dumbfounded. "Did you believe they would not use atomic weapons, that you could trust them?"

"Yes, because of the wind. We were attacking Berlin and the winds always blow toward Berlin at this time of year. We thought if they bombed us they would kill their own troops with radioactive fallout.

They dropped five bombs and the wind did not blow toward them but toward us and we were wiped out.

Windum questioned, "They rolled the dice and won."

Mueller asked Schoenrienst what that meant.

"Yes. They gambled. The way Hitler would have gambled and won. The previous Reich chancellor would never had done such a thing, so we have another Adolph Hitler leading Germany today."

"This was Loberts decision?" Allen asked.

So the American knew Lobert was the new Reich chancellor.

"Yes, Lobert."

For two hours they questioned the general. How many jets did they have, how many tanks, what was the state of satellite countries? Finally, he summarized what they were asking. The army and the air force were destroyed. The navy was intact, but of dubious loyalty. The Blackshirts had a small fanatical following that could control the country. The civilian population was in terrible shape. Many of the satellites were controlled by Blackshirt loyalists, but if the population knew how weak Berlin was the countries would throw them out like

America did. How did he know that? He had been in Spain, a country loyal to the Blackshirts. The government and the press had no idea how bad conditions in Germany were. It was a great propaganda coup for the Blackshirts to keep the rest of the world in the dark. Yes, he guessed. They had atomic bombs left, no more than five. The actual number was three.

Schultz turned to the general. "General Mueller, I'm going to ask you two questions. Answer them honestly and I believe we can work with you. While not allies, we have mutual interests. Lie to me and I will consider you like Red Harter, a man not to be trusted."

Mueller sat up in his seat. The Americans moved so fast. The moment of truth—he expected this in days, not minutes.

"How much money do you have in a Swiss bank?"

Mueller hesitated, "Twenty million marks." The mark and the dollar were equal. Schultz's expression did not change.

"If we could establish contact with the Swiss bankers, do you think they will lend us large sums of money and can you help us in this endeavor?"

Mueller answered, "I do not think the Swiss will give you money now. They are still afraid of the Blackshirts even in their weak condition. Germany and Switzerland share a border. You would have to prove to the Swiss you could protect them from the Blackshirts before they would help you."

Schultz cleared his throat. "Time for coffee. We will resume with Mr. Schoenrienst after a ten-minute break."

Mueller slumped in his chair, exhausted, relieved to have told his story and optimistic that he had a future as something more than a clerk or starving peasant. Perhaps there could even be revenge against the Blackshirts. The Americans were serious men. He judged their questions to be serious. In the course of the morning he thought they had confidence because of their military victories. And yet, not once had they talked of their victories. The big man is a born leader. He only wants to measure his enemies. He has no time for petty recriminations. He talked of the Blackshirts as if they were on the moon. If I can help him beat the Blackshirts he will use me.

Windrum and Allen were not happy to be giving what they considered enemies coffee. But they did not challenge Schultz. He had been quick to discard Harter when he could not help them, and he certainly would have executed him.

Allen said, "What next, tea and cookies?"

Schultz answered, "We are going to set the bar high for their two guys. I think we have a gold mine in these characters. They probably wondered if we are going to shoot them, and every step they are going to help us and if they cross us. . . " His voice trailed off.

Schoenrienst arose from his chair, accepted a coffee from the young lady, and walked to the end of the room, staring out at the river in the distance. He thought Harter was right, it was time to switch sides.

William Allen was standing alone staring out at the window deep in thought.

Schoenrienst approached him. The Nazis were either master or supplicant. "Mr. Allen, may I have a word with you?"

"Yes."

"I can be of service if you need someone who knows the working of the Swiss banks, and I have much knowledge of the Blackshirt leadership and I speak the language. I only ask that you let me prove my worth."

Allen looked at him through narrow eyes. The man was a killer. He had probably killed more Germans than Americans, but he was a killer. "We will set the bar high," said Schultz.

"You can prove yourself?"

"How, please let me know."

"Candor."

"Excuse me?"

"Answer all of David Schultz's questions with candor and that is a beginning, but only a beginning."

Schultz signaled they were to begin again. He opened with Schoenrienst.

"How did you meet Albert Lobert?"

The Americans asked questions like a punch in the chest. Schoenrienst knew they had heard the phone call to Harter. He had hoped they would.

"I arrested Albert Lobert in Stuttgart in 1937. I was head of the local police force but that was a cover. I was head of the regional Gestapo office.

"What did you arrest Lobert for?"

"A morals charge. He was a schoolteacher and had raped a young girl in his class."

Windum leaned back in his chair. Perfect, the head of the Reich is a sex criminal. It was only fitting. Both Allen and Windum followed Schultz's lead and said nothing.

"Go on," said Schultz.

"Albert was twenty-three and a brilliant young man with a problem—one of the smartest agents I ever had."

"Were you able to cure him of his problem?"

"No, but I didn't care. He quickly proved himself a real find for me. All went well until 1943 when he bothered a young girl on the subway and her father, an important general, had him drafted into the army. I couldn't protect him, but just before he went to Russia he was assigned to become a junior officer in one of the camps. I was not surprised. Albert had a way of surviving. I never saw Albert again but when I was leaving for America in 1954 to develop a Gestapo organization I was shocked to find out that Albert had been appointed to an important position on the Blackshirt general staff. It was just the beginning of the trouble between the Blackshirts and the Gestapo, but I knew Albert would never hurt me."

Before the next question Schoenrienst told them why.

"Albert knew I kept great records, and from his important position I'm sure he destroyed his records in Stuttgart, but he would never find my records and if I had an accident my records would surface."

Windrum knew why Schoenrienst had never been arrested.

"I have dossiers on him, with his picture the day he was arrested."

"He's very clever, with no scruples."

This was an amazing comment from someone from the Gestapo.

"Is your dossier in a safe place?"

"A very safe place."

Schultz asked either one of them. "Can you tell me about Lobert lately?"

Mueller said, "He was number three in the Blackshirts when the Reich chancellor died. Number one died very suddenly and after number two negotiated a truce with us he . . . disappeared."

Schultz called an end to the meeting. "I expect you to stay with us. We will have more meetings and questions. We're off to a good start but we have a long way to go. If you need to talk more your contact is Henry Windum." Windum would also make sure they didn't escape.

After they left, Schultz told them his plan. "I will call Mark Collins and tell him what we've learned. We have the measure of Lobert but does it matter in that country where so many have been killed? Maybe his crimes are not important." Schultz turned to Allen.

"The general will work with us. But it's possible Schoenrienst has more to offer. He's played in an arena where a mistake is death and he's still alive. He tipped us on the call to Harter. I think he might have some ideas on Lobert."

Allen asked, "How do I play it?"

"Lots of meetings, talk to him day and night. I have a feeling this wily old spy might like to show how smart he is to some new men in the business. These guys want revenge. And they know how to play dirty." Windum was sardonic. "And what do the poor Americans add to these geniuses?"

Schultz looked at Allen.

"What do we add?"

Allen smiled, "Action."

"They were stunned all day by how direct David's questions were. They were impressed when we got rid of Harter so quickly and we went right to the gut. This is not old-world style, but it worked. I don't think they intended to tell all today but they adjusted to the pace."

William Allen was right. The Germans would describe the meeting in terms of action. They would call it the American blitzkrieg, the American way.

The new Reich chancellor's first tour of the Great Domed Hall as Reich chancellor came three weeks after the civil war was over. It was a great moment for him to come to the Shrine of the Nazis. Master of the world, he entered the hall quietly with an entourage of twenty supporters. It was dark, and Berlin, wounded in agony, did not know he was there. It suited his basic reticence. Fires still smoked on the outskirts of the city and hundreds waited for hospital care, victims of the great atomic blast the chancellor ordered to destroy the army. As

Chancellor Lobert walked through the giant entrance he knew his predecessor would have entered with bands playing and a great crowd in attendance. He despised that arrogant tyrant, who loved the spotlight. Chancellor Lobert knew the man would have slurred Adolph Hitler on such an occasion. Lobert had seen him do it many times. The Fuhrer would be revered again, and Germany would return to the original tenets of the Third Reich. His predecessor called the world's greatest power the Fourth Reich after the death of Hitler. Subtly some of the Fuhrer's ideas were downgraded and his most loyal followers driven from power. How Lobert hated his predecessor, the liberal self-indulgent policies led to the civil war. Now his Blackshirts would rule with an iron fist again. The Fourth Reich would be written out of history, and especially the former Reich chancellor. Perhaps he would call his reign the Fifth Reich, for it would be difficult to go back to the Third Reich.

His entourage walked behind the Reich chancellor on his first visit to the Great Hall. He peered up at the great ceiling. Its immense size gave him the feeling of the power that the chancellor was curator of. This was his destiny. From here the world would hear their litany. As if in a cathedral, his followers spoke in a hush. This was the highlight of his career and none would attract his attention by speaking in a loud voice. None would have dared to speak of the suffering of the German people. The homeless and the hurt would not detract from the supreme triumph.

Hust, the custodian of the Great Domed Hall, hesitated wondering if it was time to escort the Reich chancellor to the speaker's pulpit. Less than two hours ago he was called and told that the entourage would visit the hall. The visit would be short. He was to escort the Reich chancellor to the pulpit and then Lobert would leave because of an important meeting. Hust was terrified of the Reich chancellor and would not consider speaking to him. Unlike his predecessor, who was a loud and coarse man, Lobert had a sinister quietness about him. The thin hawk-like face, the colorless eyes set deep under the wrinkled forehead. Despite his age and long service to the Reich he was a mystery to all but a few. Hust had served the powerful long enough to see the fear in Lobert's followers. Rumors of perverse cruelty and terrible deaths shadowed his career. Some men loved women, wine, power, the former chancellor all three. He was unpredictable, frighteningly strange. What did he love?

Lobert was the cabinet minister in charge of security under the former Reich chancellor. His misreading of the army's power was responsible for the Blackshirts' early defeats. However, he laid the blame on the others and made the decision to drop the atomic bombs on the army to break the treaty.

Lobert returned and motioned Hust to him.

"You will escort me to the speaker pulpit."

Hust came to attention. "It is my pleasure, Reich chancellor."

They rode in silence in the elevator that took them one hundred feet high to the gallery. Hust stayed outside and the Reich chancellor walked out onto the balcony alone. Only the Reich chancellor could stand on this spot and he noted that below they snapped to attention. Good, they were afraid of him. It was how he would have reacted a year ago, if he had been standing below.

He looked out at the vast area, his mandate of power. Despite his victory he felt melancholy. It was too quiet; he must fill the hall with cheering crowds. Yet, he hated the closeness of the crowd. He would not enter in a great show and walk between saluting mobs. No, he would be outside the balcony and they would all rise when he approached the pulpit. Yes, and they would return to the tenets of Adolph Hitler. The German people would have to prove themselves again. The people sided with the army during the civil war. The people would pay with blood for this crime. He did not consider that in some areas of Germany twenty-five percent of the civilian population was injured or dead. The Reich chancellor knew his loyal constituency; they were the Blackshirts and their followers around the world. Their vested interests would maintain their loyalty. He would use their ambition and with a mighty minority strike terror into those who opposed.

He thought of his challengers—the dirty jackals, the Japanese. Already with the Reich weakened by civil war, they were taking advantage. This morning an envoy politely but firmly demanded that the Nazis cede them all of Indochina. He would have to accept their demands. Someday he would be powerful enough to take it back. If only they knew that the Nazis, through a neutral country, had been arming the guerillas that tied the Japanese down in China and Vietnam. Now he would have to concede the Japanese some power in the Pacific, until he finished the Americans. The Americans surprised him with the speed they had overthrown the Blackshirt government. They were a bad example for the other captive nations. Indeed, there could be a problem with them supplying arms to other countries.

Yes, the Americans would have to be crushed. He would invade with an army recruited from the Blackshirts outside of Germany. The army would be promised great spoils for success in America. Perhaps the best way to end the American threat would be to disperse their people. Yes, the American people would be scattered to other countries and resettled in Asia and Africa. Air attacks and atomic bombs would soften the Americans and then the armada would land. Cruel and zealous men would profit from each American sold into slavery and land confiscated. He brightened, his mood excellent; now he would return to his apartment. His aides would have a young girl waiting for him. Yes, it was a good day, the thought of so much suffering by his enemies made him happy. Then his personality reverted. He darkened; there were not too many atomic bombs left and no capacity to make more. He snapped at Hust to open the door.

Warner Klaus, his trusted aide, was waiting for him. The cabinet had asked for a meeting. Lobert groaned; Hitler did not have a cabinet that could call a meeting. His predecessor did not have a cabinet that could call a meeting, but he must meet with the cabinet. They were not strong enough to accuse him of the murder of the men that proceeded him after the Reich chancellor's death, but they could force a meeting. The fat hog had planted his relatives in positions of power all over the world. He had taken larger sums of money from the military budget and yet this cabinet loved him. Lobert did not understand. They had all eaten big meals and gotten drunk with the former Reich chancellor. He was actually a friend to some of them. Lobert had no friend and had never even had coffee with anyone in his cabinet. They were used to his long rants at meetings, made worse now because he was the leader.

"Klaus, did you work on the piece about Rome I asked for?"

"Yes, Herr Reich chancellor."

"Good, I was thinking about America just now. Read it to me." They stopped in the hall; this was a piece that Lobert was to read at the meeting today.

Klaus began, "America is a bastardized nation without blood lines. A collection of the scum of Europe and the trash of the rest of the world, black and yellow. We shall plow over the land and put salt in the ground so nothing will grow again. It will be Carthaginian peace and America will cease to exist as Carthage did." Lobert would have been surprised to know his most dangerous opponent was the grandson of a German immigrant and a former Long Island fisherman.

Hindenberg, his enemy in the cabinet, would say after the piece, "Albert is very intelligent, but his education is sadly lacking. Rome defeated Carthage but Rome was a Republic at the time. They were more like America than we are. We can't even declare a national day of mourning. He's afraid we'll spend money on the people; he wants to spend money on weapons. I don't understand how man could reach so high, he has no soul, no depth."

Hindenberg would not say that in front of Lobert, but only the thought of another civil war kept him and his followers from getting rid of Lobert. Hindenberg told his friends, "One mistake and he's gone."

Erich Hindenberg was the son of the famous World War I field marshal, Paul van Hindenberg and was named after Hindenberg's all-powerful deputy, Erich Ludendorff. As the only son of a late-in-life second marriage, Erich and father grew to hate each other and Erich gagged at the familiar, "I'll make a man of you," from the old field marshal.

Sent to the army as a captain, he developed the Achilles' heel of his life—heavy drinking. This almost ruined his life. While on field maneuvers one morning, bleary from a late night, as an artillery captain he gave the wrong field coordinate and several men were killed. Cashiered would have been court-marshaled if not for his famous father. Here, fate intervened in the person of Adolph Hitler. Hitler, a rising politician, rescued Erich by giving him a staff job. This was to ingratiate Hitler with his father. The father did not care about the boy but recognized the publicity was what mattered because of the new job. After the old general died, Erich languished on the staff, considered little more than a glorified clerk. Here, fate intervened again in the person of Rudolph Janssen.

Janssen was considered one of Germany's greatest heroes because of his exploits with the German airborne on Crete. The airborne invasion of Crete was an early disaster about to become a German defeat. Colonel Janssen, twice wounded, rallied the troops to victory. But the victory was so costly that Hitler never allowed another airborne attack.

Janssen was given the highest honors and retired from the service when after three operations he lost his left arm. Erich Hindenberg was seated at the table for a dinner to celebrate the German victory at Crete when Rudolph Janssen was seated next to him. The poor man, so weak from his operations, could not stand when Hitler arrived for the dinner. Hitler, seeing Janssen, came immediately to the table, pulled up a chair and sat down. He shook Janssen's good right arm.

"My dear Janssen, I'm so glad to see you." Hitler, knowing Janssen had avoided an embarrassing defeat, felt deep in his debt and he could see how weak the man was. Hitler said to Erich Hindenberg, "Erich, I want you to personally take care of General Janssen. I consider it a favor to the German people."

And so Hindenberg became Janssen's confidant, chauffer, and secretary. Janssen was much in demand for war rallies as a great hero and the Nazi party considered him a public relations star. Hindenberg would arrive at Janssen's hotel and his chauffer and another man would help Janssen into the car. At the rally Hindenberg would open with the story of Janssen's exploits on Crete and his loyalty to the Nazi party. Janssen would stand and, leaning on Hindenberg, make a short speech. They would leave and go to the local hotel bar to celebrate their day. Janssen appreciated Hindenberg's support and one day said, "Erich, you're such a good friend and good officer." It was the first time in his life Hindenberg had been told he was important and coming from this great hero, it marked a highwater mark in his life. The two men, who also shared a common interest in drinking, were joined by a third confederate in the afternoon and nightly parties, the future Reich chancellor. After he became Reich chancellor the late evening parties continued with one of their favorite topics making fun of Albert Lobert.

"Lobert is smart but he is a squeak." This was short for pip-squeak and they would all laugh uproariously.

The Reich chancellor was a coarse man and loved to tell ribald stories to his friends. But later in the evening he would say, "Of course we're killers and brigands but we're better than Hitler." The Reich chancellor had closed some of Hitler's worst prison camps and destroyed the Gestapo, which he considered worse than his Blackshirts. Then he'd talk about his favorite subject—the weakness of the Democracies before the war. "The people could be worse off, they could be governed by Democratic politicians, chaos, depression; we at least give them order. If you want to work in Germany we give you a job."

Rudolph Janssen was a quiet man but when the Reich chancellor would ask him about Crete he would tell the familiar story they loved to hear.

"We parachuted in at the airport hoping we could bring gliders in later, but the English had us in a strong crossfire. My left arm was useless, shattered at the wrist by a machine-gun bullet. Luckily I could use my submachine gun with my good right arm. I and two others began to circle the airport perimeter knocking out English and Australian firing positions. The other two were killed and in the last position I attacked two Australians." The Reich chancellor who knew the three participants had killed almost two hundred of the enemy would interrupt at this point. "The English were no good." And Janssen would say, "Their generals were not good."

After the Reich chancellor died, Rudolph Janssen was designated his successor, but he was killed two days later. Lobert told the cabinet it was the army but Hindenberg did not believe him. Hindenberg hated Lobert and he told his aide. "If he gets a bad cold we get rid of him. He killed Rudolph."

By the end of the second week a plan began to evolve from the joint meeting of the Germans and the Americans that could only be described as audacious. Allen did not like the Germans but agreed that Schultz was right. They were very good at this type of thing. Schoenrienst and Mueller knew the Swiss bankers and the Blackshirt leadership and they said it would work. Schoenrienst said the plan was American in concept, quick hitting depending on split second timing like American football, not European soccer.

Just as the Americans were learning from the Europeans the Germans were beginning to see another side of the Americans. The guards at the headquarters were to display the spit and polish that Mueller associated with a professional military establishment. Yesterday two jets swept over New York in a flyover and the people cheered at the sight. Each day at 4:00 P.M. a different group of the American militia would parade in front of the Empire State Building and crowds would gather to watch.

The Germans noted that David Schultz and his staff always attended the parade.

Schultz questioned General Mueller on German tactics, military strength, and strategy. After four days Mueller asked Schultz if he would replay the three battles David had commanded, Broadway, Lexington, and Boston. Far from an armed rabble, as described by one of their fellow Germans where they were staying, each of these battles was different in concept, sophistication, and execution. Mueller told Schoenrienst that Schultz had a better military mind than anyone he had met at the German staff college. "He uses three different concepts, at Broadway, it is double evolvement, at Lexington attack from a defensive position and Boston a very well thought out trap."

Schoenrienst asked, "Is he Rommel?"

"No, this is Napoleonic warfare."

The general, a military professional and a recognized military historian, explained. "The Napoleon plan is to cut off from your base as the battle continues. There is always one juncture where Napoleon or one of his generals intercepts at the critical moment. An unexpected cavalry charge, a unit of cannon to blast at the enemy flank, a mass of infantry outnumbers the enemy at the decisive point of the battlefield. This is what the Americans did. The Germans had a huge advantage, but lost because they were outgeneraled."

Schoenrienst said the Americans fought with great courage and took many casualties.

Mueller pinched his monocle and said, "Schultz, where he had some firepower at Boston had few casualties, and if the troops fight with courage who is to get credit for that. It is the leaders, always the leaders." Being a general it was natural for Mueller to think as he did.

Schoenrienst asked, "What if he fought great battles with large armies." Mueller polished his monocle. "If I was on his staff he would win." Mueller shook his finger at Schoenrienst, "And most important, most important, Schultz inspires his men to do the impossible."

Schoenrienst thought our plan to be impossible. Only men who work for Schultz would try it. Then Schoenrienst thought, it is really my plan and I think it will work if the conditions are right.

Schultz and Allen met to go over last-minute details of the plan. Mark Collins had forbidden Schultz to go oversee, so it would be Allen and Windum joining the two Germans.

"This thing is so crazy I can't believe it will work, but I'll try it," said Allen.

Schultz said he thought it had a good chance. Allen responded, "If it works the general will get the ten million marks, a good day's pay."

Schultz said, "I've talked to the general. Despite our original agreement, he will not get half if it works. The general will donate six million marks to restore West Point and will become an unpaid advisor to our war college up there. Allen was nonplussed. A Nazi general at an American college. What next, Schoenrienst to the FBI?

"We will pay all our debts and show great charity to those who work with us. We will show Americans can be trusted," said Schultz. "Schoenrienst to the FBI."

Schultz laughed, maybe the first time William had seen him laugh in weeks. "Do you realize that this will make the general the biggest single cash contributor to our cause? These are strange times, William. The general ran the war college for ten years. I think we can learn a lot from him.

"But he and Schoenrienst are losers. The Blackshirts beat both of them," Allen protested.

The war is not over, I think they hate the Blackshirts worse than we do. The Blackshirts are like a disease and I don't care which set of doctors finds the cure."

Next day one of the jumbo jet tankers captured in Baltimore flew from an airport in New York carrying the four players in the drama and their security detail to Zurich, Switzerland. When they landed they immediately found that Schoenrienst's contacts in Zurich had given him excellent intelligence. There were no Blackshirt agents at the airport. Despite Switzerland being a neutral country usually there were German officers to be seen on the streets of the major cities.

Now there were none. Schoenrienst's man told him that many had been killed and others deserted. The Swiss met them at the airport and while not friendly were declaring themselves neutral. Mueller argued this was a good sign.

Next morning at nine thirty, General Mueller led Schoenrienst and Allen to the National Bank of Switzerland and presented his card with the secret number to the young vice president seated at the reception desk. Quickly they were ushered into the president's office. His name was Heinz.

Heinz came around the desk and shook hands with the general. At five feet five inches he was the same height, but weighed one hundred and thirty pounds more.

Mueller introduced Schoenrienst as an important contact from Germany and Allen as a Nazi sympathizer from America.

Heinz was puzzled. He knew that Mueller was part of the defeated army and while the Blackshirts were in disarray, was it not dangerous for him to be in Europe. Heinz was aware that the Blackshirts had disappeared from Zurich and he had not heard from Reich Chancellor Lobert in a week. Was it possible things were worse in Germany than he suspected?

Schoenrienst said, "Herr Heinz, you are going to hear of a very secret plan conceived by Chancellor Lobert, and agreed to by the army and the Gestapo." Schoenrienst showed him his Gestapo ring. Heinz knew it was authentic. He had two accounts with high Gestapo officers who always identified themselves by their rings. Schoenrienst's ring also showed he was a senior officer. But Lobert with the Gestapo and the army, that couldn't be.

Schoenrienst continued with a tone as if he was speaking from Mount Olympus. "I'm sure you were as surprised as we were how quickly the Americans defeated our forces." Heinz agreed he was surprised by the quick American victory.

Schoenrienst said to Allen, "Show him the pictures."

Allen showed the pictures of burning and wrecked Nazi jets at Houston. "Those planes were destroyed by a secret American ray fired at five hundred yards while the German guards put up a valiant fight." Heinz was incredulous. A secret ray.

General Mueller said, "A terror weapon. The planes had no chance."

Schoenrienst directed Allen to show Heinz a drawing of a jet plane. It was clearly very sleek and powerful. "This is the only rendering of this plane we have. Mr. Allen, at great risk to himself, brought this to us and showed it to the Reich chancellor two days ago. It was a great new American jet, but it would not fly for another year. Because of these terror weapons we have concluded a peace treaty—Blackshirts, Gestapo, army united against the Americans."

Heinz sat down. What were they saying? A treaty between their great antagonists?

"Herr Heinz, we have shown you these photos because you are part of a plan to defeat the Americans. We are going to combine financial resources to fund research to build our own terror weapons," General Mueller told him.

Mueller, very solemn, looked at Heinz. "I want you to combine my account with the Reich chancellor's."

Heinz almost fainted. Mueller was going to assign his account with the Reich chancellor's. This was an account that Mueller had been building for ten years. It had twenty million marks in it.

Schoenrienst thought this was an American moment. He had told Mueller on the plane when you tell the Swiss banker you want to combine the account I will follow up like the Americans do, catch him if he has a heart attack.

Schoenrienst said, "Herr Heinz, I know this is very sudden but this is the genesis of what Chancellor Lobert agreed to. I want to talk to him and then you must leave the room because we have other plans that you must not be privy to for your own security. When you return he will give you his final instructions."

Heinz was in shock. The world had turned upside down. He pointed to a red phone on a small desk next to his. He was calculating in his mind if this was really going to happen, he could delay the paperwork two days and save the bank a very tidy sum on interest.

Albert Lobert was exhausted. An all-night meeting was held because several naval ships had rebelled and the local Blackshirts had refused to fire on the crews. There was no electricity in Berlin and food lines existed throughout the country. He had won the civil war by dropping five atomic bombs despite his cabinet's protest and last night the cabinet had voted on a small issue and he had barely won. That Hindenberg, the son of the World War I general, would even challenge him showed how weak he was. If that fool had won Albert was finished. Hindenberg was a friend of the man Albert had murdered to become Reich chancellor. He knew his days were numbered if Hindenberg gained control.

The red phone rang. It was the Swiss banker's phone.

He picked it up and a voice said, "Albert what's on the menu tonight?" Schoenrienst waved Heinz out of the room as Mueller pushed him out of the door. Heinz heard a voice at the other end of the phone. He knew it was the Reich chancellor. No one would pick up that phone and Schoenrienst had called him Albert. Albert, called him by his first name.

Heinz waited outside his office. They said it was a security issue but he gathered himself. There would be no transfers unless the Reich chancellor gave him verbal orders and followed this with written instructions.

Lobert said twice, "Who the hell is this?" before the voice answered him.

"Albert, what is on the menu tonight? A young girl, hot or cold running children?"

Lobert stiffened. Not even the cabinet called him Albert. What was this voice talking about? The voice sent a chill down his spine. "Albert, you must remember me. It's Schoenrienst."

Lobert was so disoriented he forgot he was talking on a direct line to Zurich.

"Schoenrienst, where are you?"

"I'm in Zurich at the desk of your friendly banker, but he is not here now so we can speak freely."

Schoenrienst was speaking to him in the same mocking manner he used when he first met him in 1937. Lobert had almost ordered him killed three times in the past eight years. Each time he changed his mind, knowing his best agents might not find the dossier, and if one did, the agent might become the new Schoenrienst.

Now Lobert knew he had made a mistake.

"What do you want?"

Schoenrienst laughed, "I want money."

"How much?"

"All of it."

Lobert tried to play for time. "I'll give you five million marks, but hang up the phone and leave the bank and I want the dossier."

"Albert, you can't have Germany for five million marks."

Lobert tightened his fist on the phone. A foolish mistake years ago let this policeman catch him, but he was the Reich chancellor. His police could control the people; they would not believe the dossier. A filthy lie.

"Albert, are you still there? I'm not going to send the dossier where any fool can look at it. No, I'll be careful. I heard General Hindenberg has a good sense of humor. I'll send it to him. He won't use it against you."

Lobert quickly calculated. Could he cut off all of Hindenberg's mail? No. He slumped at his desk.

When Lobert didn't answer Schoenrienst knew he was beaten.

"Not the whole account Schoenrienst, half."

Lobert thought, thank God he doesn't know about the other three accounts.

Schoenrienst knew there were other accounts, but where and could he push Lobert much further? He had not even told General Mueller and he doubted that there was more room in this game. Let Lobert know he had something still to protect and while Schoenrienst was safe in America, if Lobert had money it would provide Schoenrienst with a cushion. The Americans would not love him more if the price went higher.

Schoenrienst was serious. "I'm going to put Heinz on the phone. You will tell him to co-mingle the account with the other one I have, and make me the executor of the account, and you will send the paperwork tomorrow."

Lobert knew he was beaten. "I don't ever want to talk to you again and if that dossier ever shows I'll hunt you till the end of the earth."

Schoenrienst changed his tone. "Lobert, that material is my life insurance policy. I won't cancel the policy; let me stay healthy and you'll have no problems. I just want the money. You can have Germany. Hold on I'll get Heinz."

Lobert heard Heinz get on the phone.

"Yes, Herr Reich Chancellor."

"Heinz, I'm making Herr Schoenrienst sole executor of the

account, merge it with the one he has and take all instructions from him. I'll send the paperwork tomorrow."

Lobert hung up. Could his police be in Zurich quick enough? He wanted desperately to punish that bastard. No, Schoenrienst was smart. He would get the file to Hindenberg and Lobert would be dead. Now he had another reason to regain his power. History would show that Albert Lobert paid a blackmailer one hundred million dollars to protect himself while his people starved.

Heinz, Allen, and Mueller began to prepare the paperwork. Schoenrienst would have to sign but first he excused himself and went to the men's room. He ran cold water over his face for a long time. The Americans would never see that file and if Lobert ever gained strong control over Germany he would insist that Schultz give him twenty-four-hour guard. Mueller was going to West Point; he would go with him. He looked at his face in the mirror. His information was correct. Albert was afraid of Hindenberg. He started to laugh; his last game was his best.

When they left the bank, Schoenrienst lit a big cigar. "Tell Schultz what a great actor I am and how the general and I earned a big commission."

Allen, for the first time since he met Schoenrienst, did not answer him. America had enough money for two atomic bombs.

Schoenrienst remembered what Hitler once said, "The victor will never be asked if he told the truth."

Events would move quickly for the Americans. Within a year they would have two atomic bombs. Their jet fighter, a plane that could fly higher than any other and whose speed was recorded at two hundred miles faster than the best the Nazi's had, was in the testing stage. The Swiss banks as a group gave America a loan of fifty million dollars and one heard the Americans were building a missile that could fly from continent to continent. Mark Collins, the American leader, would die and the cabinet would universally elect David Schultz the new head of the national government with general elections scheduled for the fall. The Germans and Japanese would lose some of their satellites to revolt. South of the border American intelligence was right—there would be divided rule by the Blackshirts and the German army. Both sides, militarily exhausted, would ignore dictates from Berlin.

Then Americans would begin an active program of supplying arms to satellites of the Axis powers. It was said America was the arsenal of democracy again.

In neutral England, at a cocktail party, the German ambassador would protest the supplying of arms to the north countries to Susan Tyler, the American ambassador and sister of Judy Tyler, who died at the Metro Complex.

Susan answered, "If you don't like it, try and stop us."

The German ambassador was outraged. "You will be like Carthage; we will destroy you."

Susan gave him the official American answer. "America will be like no other world power. The Atlantic and Pacific will be American lakes. We will go to the moon, invent machines that will define the information age, and set a standard for free men everywhere. To paraphrase Mr. Churchill, if America lasts a thousand years this was her finest hour."

Word reached Washington several hours later of the confrontation and Schultz spoke to Mueller and Schoenrienst. "Well, we wanted a provocation and we got one. The Tyler girls are feisty. What do you think?"

Mueller answered first. "Well, I think the fact that their submarines and naval ships do not attack our ships carrying supplies to the satellites is more important but the response to the provocation is interesting. Clearly, the German navy is not under the control of Berlin. On the ambassador response, that is pure Lobert. He gets hung up on things like Carthage. I think they do not attack us before one to two years."

Schoenrienst replied, "I'm not sure. Do not underestimate Albert and whoever takes control there. Albert or some other, they will recognize that if America fully develops its industry they are finished, I think they attack us in less than a year."

Schultz leaned back in his chair, "We will be ready!"

Book Two

Chapter I

David Schultz, president of the United States, entered the White House precisely at 6:00 A.M., as he did every morning. He was driven to the White House by his friend Abraham Chamberlain and a secret service agent. He accepted the salute of the marine guard who said "Good morning, Mr. President."

He returned the salute and said, "Good morning, Joe, how's the arm?"

Schultz knew that Joe's arm bothered him on a wet rainy day like today. Joe was wounded at the Battle of Boston sixteen months ago when he and Abraham Chamberlain were pushing an American artillery piece into position. A German shell fragment hit Joe but missed Abraham. Joe flexed his arm. "It will be as good as new some day, sir." Schultz liked to have veterans of past battles working at the White House and he remembered Joe on that glorious day the Americans destroyed the last of the Nazi tanks outside Boston. It was a happy day for Schultz, because of so few American casualties as opposed to the two battles of the previous week. Schultz's son died at Lexington just one week before Boston. He would have been one year younger than Joe on his next birthday. Freddie Schultz would have been eighteen next Friday. Schultz planned to fly to Boston on Friday and he and William Allen would drive to Lexington. Schultz made a mental note to himself to tell William Allen to include Joe on the security detail. That way he could visit his parents in nearby Concord. They would also bring Abraham Chamberlain on the plane; his two brothers were buried at Lexington.

The security guard opened the door to the president's office and Schultz could see his morning coffee and two morning papers were on his desk. During the ten years the Nazis occupied America he had never read a newspaper; now this was part of his daily routine. Work usually started at 6:30 when William Allen and Henry Windum arrived at the White House. Allen was head of special projects and important personal decisions. This was the man they called the historian but his true calling was his ability to pick people for tough jobs with a track record that was outstanding. Henry Windum was head of national security. A great shot, he was in the middle of the three victories that freed the Northeast from the Blackshirts. Just as active in protecting America against spies and traitors he had arrested Red Harter and cleared the Northeast of the many collaborators of the Fourth Reich.

Schultz was opening the second paper when the phone rang. It was the White House switchboard. "General Mueller calling from West Point, sir." Mueller was the former number two man of the German army and was now an unpaid advisor to West Point and a new American citizen.

It was strange for Mueller to be calling so early. Schultz shifted the phone to his good ear and stiffened as Mueller said, "David."

Mueller always addressed him as Mr. President; he knew something was wrong.

"Schoenrienst was strangled last night; we just found the body ten minutes ago."

David Schultz immediately questioned the general. "Do we know who did it?"

"No, I'm in General Howard's office. They called me when they found him. The general is on the phone sealing off the Point from all traffic in or out."

Schultz uttered the name that everyone mentioned when they heard of Schoenrienst's death, "Albert Lobert."

Muller answered, "My first reaction too. We had two M.P.s at the house; whoever did this was very clever to get past them."

Schultz knew the process of investigating Schoenrienst's death would affect national security, for if Albert Lobert had killed Schoenrienst that meant conditions in Germany had changed and Lobert was a much greater threat to the United States.

General Mueller, resourceful as ever, suggested the beginning of the investigation. "Mr. President, when Schoenrienst asked for two M.P.s to guard his house he wrote me a letter to be opened on his death. I have the letter at my cottage next door. Let me get it and with General Howard call you back. We don't know much now, but in ten minutes we may know more."

Schultz said, "Make it fifteen, William and Henry will be here by then. I want them to hear the call."

Schultz buzzed Joe at the front door. Sometimes William would go to his office to get papers before he would come to Schultz's office; this was a crisis. Schultz, a man of action, wanted instantaneous reaction from his team. He felt very alone for the moment. Schultz knew when Henry and William arrived the machinery of solving the problem would begin and he would feel better.

Joe answered the phone. "Yes, Mr. President."

"Joe, when Mr. Windum and Mr. Allen arrive tell them to come directly to my office; I want to see them as soon as they arrive."

Joe had rarely heard David Schultz speak in such a serious tone. He snapped to attention. "Sir, I see the car coming up the drive. I'll send them to your office immediately."

Schultz thought back to the three battles they fought together. At Broadway, Henry Windum was a sniper and his shooting started the battle and with others he drove the Blackshirts infantry back and was the most effective firepower the Americans had that day. William Allen had gone to the Blackshirts headquarters and obtained the critical information the Americans needed and after the battle became Schultz's aide.

At Lexington Windum's shooting kept the American cause alive during the critical stage when it appeared the Nazi tanks would drive the Americans from the field. Allen had directed reserves at the close and showed his mettle as a leader.

It was at Boston they really came together as a team. Windum found the German 88 artillery tank killers and helped with the training of the men. Allen worked up the plan that won the battle. The Germans would expect a suicide infantry attack. Instead the Americans faked such an attack, and drew the Blackshirts into a trap.

Allen had a map of the area. He cut out cardboard pieces of the tanks and artillery and placed them on the map. The next day the actual weapons were hidden in the trees. General Mueller said a successful battle was like a blending of the instruments of a symphony. The calliope of the American army that day struck with perfect timing, Schultz, Allen, and Windum responding to each other's moves won the battle. This partnership continued into the peace; David Schultz would no more move without these men than read with his eyes closed.

Henry Windum entered the room, Allen right behind him.

Schultz announced, "Schoenrienst was murdered!"

Henry sat down. "Where? How?"

"At West Point; he was strangled last night."

William Allen asked, "Lobert?"

Schultz just shook his head. Lobert was his choice too, but it was almost too early to speculate. "We don't know."

Henry questioned, "How did they get past the guards?" Henry had signed the order when Schoenrienst requested full-time protection two months ago.

Henry continued, "I think he must have suspected Lobert was growing stronger in Germany and that his life was in greater danger."

Allen said, "I changed my mind about Schoenrienst. When I first met him I thought he was just a murderer and jailer but he proved he was more a master spy. You were always right about him, David."

Since they had traveled to Switzerland and met the Swiss bankers, it was Schoenrienst's contacts who had given them the best information about Germany.

The phone rang. It was from West Point. Schultz switched on the conference phone.

General Howard began. "Sir, we have little to tell you. Schoenrienst must have died at 3:00 A.M. I have sealed off the Point. We show only three cars left from the central gate around that time. Two cars can be accounted for. The third car was driven by a white man in his thirties, but in checking we can't see where that car entered the Point. I've got the provost marshal investigating. The two MPs guarding the house were good men; I can't see how someone slipped past them."

Henry Windum spoke. "General, I just talked to the FBI. They will have a team at the Point within an hour."

217

General Mueller cut in, "Let me read Schoenrienst's letter. We may have to act quickly."

> *My dear American friends, if you are reading this I am dead and this letter will be my last act as an operative. President Schultz always called me "The Old Spy" and I want to tell you that David Schultz treated me with the greatest respect and honesty of any man I ever worked for. You let me do things my way and respected my wishes to keep the Lobert document secret.*
>
> *Now if my death is not natural you must believe it was Lobert; and as I have told you, do not underestimate him. Albert is resourceful and clever. So the first thing you must do is check if Albert has gained complete control in Germany. Second, the names of my operatives in Germany and the Lobert document are in a safety deposit box at the Bank National in New York #586719. Let me warn you—if that box has been compromised, do not trust the three men named; they may have been turned by the Germans.*

Schoenrienst always said his safety depended on the Lobert document not surfacing, and Lobert not gaining complete power in Germany. If ever the document was released he could suppress it. The document proved that Lobert was guilty of moral charges against young children.

Mueller stopped reading. "I suggest that General Howard call the bank right now and have guards posted in the vault until I can go there and check the contents."

David Schultz ordered it and General Howard left the room to make the call.

Mueller continued reading.

William Allen and Henry Windum, do not be mad at me. You will find in the box the name of an American working for me in China. I never told you about him, but you know the president said we knew little about the Japanese and we still don't, but I hoped this fellow could get us started.

Henry looked at William. "He must have laughed when he wrote that part. Starting a spy ring in Asia without telling us."

Allen shook his finger. "The spy master until the end."
Mueller continued.

Now William, remember you told the greatest lies when you told the Swiss banker about America's secret weapon? You are a better spy than you give yourself credit for. That was a great day, my greatest game. [Schoenrienst was pleased when he had fooled the Swiss bankers and blackmailed Albert Lobert.]

My last information to you all—I was saving this for last—but now I give it to you for free, the last secret of a master spy. Lobert is very smart and diabolical and ruthless. He will go off on a wrong idea sometimes, but we all do that. His greatest weakness is not that he bothers children, but that he is a physical coward. I have seen him several times when confronted with danger tremble and break down in tears. Once we were being bombed and he wet his pants. General Mueller, when the Americans fight him perhaps you can use that. His greatest strength— he never seems to play the card you expect. My friends, be very careful when Albert is dealing; don't watch his hand, watch the cards.

General Howard came back on the line. "I just spoke to the bank. They had a robbery. All of the safety deposit boxes are gone. Schoenrienst's material is gone."

Allen was the first to speak. "Well, a voice from the grave warns us. Lobert had the man killed and also broke into a bank. He's right; Lobert is dealing the cards."

Schultz had digested the information now; it was time to go to work. He ordered General Howard to investigate with the FBI at the Point, then he told General Mueller to come to Washington and to bring his book with him. Mueller was working on a history of the Second American Revolution, but beyond that he told Schultz that he had traveled around the country speaking to leaders of the war, so that he could pinpoint men who could lead in the war with Germany that they expected.

After they hung up the phone, Schultz turned to Henry and William.

"Assume we are going to be attacked by Germany, we can't use Schoenrienst agents anymore, but William, we've got to recruit new agents. I want you both to double your security. We've got a killer loose and Lobert has the initiative at the moment. This was always coming and we've had a year and a half to get ready, so let's go to work.

Henry spoke. "If Lobert is averse to physical danger this will only benefit us if we meet him in battle, something that is not likely to happen."

Allen responded, "A man who will take great political risks, but I wonder if he can inspire anyone to trust him. I think his weakness is that he has a great many enemies; we have more friends out there than we know his enemies."

This last statement by William Allen would prove to be an enduring theme of the next few months.

Chapter II

He was tired.

Albert Lobert, the Reich chancellor of Germany, like his role model Adolph Hitler, did not sleep well. He seldom went to bed before 2:00 A.M., and most nights it would take one to two hours before he could fall asleep. He used a great many tranquilizers, switching from one to the other as his mood or health demanded. He ignored his doctor's advice that simple exercise would help. Unlike Hitler, who did not use alcohol or drugs, Lobert used both, especially since he had assumed control of the German government after the civil war between the Blackshirts and the army. The pressure was enormous. This contributed to his nasty disposition and fits of temper. Since his staff was in constant disarray and fear of him, their performance suffered. He did not trust them. All conceded that Lobert was smart, but his logic was convoluted. He looked at the world through a prism of hate and fear. His enemies had always underestimated him and missed his outstanding strengths in the political arena. His outstanding attributes included his timing of when to gamble and a pathological ability to exterminate his enemies. In a culture of destroy or die he was the unsurpassed master of survival. There was no price he would not pay, of friends, constituents, and safety of the group he belonged to, to save himself. It was Lobert's job, as head of intelligence, to determine the strength of the German army and the mood of the people when the civil war started, and he failed. Yet he was able to shift the blame to others and eliminate his two chief rivals from the chancellery of the country. Then he took the great gamble of his life, dropping atomic bombs on the army when all logic said he should not since the wind was blowing to Berlin and would destroy his followers. The wind shifted and his gamble worked. His followers did not know that he had abandoned Berlin and did not share their danger.

His victory was bittersweet as it brought him the power he wanted, but also much greater problems than he anticipated.

Not since the great religious wars of the Middle Ages had the German people suffered so. Berlin, the capital, would go for days without electricity. Medical supplies in all parts of the country were in short supply, and no family in the country had escaped the tragedy of the civil war. It was far easier to be a member of the Blackshirt cabinet under the former chancellor than to deal with the day-to day problems of Germany. So Lobert took a classic response to the problems; he ignored them. He had two great obsessions. The invasion of America and the death of the only two men who truly understood him.

Schoenrienst, the Gestapo spy, who was his first boss in the game of intrigue and had blackmailed Lobert through the Swiss banks and shifted millions of marks to the American cause. Schoenrienst was in America and appeared safe from Lobert's revenge. Schoenrienst had the dossier that proved Lobert was a child molester.

The second man was General Hindenburg, his rival in the Blackshirt cabinet, who hated Lobert because he had killed Rudolph

Janssen, his friend. Lobert knew he must kill both men and get the dossier before he could move against America. While Lobert was telling the cabinet of his plans to help Germany, all his interest and energy were directed toward his personal goals. Six weeks before the death of Schoenrienst, Lobert initiated the first step in his master plan.

A man was brought up the private elevator to the Reich chancellor's office. It was a private meeting in the very large office with a high ceiling and dark heavy drapes covered all the windows. The chancellor sat at a desk that Adolph Hitler had used. Lobert forced himself not to smoke. He wanted nothing to break his concentration. He favored the dark foreboding room with heavy rugs for he thought that secrets revealed here would stay secret. This man was perfect for his plan and meticulous research had gone into his choice.

Lobert spoke first. "You can smoke, I have need of a man of your talents."

The stranger uttered an affirmative response, but said nothing further.

"I want you to go to America and kill this man." He handed the stranger a picture and the details of where the man lived and how well protected he was.

The stranger, of medium height and slender build, had been released from prison two weeks ago. He was a former college professor with a very high IQ, and had killed eleven people, six by strangulation. The only reason he was caught was because his last employer had traded his name to the police for a lighter sentence in the employer's case.

"After you kill him you must call a phone number in New York. He has a secret security box in a bank vault, and my men will break into the vault when they know he is dead."

The stranger asked, "How do you know what his box number is?"

Lobert responded, "We will open all the boxes. But only if you make the call. We have followed the man; we know this is the right bank.

"Then your contacts in America will lead you to a second man. I don't care how you kill him or who does it, but I want the first man strangled."

Lobert repeated the price for the two deaths and added a great incentive. "When we conquer America I will make you Reich protector of the Northeast and you will be a rich man. You can do with the men and women and children what you want."

He emphasized the word children.

"Your code name will be Assassin."

Lobert thought to himself, that is of course if you survive the atomic bombs we will use against America.

In the elevator on the way down the Assassin opened the file folder. This would be a difficult assignment, but doable.

The research was very good, clearly the Reich chancellor had good agents in America and someone in a high place in the American government. The Assassin had been to America before. A man named Red Harter used him to kill an Underground rival and insisted on a foreign agent so he could not be traced. He looked at the suggested schedule. It was very well planned. There was no question in his mind that he could do this, and the reward would be great. Why did he feel uneasy. The plan assumed the Americans were incompetent. The second murder would be difficult, perhaps more difficult. He looked through the sheets. There was no assessment of police or American security. His patron was too overconfident. He would take the risk; they could afford to be overconfident.

Then, because he was a very intelligent man, he realized it was not overconfidence as much as hatred. The architect of the plan hated the Americans. The plan could not conceive that they would react and foil the scheme. He realized he must be more flexible; he would not assume anything, but execute his specialty. This was vintage Albert Lobert; his judgment and audaciousness was correct with the Assassin. His hatred could be a fatal flaw, because he was an absolute dictator. No one would change him, right or wrong.

The second part of Lobert's plan was a much greater challenge. To destroy the Americans he must use the navy.

Lobert's meeting today with Admiral Hans Heidel was their second encounter. Heidel's superior was in the cabinet and a supporter of Hindenburg.

The admiral was a member of one of Germany's oldest families. It was unusual that he was in the navy rather than the army. As the youngest son in the family the admiral father did not care that Hans had not followed in the footsteps of his brother in joining the Wehrmacht.

So Hans, not supported by his family and behind a man who was clearly past his peak, had decided, at the age of fifty, it was his time to take control of his life.

Hans did not like Albert Lobert and considered him dangerous but he told his staff, "Let us find out what he wants, we are ready to be the kingmakers in Germany. They need the navy; we can't pretend to be disinterested anymore." The navy had languished on the sideline during the civil war supporting neither the Blackshirts nor the army. This was a good decision because some had argued to support the army, which lost.

After the disaster of the civil war the navy was the strongest service, since the army and the air force suffered fifty to seventy percent casualties. Then all the plans of the navy unwound when it was rocked by strikes and the revolution of the rank and file. Heidel and his superior were stunned by the disloyalty of the sailors, who in many cases had imprisoned the officers. His superior retreated to a cabinet meeting and left Heidel to deal with the revolution.

So in the most distasteful episode of his life Hans Heidel had to negotiate with the strike leaders. They wanted pay raises, better working conditions, and above all no battles with any foreign countries. They did not want to risk their lives for a Blackshirt government. When the Americans began to send arms to neutral countries and fomented revolution in the satellite countries, Lobert tried to force Heidel's superior to attack the American ships but he was rebuffed.

Heidel and Lobert met in a secret meeting and again Lobert asked for the navy to attack American ships, but Heidel explained, "I have come to an accommodation with the strike leaders and however distasteful, they have agreed to serve their officers again. But if you force us to attack the Americans I can't guarantee the men will not turn against their own government."

Lorbert was moderate in his reply.

"In the future if we guarantee financial reward will the navy support me; do you think you can control them?"

Admiral Heidel said he thought this would work. Lobert promised, and kept his promise to give the navy a large sum of money directly controlled by Heidel. The money was from the former chancellor's secret bank account, not even known to the cabinet. Lobert said, "You know, Heidel, you should control the navy; you are doing all the work."

Today would mark the second secret meeting between Lobert and Heidel.

Heidel, dressed in civilian clothes with a hat pulled over his eyes, was driven to Lobert's office building and came up a back elevator to meet with the Reich chancellor. Admiral Heidel was a stocky powerful-looking man, his upper chest dominated a tight fitting uniform. Lobert judged him not to be very smart, a man better to always be number two to a strong leader.

Lobert said, "Tomorrow I am to join the cabinet in a tour of southern Germany where the destruction of the country is most acute. I will somehow miss the plane and it will take off and have an accident and crash, killing everyone aboard. Since your superior will be dead you will be in charge of the navy and a member of my new cabinet."

Heidel did not blink an eye. He had expected something like this.

"Do you want my loyalty to the new cabinet?" he asked.

"Yes, I do."

"It will take money."

Lobert knew that Heidel did not mean this for himself. He was gaining control of the navy and it was not a given, yet he needed money.

Lobert pulled out a piece of paper and wrote a figure three times. The money he'd given Heidel two months ago.

Heidel looked at the piece of paper and said, "Yes, this will work."

Lobert leaned across the desk.

"I have an army; it will embark for Mexico and meet with the joint military and Blackshirt group in Mexico who have agreed to join us to invade the United States. I need the navy to take my army to America from Europe.

Heidel asked, "How big is the army going to America?"

"Two hundred and fifty thousand men," said Lobert proudly.

Heidel looked puzzled. He knew Lobert could not raise that amount of men in Germany.

"Can you raise that army in Germany?"

"No, this will be like the conquistadors from Spain when they went to the New World, only this time they will conquer North America, not South America. Our army will be made up of soldiers of fortune; all will be promised a share of the profits, paid for by the Americans. Lobert handed Heidel another piece of paper with the figure 250,000. It did not show that some Blackshirts from Germany would join with soldiers of fortune, mostly released from the jails of Europe. In addition, fifty thousand men were from the satellite countries.

Heidel looked at the sheet.

"Only five thousand from Spain. Does not the Caudillo share the enthusiasm for the venture?"

Lobert was disappointed with General Franco, dictator of Spain's lukewarm response to the venture, but in the interest of secrecy, Lobert had accepted the number of men from Spain and even accepted hypothetical numbers from other countries. The sheet had been typed only this morning.

Heidel answered, "We can convert some warships to troop ships. We can transport that number of men to Mexico. But do not the Americans have atomic bombs?"

Lobert answered, "The Japanese have agreed to a strategy with us. Two Japanese carriers will attack the west coast of America. They will bomb American cities and pretend to have an invasion fleet to attack the west coast of America. When we win the war the Japanese will occupy all of America west of the Rockies. We have an agent at the highest level of the American government. He assured us if the Japanese menace the west coast, the Americans will move their bombs to the West.

Heidel questioned, "Do you think you can vanquish the Americans with half a million men?"

Lobert explained the rest of the plan and Heidel agreed the navy would cooperate. The plan was the destruction of two American cities, but Lobert did not tell him submarines would be used.

The next day, Tuesday, at 9:00 A.M., the Blackshirt cabinet boarded a large commercial jet liner at the Berlin Airport for southern Germany. They saw Albert Lobert board the front of the plane for his private cabin. What they and the crew did not see was two Blackshirt security men quickly give Lobert the jacket and the cap of a baggage handler and all three got off the plane.

One hour later the commercial liner blew up over southern Germany. Berlin radio reported the accident and that by good fortune the Reich chancellor had missed the plane and would form a new cabinet.

Chapter III

William Allen never forgot Judy Tyler who sacrificed her life so he could escape from the Metro Complex. He visited her family in New Jersey and met her sister, Susan Tyler. As Mrs. Tyler made supper, Allen and Susan walked and talked and he was much impressed. She was an assistant to the head of a college in New Jersey. Her husband was killed during the uprising and she had thrown her life into her work. At five foot nine inches, she was taller than her sister, but had the same high cheekbones and long black hair. Before Allen left he offered Susan a job at the State Department. Susan was an instant success at the State Department; she became liaison to William Allen at the White House and he knew she was a great choice. Suddenly foreign policy decisions at the White House were quickly and efficiently implemented. At the State Department, Susan was a born executive, she had a knack for getting people to work together. Allen decided that she was a candidate for bigger jobs, since America needed people who could handle more responsibility, especially in the diplomatic field.

William Allen appointed Susan Tyler assistant to the ambassador of the American Embassy in London. Neutral England was more independent of Germany since the civil war and at the crossroads of the battle of diplomacy and espionage between America and Germany.

He began by explaining his judgment. "Susan, you're an excellent organizer and you've shown great ability for the State Department and I'm going to miss your work at State, but England is the most important overseas post we have. All of Europe is watching America and Germany through the window of London. You're like your sister Judy; you have spunk and brains. I want you to recruit someone over in Europe who can give us high-level information about Germany. The English have important business ties with Germany; their people move in high circles. We have contacts in Germany but they tend to engage in grassroots stuff, cloak and dagger. None of our people have been able to tell us why the German navy is so quiet or what is going on in the German cabinet. There are rumors about new German weapons systems. You'll be moving in high diplomatic, financial, and political circles. You may meet people who can help us. Now, I don't want you to take any risk; you'll report to me directly and I'll support you with whatever funds you need. Money talks in London." He left unsaid that she was so attractive this would help and that he truly didn't want her to take any risk because he could not forget the death of her sister. Susan had respect for his judgment. If he said she could do this she would try to succeed.

Two weeks after Susan arrived in London she attended a party and met Lord Justin Oliver, the English ambassador to Spain and a close personal friend of the Spanish dictator, General Franco.

He invited her to go to one of London's gambling halls with him the next night. In an elegant gambling casino she sat quietly as he drank and gambled away a large sum of money. In his car he invited her to go home with him, but she refused and invited him to breakfast with him the next morning. He accepted. She was beautiful, intelligent, and had politely watched as he gambled; not all his dates were so charming. He loved to gossip and began breakfast telling her that the bookies in London, who would bet on anything, had made Germany a seven-to-five favorite in a war with America.

"Actually, the odds would be a great deal higher except your president, Mr. Schultz, is building a reputation as a very strong chief executive."

She did not understand gambling and had been waiting to talk about a more serious matter.

"Do you need money?" she asked.

He stroked his beard. This was consistent with the reputation of the people she worked for. Direct almost to the point of rudeness.

"My dear one does not ask a gentlemen a question about his finances."

Susan had rehearsed the next line all morning. "Lord Oliver, you must excuse me; I'm an American and we are too impatient at times, but you clearly are a very impressive person and I've heard you are one of the most knowledgeable people in the world of diplomacy in Europe."

He stroked his beard. Yes, she was very intelligent and charming. Susan could tell he liked the last compliment, especially since it was true.

Susan continued, "You have a knowledge and insight to the governments of Europe that my government does not have. If you can help us it is only fair we reciprocate with financial support of your efforts."

He thought that was one of the most diplomatic statements to justify a bribe he had ever heard. He sipped his tea and asked her, "How appreciative would you be?"

She saw him lose twenty thousand pounds last night. That number had stuck in her mind.

"I think I could convince my government to pay twenty thousand pounds per quarter for top-level information especially about the Fourth Reich."

Lord Oliver owed his bank two hundred thousand pounds. He needed money and she was right to come to him. He could tell things no one else in Europe knew. Yes, it would be fun to chitchat with this young woman. Oliver was the de facto advisor to General Franco. This would be amusing to share all he knew.

He leaned forward. "My dear, you know about the 101?"

William Allen had briefed Susan about the 101, America's super jet fighter. "Yes, our jet fighter."

"Well, the Nazis have heard about it too and they have developed and tested a ground-to-air missile that will shoot down the 101 if it flies below ten thousand feet. Only one other person outside of Germany knows about the weapon."

She guessed he was talking about the Caudillo of Spain.

He leaned back, pleased with himself. "Now would you call that high-level information?"

Susan questioned, "You have seen the missile operate?"

Lord Oliver was Spain's representative to the test, for the Germans needed money and wanted to sell some weapons to friendly governments, like Spain.

"Let's say I was invited to the test, as my judgment would influence the ultimate buyer, and it works."

Susan thought, I'm glad William Allen briefed me on the 101.

She reached for her pocketbook and pulled out her checkbook. Her account held one hundred pounds. She wrote him a check for twenty thousand pounds.

Susan said, "Please hold this for three days."

He took the check, folded it, and laughed. "My dear, we have to be more discrete next time—phone calls, dark corner meetings, spy craft, and all that." Yes, but this check would hold the bank nicely.

Susan remembered William Allen had said, "Be bold, America needs your courage." She took a deep breath. After all, she was Judy Tyler's sister.

"Lord Oliver, how much do you think it would cost to obtain such a ground-to-air missile?"

Lord Oliver greatly admired General Franco because he had brains and courage. This girl had brains and courage too. He pulled on his beard again. He took out his pen and wrote some numbers on the tablecloth. There was a general in Germany and it would cost to transport the weapon to Spain, where it could safely be brought to England. He quoted her a number, thirty-five thousand pounds, expecting she would tell him she had to check with her boss. She did not flinch.

"Yes, I think that's fair. How do we do this?" Lord Oliver's judgment was correct. She was like General Franco.

Lord Oliver said, "Half next week and the balance when I give you the weapon in three or four weeks."

Three hours later Susan Tyler called William Allen on a secure phone. He listened intently as she explained about her meeting with Lord Oliver. William Allen knew Lord Oliver was an important contact and he was disturbed to hear about the missile. They thought the 101 was inviolate. Yes, she did the right thing; they had to see this weapon.

"Susan, this is brilliant. We did not know about the weapon and clearly we have to see it. I'm proud of you; you've handled this better than we had the right to expect. I'm going to speak to the president

235

immediately. We will have a plane in London when you get the weapon and bring it to Washington so our scientist can look at it.

"Now I want you to be careful, I'm sending a note to the security detail in London. We are doubling your security; be careful. We need you, Susan. Your country needs you."

Susan hung up and sat at her desk. William Allen's judgment was correct. She could do this. She spoke to someone who was not there. "Judy we promised Dad we would fight them and you did, and now I am fighting them too."

William Allen walked next door to David Schultz's office, closed the door, and told the president the story.

Schultz said, "We had no idea about this weapon. Thank God Susan had the brains and the guts to do what she did. We owe that lady."

"You deserve some credit too, William. Good appointment." Schultz had seen Susan just before she went to London. She was tall and attractive but he thought very quiet, maybe too quiet at the time. He was wrong, just as he had been wrong when William Allen said someone in the administration should be appointed political consultant and Schultz had rejected this idea. He found out this was a mistake when political pressure forced him to accept Alex Livas in an important security job. Schultz hated Livas. He blamed him for not supporting the New Yorkers at the Battle of Lexington and for the death of many of the New Yorkers, including his son.

The president's final words, "We better keep an eye on Susan; she may be heading for big things for us."

That night in London the Caudillo called Lord Oliver. Ostensibly the call was about an over and under shotgun rifle that Oliver brought to be fixed at a gun shop in London. Then they got down to the real reason of the call. He asked Oliver how the test went and what conditions in Germany were like. Oliver told him the ground-to-air missile would work and that conditions in Germany could not be worse. A Blackshirt general had told him they should make peace with the world and withdraw all their overseas troops.

General Franco said, "Lobert called me; he wants troops. I'll have to give him some. What do you think, Oliver?"

"I think he's on very weak grounds, general. Do not give him more than you want to."

They hung up and Lord Oliver thought of David Schultz and Susan Tyler and the people of Germany. He would give his butler five thousand pounds to take to betting shops tomorrow to bet on the Americans. The Americans were a live underdog. Not only were the Americans a live underdog, but if Susan Tyler was an example, they were full of fight. Yes, he would get Susan a ground-to-air missile and the next time he saw the Caudillo he would suggest it might be time to hedge bets on the Blackshirts. He thought of Albert Lobert, a strange man. He decided to bet ten thousand on the Americans.

Four weeks later scientists in Washington examined the German ground-to-air missile. It was a splendid piece of engineering. With only one glitch in the weapon it would take two minutes to adjust the height of the weapon to explode from ten thousand feet to a hundred feet high. At the lowest height the explosions were erratic. Clearly, if the pilots could attack at a very low level there would be less danger. This fact would save many pilots' lives, thanks to Susan Tyler.

The ambassador to England had a heart attack and Susan Tyler was appointed ambassador of the American legation. Shortly after that, at the direction of William Allen, she confronted the German ambassador at a party to test the German reaction.

Next day, the embassy switchboard rang Susan's phone. "Miss Tyler, there's a man on the phone. He won't give his name but he wants to talk to you."

Susan waited for the strange voice.

"Miss Tyler, I was at the party last night and I heard what you said. You are right. I want to help you, but I can't come to the embassy. Can we meet in a neutral place?"

Susan was on guard, she knew her life could be in danger.

He said he had information that would help the Americans, but that he had to be careful. Could they meet in a small restaurant just off Picadilly? It would be almost empty at 4:00 P.M.

She could not be like Judy and carry a gun. She didn't even know how to load a gun. Susan called security and arranged for two agents to follow her to the meeting.

Susan was very tense and excited as she entered the restaurant. It was almost empty and she saw a tall man in a green raincoat at the back wave to her. She walked to the back and he looked tense too. They both sat down. "Thank you for coming," he said.

"I must tell you I'm not betraying my country. The people who run my country have betrayed it. You can not know how the German people have suffered." He was extremely nervous and talking so fast she could barely follow him.

"When I heard you last night, I knew you were right. America and Germany should be talking peace, but Albert Lobert will never do that. He is a swine."

Susan realized he was an official of the German government and it was best to let him continue.

The man pointed to a briefcase under the table. "In the briefcase is a cipher to the German naval codes and the frequency they are transmitted on."

She finally spoke. "You are very brave to do this."

He fidgeted with the button of his coat. "I wanted to meet you, but we can never meet again. It's too dangerous. The navy has been neutral but I sense they are turning to the Blackshirts. You must realize the storms are gathering over Europe and will be coming America's way."

Now he was calmer.

"If I have more information for you in the future I will call your embassy from a pay phone and say, 'the weather is warm.' I will be at this table one hour later. You should send someone, not yourself. The man should carry a briefcase and the *London Times*. He should sit at that corner table.

He pointed to a table at the far left.

"I will go to the men's rest room and leave the material in a basket next to the wash basin."

She knew she should not offer this man money. He was a patriot.

"We will have someone man the switchboard twenty-four hours a day. We thank you very much. I will not ask you to tell me who you are, but can I ask why you think the navy is changing?"

He was very calm now. This woman was sympathetic, different from the other night. "The former head of the navy hated Lobert. The new man is not a Blackshirt, but I think he takes Lobert's money to unite the navy. The navy is going to start intercepting American ships. Be careful how you monitor the code signals. If you warn all your ships they will know you have broken the code."

Susan knew she must ask this man to do more. "We want peace too, but peace will only come if we can defend ourselves. If I need your help, can I get in touch with you? I will never do it unless it's a life-or-death situation."

Before the meeting the man vowed he would never expose himself to the Americans, but this woman was so reasonable and calm, he trusted her.

He wrote down on a piece of paper two short sentences.

"Put this add in the *London Times* and I will call the embassy."

She shook his hand. "May we meet in a different time and different circumstances."

He answered, "Your Thomas Jefferson said it best. The tree of Liberty must be refreshened from time to time with the blood of patriots and tyrants; it is its natural soil."

Chapter IV

At the President's request General Mueller moved from West Point to an office at the White House. He was in his office a short time when he complained to William Allen about the poor performance of the White House staff. William Allen agreed and the two went to see the president.

"David," began William, "The general and I believe the White House is not functioning at the level it should. On this wing people work hard and almost everyone is here before seven in the morning, but in the other wing many people don't get to work before nine o'clock. I know you've complained about too many meetings starting late, and you can't get information and reports on time, and frankly, you see a lot of people standing in the halls talking in the other wing.

The President said, "What do you want to do?"

Allen responded, "We need a new chief of staff, and I suggest Susan Tyler."

"Susan?" the president asked. "Don't we need her in London?"

Allen said, "We don't; she recruited the people I was looking for. She's done a great job, but now its too dangerous for her to contact these people. We are using other agents for the contacts. Susan is the most qualified person I know for chief of staff at the White House; I know she can do it."

Mueller agreed. "I've looked at this young woman's record. William is right; we need her here. The White House is the heart of the republic; it has to function at a high level. We need our best people working here.

The president supported the proposal and once again Susan was given a job by William Allen. She returned, and quickly began to make changes. She wrote a memo that said work began at 7:30 A.M. and if anyone had a problem with that they should speak to Susan and she would attempt to relocate them. Only one person could not meet the requirement and was transferred to another position in government. A noticeable pickup in the tempo of work ensued.

Susan was given an additional request by her mentor, William Allen.

"Susan, the president works too hard. He's here seven days a week. He'll burn out at that pace. About once a month he goes sailing with Abraham Chamberlain, and he visits his son's grave, but the rest is work trips or he is in his office. See if you can get him out of the office to relax."

It was Sunday. The president was working in his office. He had a two-foot stack of executive orders he had to sign. Susan Tyler entered the office. She had on blue jeans, a checkered shirt, blue and white boating shoes, and her hair was tied up in the back with a gold comb. She looked elegant.

"Mr. President, it's a beautiful day. Abraham has promised to teach me to sail, but he said you have to put up the sails to start."

Schultz knew she was right. Abraham, with his bad foot, always had trouble putting up the sails.

Schultz pointed to the pile of papers. "Susan, I'd love to come but I've got to sign these."

Susan began loading the papers in a briefcase.

"I know what. You put up the sails, get us away from the dock, we will sail, and you work on your papers."

It was an argument that Schultz was quick to agree to. He stood up and pulled off his tie.

"I guess the republic is safe for the rest of the day."

She pointed to a wicker basket.

"Mr. President, that's our lunch; can you carry it?"

Abraham and a Secret Service man were at the car. Joe held the door for the president and Susan. She said, "Thanks, Joe. How is the arm today?"

"Real good, Miss Susan."

Technically, Joe was part of the White House staff, but he had helped her move her boxes the first day she came to the White House and Susan told him to call her by her first name. He worked for her, but he thought of her as a friend.

As they rode along listening to music, Susan found out the president had a sense of humor, and he insisted she call him David out of the office.

"David, William Allen said the time he went sailing with you, there were people shooting at you!"

Schultz remembered before the Revolution, a German boat had chased them on Long Island. "Susan you are only allowed to shoot at sailboats on Long Island. The Chesapeake is a much more gentle place, no shooting allowed, and no clamming either." Abraham Chamberlain had brought along a clam rake one time and Schultz told him you either sailed or clammed, not both.

In an hour they arrived at the Chesapeake Bay, the sailboat at the dock with a motorboat of security men. Schultz recognized this was planned, but he didn't care. It was a beautiful day and he was having fun.

Susan squealed with delight as the boat slid swiftly away from the dock in a stiff breeze.

First Susan worked the jib sheet and within an hour she and Abraham shared the tiller. Schultz could see Abraham was mesmerized by Susan. He never took his eyes off her and laughed at all her jokes as she giggled at his. Schultz was so relaxed he almost fell asleep. Abraham was talking more than Schultz had ever seen him. After two hours, Susan offered them sandwiches. David thought it was the best sandwich he ever tasted.

He asked, "What kind of bread is this Susan?"

"French bread with a hard crust, it's brick oven baked." He loved the sandwich and had a second. "Is this provolone cheese with ham, great dressing?"

Susan said, "I'll have you know that dressing is Tyler's special mustard, a secret recipe from my grandmother."

Schultz thought, is there anything this woman can't do? She had organized the greatest espionage victory of my administration with her buy of the ground-to-air missile, and she was fun to be with. They talked and talked. Schultz and Abraham explained what a Maine clambake was—lobster, clams, and corn in seaweed cooked over hot stones. Susan told them some of the gossip of the White House. General Mueller scared the White House secretaries with his gruff Teutonic nature but he had a sweet tooth. Susan would bring him chocolate cake and he would tell her stories of the war and military organizations. She thought she had learned a great deal from him.

Abraham ate another sandwich, but the basket was still half full.

Susan said to David, "I made too many sandwiches, can we give some to the security men?"

"Yes, good idea."

She waved to the motorboat to come close. "Guys, we've got a ton of sandwiches, anybody hungry?"

The chief looked at Schultz, who nodded it was okay.

As Susan leaned over to hand the basket to the security men David Schultz realized that Abraham Chamberlain was not the only man on the sailboat who was in love with Susan Tyler.

They sailed until dark and then drove home. Susan made an excellent suggestion. "Mr. President, I would think it possible someone else could sign a lot of those papers. William Allen told me one of my jobs was to relieve you of some of your paperwork. Can I check on this for you?"

Schultz walked into his bedroom, tired but very happy. It had been a great day. He looked at his picture of Freddie and spoke. "Freddie, I've met someone special. You will always be in my heart, but I think I have room for someone else."

Chapter V

William Allen walked into the president's office. "Any further news?"

The president had called at 2:00 A.M. There had been a Japanese bombing attack, but it appeared little damage was done.

Schultz said, "I've had another call from the navy. They see little damage on the West Coast, but they said a complete assessment would be on the wire. It's only 4:30 Pacific Coast Time."

"Where is Henry?"

Allen said, "He told me he was working in his office at the State Security Building, but usually he would call by now or be here for the meeting. Let me call him."

As William went to the president's secretary's desk he asked them to track down Henry Windum; it was important.

Susan Tyler and General Mueller walked in. Susan had the teletype message from the navy and handed it to the president. Susan was now a full-fledged member of the president's crisis council of Allen, Mueller, Windum, and Tyler. She kept the notes and within thirty minutes of a meeting all the members would have a summary of the current problem. Susan would not speak often but she asked great questions and was brilliant in summarizing the salient points to a problem and suggesting language that all would agree on.

The summary points were clear and concise.

William Allen came back in the room and the president said they would start. Henry would have to catch up.

"Japanese planes bombed the area of three West Coast cities, Seattle, Portland, and San Francisco. This happened just before dark last night. Not one bomb landed in the city limits of any of these cities. There are no reported casualties, and no real damage. The plane came from two carriers who now appear to be headed away from the mainland. In addition, the navy does not see any evidence of troop ships or possible Japanese landings."

For days the navy had been saying they saw no evidence of a Japanese invasion fleet. Because two carriers were seen heading for America, the president had approved the moving of American's two atomic bombs to the West Coast to be used if the invasion took place.

William Allen said, "What are the Japanese doing? They send two carriers halfway around the world, bomb some woods and pull out right away?" Because America lacked even basic information about Japan, the problem seemed even more confusing.

Muller said, "It sounds like a feint. They can't know our carriers will not be ready for several months. They bomb and then run away to protect their ships. I suspect Lobert asked the Japanese to distract us while he prepares his forces in Mexico. He gambles we move our atomic bombs to the West Coast."

The president said, "The Japanese have never fully rebuilt their navy since the war, but two carriers sounds like a token force."

The president's phone rang. Estelle, his secretary, would never interrupt this kind of meeting unless it was important. It was the head of the FBI. The president listened, did not speak, and put down the phone. His face was ashen.

"Henry Windum is dead. He was shot in his office during the night; they are sure it is the assassin."

William Allen came out of his seat. "Henry. My God. Henry told me he was working on the intelligence problem in the Pacific. Do you think this has anything to do with the Japanese carriers?"

Both Allen and the president were shaken. A comrade—a friend—dead. Words could not reflect their feelings. They would mourn a friend, but just as important, what did this mean to the security of the American people?

Susan and Mueller were silent. They knew what this man meant to David and William. The president stood up. "America has lost a great man." He could see Henry firing his rifle at Broadway and Lexington. There would never be another like him.

Allen said, "He brought us a cold beer just before Lexington; the man was a rock. I feel like the bottom has just dropped out of my soul."

Estelle opened the door and signaled Susan to come out of the meeting. Susan came to Estelle's desk. Estelle said, "It's General Quotoius, he said he had to talk to the president. I told him the president was under heavy fire today and he said he would speak to you."

Susan knew that General Quotoius, head of the air force, was one of David Schultz's favorite people. Quotoius had flown B-17s during the war and when England declared a truce he had gotten a boat and sailed to America the same as David Schultz had done.

Susan picked up the phone.

"Susan, I know he's busy but I've got to tell you some bad news. Another 101 has crashed."

The 101 was the jet they were counting on and this was the third crash in two weeks.

Susan asked, "General do you feel you must talk to the president?"

"No, it only just happened ten minutes ago. I have no details yet. Let me go to the crash site. I'll call in about an hour. You better inform him and tell him Archie will call in an hour."

She could tell from the pain in his voice that the pilot was probably dead and the problem was the plane could not attain maximum speed and evade the German ground-to-air missile

She had talked to the general once before when she arrived at the White House. He called to thank her for obtaining the weapon so they could study it and he said she had given the air force critical help for the coming war. It was only her second day at the White House but she thought she was talking to an old friend, and he made her feel extremely welcome.

Quotoius didn't want to hang up.

"Susan we talked about the problem if that plane can't obtain maximum speed."

Quotoius explained, "The goddamn engineers have told me this couldn't happen. We've lost three good pilots in the last two weeks and the engineers would say that from their specifications it couldn't happen. David Schultz doesn't need any more problems."

He was beside himself with anger and the pain of losing another brave young pilot. Susan knew his heart was breaking, but he was expressing concern for David Schultz.

She thought, I've got to put a positive twist on today. "General, we've got good news from the West Coast. The Japanese carriers are leaving with absolutely no damage to us. If you will, call the president when you can." She did not mention Windum's death.

Quotoius thought, this lady has spirit. She's trying to buck me up.

"Okay Susan. You tell David I'll call and you tell him the plane is going to fly if I have to carry it on my back." She could hear the pride, toughness, and courage in his voice. "Yeah, I'll make the plane fly, you tell the president that."

"I will, General." And she hung up. Susan looked at Estelle, who seemed on the verge of tears. She knew what was going on. Time to keep everyone busy. "Estelle, order an urn of coffee and some breakfast things. It will be a busy morning here. I'm going to make the president a special cup from the new coffeemaker." David Schultz loved his morning coffee. Then she wrote a note. "Another 101 has crashed. General Quotoius will call in an hour, but he says he will make the plane fly." She canceled all the president's appointments. Susan went into the office and said. "We have coffee and breakfast coming, but this is a special cup from our new coffeemaker for the president." She handed him the coffee and the note.

The president and Allen had talked about Windum's funeral. They felt the news from the West Coast was positive.

The pursuit of the assassin was the job of the FBI. The president opened the note and read it. For a moment he did not speak, then he handed the note to William Allen, and he said to no one. "We're going to earn our pay today." He went to the window and looked out. It was starting to rain. Susan followed him with the coffee. He sipped and said, "How did Archie sound?"

"Like he's mad, but determined to make the plane fly."

The president responded, "That's Archie."

Schultz tried to lighten the mood.

"Susan, do you see what you've gotten yourself into? You should have stayed in London. William pretends to be your friend, but what kind of a friend would bring you to this firehouse? All we do is fight fires around here."

251

She caught the ball and threw it back with a smile. "A good friend—and I wouldn't miss it for the world." Mueller thought the best decision Allen ever made was to bring that lady to the White House.

In an hour Archie Quotoius called.

"David, I've been to the crash site. We've got a hole thirty feet deep. Same problem when the pilot took it to max speed. It spun out of control and crashed.

Schultz asked, "Did the pilot have a wife?"

Archie was beyond grief. It was all about making the plane fly. He ignored Schultz's question. During the war he had seen many good pilots go down. This was like the war, only the mission counted.

"David, I've let the engineers run this project; now I'm taking over. I'm going over the plane wingtip to wingtip. I promise you, I'll make it fly. I scheduled another test in Washington next week. I'll let you know when we're ready to go." He hung up.

Schultz thought, "We're not having a good day, but my job is to keep everybody working. I'm going to leave the two atomic bombs on the coast. I don't know what the Japs are doing and if the 101 works and we get our elite units together we can beat the Germans.

"I've got three problems. The jet doesn't work, but I believe in Archie. If he can't do it nobody can.

"The FBI has to catch Henry's killer and finally someone has to shape up the elite units. Mueller thinks Mitch Iberson can. God he would miss Henry."

It was raining harder now. He looked out the window. Joe was in his raincoat. He was directing a car to move under the portico. His arm must be hurting in this weather. Joe and Freddie would be about the same age. Joe was a nice young man. He and Freddie would have been friends.

Schultz turned to Susan. "Joe's getting pretty wet out there today. Can we send him a cup of coffee?"

She said, "He drinks cocoa. I just sent a cup out to him."

She knew he was thinking of his son. He identified his son with Joe and now he lost Henry. He has all these problems, but he's thinking of Joe. That's why we're going to win; we think of the Joes of the world and they don't. Albert Lobert doesn't understand the we and all, the Joes are going to beat him.

Archie Quotoius was sitting in a chair smoking a pipe looking at the 101 jet fighter plane. He had been sitting there for two hours. He would go to Washington and fly the plane at max speed. In the last two hours he had walked around the plane three times, touched it and rubbed the wing and climbed in the cockpit. He had one hundred pilots who were cleared to fly the plane, but it crashed when you took it to max speed. The general hated only one thing about the 101, the special flap. The extra flap was to slow the plane for strafing ground troops. Quotoius didn't think that would work with the new German ground-to-air rocket and the damn engineers always had to junk up a plane. They loved to add things to make it more complicated. The special flap worked. They had tested it many times. Archie conceded it worked, but they didn't junk up the lady.

The lady was what he called the four-engine World War II bomber, the B-17—the best plane America ever built. Drafty, noisy, slow, that plane could fly to hell and back. Quotoius had flown thirty missions over Germany. Four times he came home on two engines, once on one engine with another engine on fire. After many missions he couldn't count the number of holes in the plane. He had one copilot dead and another one so shot up he never flew again, but the lady always brought him home. The young engineers all laughed when he talked about the B-17, saying the jets made the plane obsolete. Archie had ten B-17s built. New beautiful planes, and it never showed in the budget, and even David Schultz didn't know about the planes. Archie didn't know how he would use the planes. They would be no good against the Nazi invasion fleet. The plane was ineffective against moving ships. Once the German army landed and was strung out it would make poor targets from the height the planes would fly to avoid the ground to air. In addition if the 101 couldn't drive off the Nazi jets, they couldn't get close enough to bomb anyhow.

But if the 101 could fly and drive off the Nazi jets and the army bunched up he could do a lot of damage. There was one other option. If the Nazi army got close to an American population center he would double the bomb load, carry a minimum gas load, for they would not be coming back, and lead ten planes in a low-level mission and the Germans would see what Hades looked like. Archie puffed on his pipe and stood up to his full five foot four inches height. He would walk around the plane again. He rubbed his brush haircut and looked at the wing.

Ten days later the president's car pulled up to the main hangar at Washington National Airport at 8:30 on a bright sunny spring morning.

Archie's assistant and the designer of the 101, a man named Pullum, was waiting for the president. Pullum, a young man of thirty-two and considered brilliant, was as tall as David Schultz. Pullum was highly agitated and complained to the president, "General Quotoius has taken off already and I was not able to inspect the plane. The agreement we had was I was to arrive today and look at the plane and brief the general on the test. I protest the way this is going."

The voice of the general could be heard on the radio inside the hangar.

"Mr. President, I understand you are at the hangar. I've been up for about twenty minutes. I'm at twenty-five thousand. The plane is handling fine. I'm going to put her into a dive and see if I get it to max speed.

A moment later they heard the jet and a loud boom. Schultz tightened his hand on the lucky coin Estelle had given him. My God not Quotoius. Then they saw the jet at five thousand feet. They heard Quotoius's voice.

"Smooth as silk. Well over a thousand miles per hour and no buffeting. She performed like a pro. I'm going up to ten thousand feet and do it again."

Three times more the jet dove, and loud noise and Quotoius's voice on the radio, telling them the jet was fine.

Finally Quotoius came on the radio. "Mr. President, I can report the 101 is combat ready. There is not a plane in the world that can touch her."

The president was so happy he wanted to sing, but he patted Quotoius's assistant on the back.

Quotoius told them he was bringing the plane back. They saw him bring the 101 in a wide arc and go so low he disappeared over the horizon. Suddenly he was buzzing the base at four hundred miles per hour, flying upside down. He flashed past the hangar perhaps a mile away, turned the plane right side up, and wiggled the wing and then did a victory roll. The president had his great plane. Nothing the Germans could do would beat them now.

He said to the group, "Archie would make a pretty good fighter pilot."

They moved out to greet him as he taxied to the hangar. He was on the wing dropping his parachute, and stepped down to congratulations from all the men.

He shook the President's hand and said, "She's ready to go; best plane in the world; second-best plane I ever flew."

Pullum was under the plane. "Where is the extra flap? You took off the extra flap! You had no right to do that without checking with me." He was screaming.

Quotoius's right hand flashed. He seemed to leave the ground as he punched Pullum in the face. At five foot four inches, he floored the taller man, who fell in a heap, blood spurting from his nose.

Quotoius was standing over him. "You killed three of my pilots. Your damn extras. I said keep it simple. Damn engineers, it blows off at high altitude and high speed, and foils the engine.

Quotoius motioned a mechanic to help him pick Pullum up. They led him away, blood all over his shirt.

Quotoius said to the president, "I tested without the flap for two days. The flap killed my guys. I'll probably apologize in a couple of days, but they better not junk up my planes again.

When they got to the White House Schultz had one of the Secret Service men show Allen Quotoius's right hand blow in slow motion. Allen knew the president was in a great mood; they had just put out a fire.

Chapter VI

One of the strangest employees of the White House was Dan Ryan.

Dan Ryan was David Schultz's uncle. At one time Dan was the best detective on the New York City police force. He was dismissed when the Blackshirts took over and as his wife said, "Dan missed the next ten years. He was drunk the whole time."

When David Schultz became the president, Dan's wife asked him to take Dan to Washington with him. "David, you're the only one who can stop Dan's drinking. If he is with you he won't embarrass you. He'll stop; and if he doesn't stop, he'll die."

So David took Dan to Washington with him; and he teamed up with Abraham Chamberlain to run errands for the White House. When Susan arrived at the White House, their value jumped. At her direction, they could get reports much quicker than the previous chief of staff had been able to.

When the president asked in the morning how much fuel there would be for the new jet fighter 101, he had the report by noon from the Energy Department. The president didn't care how it happened. He wanted to be able to tell General Quotoius to go ahead with practice missions or hold. While people were working hard the human element was alive in the machinery of government. Instead of screaming phone calls from the White House, two older gentlemen would arrive from the White House with jokes and occasionally candy and flowers for rush jobs. As one department head told Susan, instead of those jerks threatening us, Dan and Abraham treat us like real people, anything you need, call me or my assistant.

When Henry Windum was murdered a deep gloom descended on the White House, the only one not to look depressed was Dan Ryan. Susan who could see him talking to the FBI liaison man, and she wondered what he was up to.

Finally Dan asked Susan if he and Abraham could have a meeting with the president. She spoke to the president, who said, "Susan, he wants to work on the Henry Windum case. At one time he solved forty murder cases, but that was ten years ago. I know the FBI doesn't want him involved. You get the file on the assassin and I'll talk to them at 4:00 P.M."

Dan heard rumors around the White House that the FBI was stuck on the case. A veteran police detective, Ryan knew it was much too early to make a judgment about the status of the case, and he also knew it was his kind of case.

A gunshot homicide, no robbery, no clues, the killer known to the deceased, Windum had opened the door to the killer late at night, the victim shot at close range. Dan had other facts from the FBI man that were not in the papers. He had solved this type of crime many times. Dan rubbed his chin, a nervous habit, and straightened his tie as he walked toward the president's office. He had the Dan Ryan technique; he had used a set of rules for his investigation. Last night he wrote out the Ryan technique. He and Abraham would make a good team.

Dan was the Boston terrier type, nervous. Abraham was quiet, but observant. He would handle the tape recorder as Dan asked the questions.

He must get David to let him work on the case. He would use a fall-back position, that any notes he and Abraham would develop would be given to the FBI to help them with the case. Dan felt more alive in the last two days than he had in years.

Susan saw the bounce in his step as they came down the hall and felt good about the meeting.

They arrived at the office. Dan suspected that Abraham had mentioned to the president last night the purpose of the meeting.

Dan started, "Mr. President, Abraham and I would like to work on the Henry Windum case as your special investigators."

David Schultz sat straight up in his chair. "You know, Dan, the FBI is working on the case. They have no leads; it's very early."

Dan looked at Susan sitting to the right of the president. "The FBI is very good and we would certainly not interfere with their case. Abraham and I would like to interview all the people that met with Henry Windum the last three weeks of his life. If we find nothing we will turn our notes over to the agency. He sounded so logical that Susan thought the president couldn't turn him down. David Schultz had grown to be a top executive by challenging people who wanted his support. He asked Dan how long he wanted to work on the case.

"I expect Abraham and I could conduct all the interviews and the follow ups in less than a month's time."

Schultz had talked to the head of the FBI this morning. They had twenty agents on the case and he was not happy a retired NYC detective would be involved, but admitted they had no leads or clues in the killing of Schoenrienst at West Point.

The president respected the man but asked, "How many murders have your agents solved."

There was a long pause. "Not many."

The president told the head of the FBI that Susan Tyler would call him back with the president's decision.

David turned to Susan Tyler.

Susan put on her reading glasses and opened a folder.

"From our agents in Europe. The Nazis sent an agent here two months ago, code name assassin. His job was to kill a former Gestapo officer who had come to our side and to kill a top official in the American government. The first murder was at West Point five weeks ago. The FBI believed the same man killed Henry Windum. Getting past the guards was the same. Also this was a man released from prison. He had killed many times before, always at close range, strangulation or gunshots."

Susan talked of agents but only one agent helped on this—the naval attaché in England. The rest came from breaking the German code. Only three people knew the code was broken: the president, Allen, and Susan.

The president spoke.

"So Dan, this could be more than a homicide. Not like your former cases.

Dan answered, "A man is dead. Everything about this case tells me he knew his killer." The FBI agent had told Dan the bullet was fired from close range, but that Henry was reading when it happened.

"Henry worked on counterintelligence. He may have met the assassin in the last few weeks; maybe he suspected the man. The FBI will be working on the theory the assassin killed him, but I would be working on the theory that I don't know who killed him."

Schultz liked that idea. The FBI did not seem to have clues; maybe a different approach would help.

The president asked, "Dan and Abraham, what do you need?"

Abraham pointed to Dan; he was doing all the talking.

"First, we need to look at the dossier that Miss Tyler has and all the information the FBI has on both cases. We need Henry Windum's phone records, his appointment book. We will build a list of names. Then we need a letter from the White House that we are your special investigators sent to the list of names we draw up. These people by order of the president are to speak to us. Finally a letter with your signature that everyone is to cooperate with us. That will get us in all the doors we need to open."

Schultz made an instant decision.

"You got it. It's your case working, parallel with the FBI. Susan is your contact; go to work, good luck."

Dan spoke to Susan for a moment and then he and Abraham went to their small office.

Abraham had confidence in Dan, but this was a great responsibility. "Dan, how are we going to do this?"

Dan said, "We are going to listen and ask questions until we drive somebody into the open. It's not easy to kill someone and not make a mistake—even for a pro. First, get us two cots. Susan will give us twenty-four-hour typists. You run the tape recorder and control the color-coded files, a file folder for each name. First interview white, second blue, third red. We will narrow the field and conduct two nice interviews and when we get to the third interview we won't be nice.

"Are you sure this will work?"

"I've never worked on a case where the killer didn't make a mistake, the pressure on us is to make sure we don't miss it."

Abraham picked up the tape recorder. "How many cases did you solve this way, Dan?"

"All of them."

Dan and Abraham worked all night to get the list of names. At 7:00 A.M. Abraham gave the list of people they were to interview to Susan.

Susan looked at Abraham. "You look terrible; did you get any sleep last night?"

"I got an hour but Dan never closed his eyes. And the worst, when he works if he finds something he likes he hums."

Susan told Abraham she would send breakfast over from the cafeteria. She told him she bet William Allen they would solve the case before the FBI.

Abraham responded, "Good, William Allen is on the list."

Susan expressed surprise. "You're going to interview William Allen? You can't believe he killed Henry."

"No, but he may say something that implicates someone else. Dan's theory is to cover everyone; it's hard work, not brilliance."

So the two special appointed agents began their work. They knew the FBI did not approve. For the president's agents were leaving a cabinet office, when FBI men were entering. The FBI agents started to laugh when they saw Dan and Abraham. Dan did not seem to notice or care. Dan was in a zone—he worked day and night and slept only three hours a night.

On the fourth day, Abraham awoke to see Dan looking out the window of the office. He was waiting for Abraham to awake. He was excited.

"Abraham, I've been listening to this guy's tape for four hours, he goes to the top of the list for second interview tomorrow. I'll call and make the appointment."

"Dan, we still have a few names for first interviews."

"I know, but we got six people for second interview, and this guy goes to the top of the list."

Abraham pulled out the man's file.

"Dan, he's a former policeman."

Dan pulled out the FBI file on Henry's death. "Yes, and do you know what kind of gun was used to kill Henry?"

"A .38."

"Yes, and cops in his neck of the woods carry .38s."

Dan turned to Abraham.

"Now calm down; until we do the second interview this means nothing."

Abraham was calm; he was still half asleep. He knew Dan was talking to himself. "Keep calm." What he did not know was that the suspect had made suspicious body motions during the interview that peaked Dan's interest.

Four days later Dan called Susan. Could he and Abraham come down and visit the president? They sat around the president's conference table; Dan read from a typed statement. "We interviewed forty people, we conducted a second interview with six people, and interviewed one man for a third time. We are convinced this man killed Henry Windum. He is a member of the president's cabinet."

David Schultz did not say anything, but Susan could see from the look on his face this would be a blow if it was true.

"We will play excerpts from the audiotapes we have; we will also read from transcripts as we go along. We will build our case."

"We interviewed this man for six hours, approximately two hours each time."

Dan read from a transcript. "Question, can you tell me where you were at the exact time of Henry Windum's death." Dan signaled Abraham to start the tape.

"Oh, that was Tuesday, 9:00 P.M.. I was in my office. I remember I was working on budgets, defense budgets. I didn't see Henry that week."

The president recognized the voice, but was silent.

Dan started again. "This was the second interview. Question, as near as you can, where were you at the precise time of Henry Windum's death?"

Abraham ran the tape. "That was a little after 9:00 P.M. I was in my office. I was working on budgets, defense budgets. I didn't see Henry that week." Abraham shut off the tape. Susan was puzzled.

"There was nothing inconsistent about that," she asked.

Dan looked up from his notes. "Not only consistent, but word for word the same answer. Also he started out strong and his voice trailed off at the end both times."

Susan again didn't know what he was getting at. "So?"

"We asked him one hundred questions, six questions were directly related to his possible involvement with Henry's death. To all six he gave the exact same answer. He had rehearsed the answer in anticipation of being asked the question. When you conduct a murder investigation people are nervous, forgetful, confused. Innocent people will give different answers, sometimes contradict themselves. They are not lying, but the pressure of this type of interrogation is not fun, so you get different answers. The man's body language was in total contradiction to his measured answers. He was extremely tense sitting in the chair in his office. In fact, I think he murdered Henry, but also he is hiding other things. This man is a very troubled man. The first two interviews we did were very low key. I was purposely adversarial when I called for the third interview. He didn't want to speak to us.

"Listen to his third answer to the same question."

"Oh, I don't know. You can look at your notes!"

"Alex Liva is now very defensive; he knows I don't like his answers. He is scrambling to change his story."

Abraham hit the tape. "I didn't leave the office until 11:00 P.M. I can't remember the type of work I was doing. No, I didn't call anyone at that time."

Dan said, "He frequently placed his hand over his mouth or he mumbles. He is lying."

Now they heard Dan's voice.

"You were a policeman in Connecticut. You carried a .38. Windum was shot with a .38."

On the tape, Liva said, "I didn't shoot Henry Windum. I'm right-handed."

Dan said, "He really is panicking now. The only thing as a policeman he remembered the killer shot Henry with his left hand. What he forgets is that only the killer and the police know a left-handed shooter killed Henry."

"This guy is ready to break if the FBI interrogates him."

The president finally spoke. "There is one problem, Dan. He has an alibi. He was with me and twenty other people at a dinner the night of Schoenrienst's death. He was drunk at 1:00 P.M. No way he could sober up and get to West Point in two hours. He's not the assassin."

Dan slumped in his chair. They were silent for a moment when Abraham Chamberlain spoke for the first time.

"What about two killers? This guy killed Henry. Someone else killed Schoenrienst."

The president said, "The FBI theory of the two murders, the assassin profile, he kills up close, strangulation or gunshots; also he's left-handed. But what really convinces them is how in both cases he got past the guards. Two MPs at West Point, and the guards at Henry's building. It took a pro to do that; Alex Liva is a lightweight. He could never figure out how to sneak into the building around the guards.

A moment of silence and Abraham Chamberlain was pulling out the huge briefcase under the table.

"Wait a minute, wait a minute; I've got William Allen's file."

He pulled out William Allen's file. How could this file possibly relate to the murder?

Abraham ran his finger down the questions and answers.

"I've got it." His voice filled with excitement.

Dan's question to William Allen: "When is the last time you saw Henry Windum?"

"I called Henry. The president was after us to set up an espionage ring in the Pacific. We had no intelligence on the Japanese. I had two men I was working on and I wanted Henry's thoughts."

"Now here is Henry's answer."

Abraham was speaking much louder.

"The president spoke to me, come right over, park your car in the back, don't go around the front. It will take you ten minutes to get past security. I'll go down and unlock the back door; it's only two flights up. We've got to get on this quickly."

Dan realized he had missed this because no one could seriously believe Allen was a suspect, but Abraham had been listening.

Dan said, "If Liva called Henry and said 'I've got information on the assassin,' would Henry have told him to come up the back way?"

David Schultz said, "Yes, Henry was a man of action. He hated the delays of security checks. That is exactly what he would have done."

"So, there were two killers."

The president dialed the head of the FBI. "Arrest Alex Liva immediately. Suspicion of murder of Henry Windum."

The man could tell from the president's tone he was serious; the head of the FBI responded. He had made a joke about the two detectives. If the FBI had blown this case, he better get on the right side, quickly.

David Schultz said to Dan, "How did the FBI miss this? They were so sure it was one man."

Dan said, "For the past ten years all the murders in this country have been the Blackshirts. We're out of practice. Hey, I blew it too. I should have interviewed you. You were Windum's friend; it might have helped."

The president called William Allen, and when Allen came to the office he explained to him what had happened.

Allen asked, "Why did he do it?"

The phone rang. It was the head of the FBI. When they got to Liva's house he was packing his clothes. He was leaving town. They arrested him and all he would say was, "They made me do it."

David Schultz said, "Nobody goes home or goes to bed until we know what this is all about." His tone was harsh.

The head of the FBI knew his job was on the line. They would not beat Liva, but he was going to get answers for the president.

For two hours Alex Liva refused to answer any questions. He had composed himself on the car ride to the FBI headquarters. He was more afraid of his conspirators than the FBI.

The head of the FBI waved the interrogators out of the room.

Liva said, "I want a lawyer."

The head of the FBI said, "If you're more afraid of your friends than you are of me, your betting on the wrong horse. You may have cost me my job. I said when we arrested you, no one touches him. Now I realize we're in the same boat. I'm lucky if I save my job; you're lucky if you save your life. David Schultz hates you. He blames you for the death of his son, and now the death of his best friend. I hate you for putting me in this position. If you talk, I'll say you confessed everything; you're full of remorse. Show mercy. I'll really try and save you. Lie to me or don't talk, and I'm not going to worry about what some court or some judge will do to me in the future about how I questioned you. Your friends don't worry about the rights of a prisoner. I'm going to treat you like your friends would."

The head of the FBI called the president one hour later.

"Alex Liva has signed a confession. He killed Henry Windum because he had been blackmailed to do it. He did two drug deals with a man named Red Harter. Harter's in prison but he sent a man to Liva saying he was a cabinet minister, but he could be prosecuted for the past so Liva passed state secrets to the Nazis through Harter. He told them about our sending atomic bombs to the West Coast to stop the Japanese. The assassin came to Liva last week, said he thought Windum was on to Harter, and the drug deals. Liva was to kill Windum or he would be turned in to us. The assassin will be arrested immediately. He's staying at a hotel in Washington. My men are on the way."

The president was silent then he said, "Let me know when you've arrested the assassin. William Allen will convene a small committee to investigate this whole affair."

The head of the FBI hung up. He didn't know if he had saved his job. He didn't expect any congratulations from Schultz and he didn't get any. He would demote his top detectives. They were playing in the big leagues. Good tries were not enough. They only paid in wins in this league. He had not mentioned mercy for Liva.

The president said to William Allen, "The FBI missed this one. You've got to see what mistakes were made. We can't say it's okay. We owe it to the people who pay our salaries to do it better."

Allen had seen Schultz growing harder and tougher. It went with the job.

Allen said, "We missed it too; I think there are some things we could have done better. Thank God for Dan and Abraham. What do you think Henry would have said about this?"

The president said, "Henry was a realist. He would say you're going to make mistakes, but you've got to keep trying, and at some point you've got to prove yourself. I don't want heads to roll at the FBI, but they have to get their act together, and if they don't do it, the American people have the right to say what's wrong with the president."

Allen said, "I was interviewed by a young man from the FBI. I should have pressed him about Henry letting me in but I thought he understood. I also think this is the last straw with Red Harter. This goes beyond jail time. He assisted in Henry's murder. This time he pays."

Chapter VII

The main fleet for the invasion of America was assembled at Bremen, Germany.

Admiral Heidel invited Albert Lobert to an inspection of part of the invasion fleet. Two great battleships rode at anchor surrounded by many transports and smaller vessels. All preparation for the sailing was working at a fever pitch. Draft boats were transporting men and materiel to the larger ships for Albert Lobert's great adventure. Next week they would sail and Lobert was very impressed with the great ships and the energy he saw. Reich Chancellor Lobert was ushered into the state room of Admiral Heidel's flagship, a battleship.

He was pleased that Heidel had gained control of the navy. If the venture bogged down he was sure the navy might offer more support than he originally planned.

Lobert wanted to impress Heidel's senior staff with his vision of the venture to America. They would all profit by his great idea. He looked at Heidel and his four chief officers across a great oak table in the state room. He thought, I should have a great table like this. He began with his now familiar litany that his people had heard many times.

The conquistador of the Fourth Reich was going to the New World, like Pizzaro and Cortez leading fierce soldiers of fortune. They were cruel and ruthless men who would sweep the Americans away. The Americans were weak. He was not sure they would fight; but it didn't matte. The American would pay for the expedition. Yes, the Americans would pay like Hitler's legions made Europe pay for the beginning of World War II. If the Americans thought the Blackshirts were harsh in the ten-year occupation, they would learn what cruel could really be like. He returned to his theme that American cities would be like Carthage. They would be destroyed and the Earth salted so nothing would grow again. He was working himself up, his own people would react to these comments, but the naval officers sat quietly.

"America will be an agricultural country. They will work on the giant farms to grow food for the new world order, and many will be sent overseas never to return again. And there will be great profits for the Blackshirts, including the navy." At this point usually his followers were clapping and cheering, but the five naval officers sat impassively and did not move a muscle.

He was disappointed and trailed off with his final words, puzzled at their reaction.

Once Heidel was sure Lobert was finished he spoke. "That was an inspirational talk, Reich Chancellor." Heidel pulled his chair closer to the table to be sure his words were understood. "I know your plan is for General Messinger to lead the expedition, and that he will meet with the troops in Mexico and form one great army. But we are troubled. You are the brains and heart of the expedition. This is your brilliant project and we think you should lead it."

The other four men finally spoke up agreeing with Heidel. Lobert should come with them and lead the venture.

Lobert was speechless. How dare they suggest to him to go to Mexico. He was the Reich chancellor, not some common soldier. Others would share the glory and hardships of the venture; he would be in Berlin, the supreme commander.

He was so upset that he could not talk. He sputtered, fighting to hold his temper. He could only say, "No, that was impossible. General Messinger had his orders. All the plans were set." Now he was emphatic.

"I will not lead."

Heidel, again clearly in charge, brushed aside Lobert's declaration.

"Reich chancellor, this is a great challenge from all of us. I speak for my fellow commanders, you have entrusted us with the army. We sail with a navy that has just begun to function at our direction. We do not know what the Americans will do to try to stop us. This is a mixed army; many are not Germans. It needs your enlightenment."

Lobert's mind was racing. Heidel was challenging him. Was this some form of blackmail? What did they want? He fought to control his temper. "Gentlemen, I am the Reich chancellor. If I order the navy to sail, it will sail without me."

Now Heidel's second in command spoke up. He was not as diplomatic as Heidel. "If you do not agree, the navy will never sail. We control the navy and we will not take the ships to sea without you."

He did not even try to be diplomatic. This was a blunt challenge. It was mutiny.

Albert Lobert had fooled many people and schemed and doublecrossed and killed other good men. The five naval officers were not risking their lives with his promises. If he stayed in Germany and the expedition failed they would have families at risk. If the expedition was a success, how did they know they might be in a plane crash when he didn't need them anymore?

Heidel tired of the game. They had reasoned with him because one of the five had insisted they try. Now he would dictate the terms, which he always intended to do.

Before he could speak Lobert said, "I can see you gentlemen are set in this. I will return to my office and review your thoughts with my staff and we will get back to you."

He would try and maneuver around them. His security guard was two hundred yards away on the dock. He cursed to himself that he trusted them.

The youngest of the five got up and took his chair and sat down against the door. Sweat appeared on Albert's brow. He knew they were going to kill him if he did not follow their orders.

Heidel spoke, "You will sign a simple agreement. You are going to lead the expedition to Mexico. Then a cameraman will film you reading the statement and both will be released to the public. In addition, you will designate five men to govern Germany in your absence. Three of the five are with us. We want no civil war, but you do as we say or we kill you."

Lobert half rose from his chair. "My followers?"

Heidel interrupted. "Your followers will not move without you and if they do we have two battleships and two heavy cruisers in this harbor—more firepower than all your followers combined."

"My jets?" Lobert countered.

"All your jets left last night for America."

Lobert looked at Heidel. "Why are you doing this? I saved the navy."

"Germany is tired of war, the people you are taking to America are your people, not Germans. We will fulfill our contract and take that rabble to America and leave you and them to fight as you will."

Two sailors were already dead because of the rabble and Heidel had every sailor of the fleet carrying sidearms for his own protection.

And so the most unenthusiastic soldier of fortune ever to go to the New World, Albert Lobert, signed a paper that said he was the leader of the modern conquistador.

He was placed under guard and when he reached his cabin he thought, I will land and turn my jets against these swine. No, he could not do that. The naval guns and their ground-to-air missiles would shoot down too many of his jets. He would need the jets against the Americans. But his other plan would still work against the Americans. These deepwater sailors did not know about that; he could still win. But he lapsed into a deep depression. He had been undone by a double cross.

What did William Allen say? We may have more friends than we know because people do not trust Lobert.

Chapter VIII

One of David Schultz's fires was his elite unit. It was the problem he worried most about.

David Schultz called General Mueller to his office. The elite American unit was floundering; they were expected to meet the Nazi invasion from Mexico and they were not ready. Schultz and Mueller had talked about this and they knew it was a time to change the leadership of the group.

Mueller liked to illustrate his suggestion with a past experience. Allen called them Mueller parables.

"I first met Erwin Rommell in 1940 in France. I was a captain and we surprised the French by coming through the Ardennes at the Meuse River. They thought they could hold us for four weeks. On the second day I was standing on our side of the river and I could see our engineers paddling for the other side against murderous French fire. Rommell was on the other side with perhaps two hundred men. He was everywhere urging the men on. We were taking casualties. But still the men responded to his orders, and two hours later we had a bridge built and our tanks started to cross.

A few days later Rommell was leading twenty tanks and some 88 guns. At the time the 88 was used only for antiaircraft fire against planes. Suddenly the French counterattacked us with many tanks and infantry. I thought they were too many for us.

Suddenly Rommell was yelling, 'Form a gun line, form a gun line.' He got the men to turn the 88 into artillery. We didn't have the right shell for tanks, but the French tanks were not heavily armored and we were doing damage. All the gunners were engaged. Rommell was up and down the line getting the rest of us to carry ammunition. I fell in the mud and lost my cap and my monocle. I was struggling with a shell and Rommell was at my shoulder. 'Well done, Mueller, keep working—we have them.'"

Mueller's eyes were closed. He was in France. For this man whose whole life was war, this was a religious experience.

"I shall never forget him saying to me, 'Well done, Mueller; we shall have them.' I have been a general for a long time, but I could never inspire captains to carry ammunition." He opened his eyes.

"Yes, we drove them off. To lead the elite unit you must get a man who can inspire captains to carry ammunition and you have such a man. Mitch Iberson, the hero of the Golden Gate Bridge."

Schultz said, "He's very young."

Mueller answered, "He's a born leader; he's the one man that can turn this unit around."

David Schultz was reading from General Mueller's book when William Allen brought Mitch Iberson and his twin brother Richie and General Mueller to the office. The president had met Mitch many times at cabinet meetings, but only spoke to Richie once before, so Schultz spoke to Richie first.

"Richie, just reading General Mueller's report on your attack on the Golden Gate Bridge. You landed a glider on the entrance to the bridge on only your third time flying a glider."

Richie sat down. "Yes, sir, it was my third try at the controls of a glider."

Schultz signaled his approval. "I flew gliders during the war. I don't think I could put a glider on that bridge my third try out."

Richie raised his right hand.

"Well, there was no wind and we had a light load."

Schultz turned to Mitch. "Would you go up with him in a glider again?"

Mitch answered, "Sir, I don't want to drive with him in a car again."

They all laughed.

Schultz moved to the business at hand.

"Mitch and Richie, I've got a tough job for you. It's almost not fair to ask, but General Mueller and I think you're the logical team to take it on.

"The Germans are loading their troops in Europe to invade America. We project they will bring two hundred and fifty thousand men to Mexico. They will be joined by about the same amount waiting for them in Mexico. A mixed group of Blackshirts and army, with some South American recruits. So a total of half a million men will march on us in about seven weeks. We have always planned to meet them with our elite units being trained in Virginia, but there is a problem. They are not ready. He took out a sheet of paper with many statistics. Absent from practice and training, fifteen percent. All the experts tell me anything below ninety percent effective and ready is bad."

"Equipment ready to fight about seventy five percent, a terrible figure. This outfit has more colds and flu than any group we have. In short they could meet the Germans and embarrass us. This is troubling because we spent more money on this group and they have the best equipment we have. If they don't perform we could be in trouble. I know what you were up against in California and this outfit has twenty times the firepower you had."

The president rubbed his hands together. "I think of what William and I had at Lexington—brave people with rifles and guts—and I'd like to go over to Virginia and knock some heads together. General Mueller has an explanation why all the training and resources have been wasted."

The general knew that Schultz liked to get right to the point. He polished his monocle and began.

"It's the leadership." Consistent with his feelings, it was always the leadership and he was almost always right.

"The leader is a man who wants to be friends with everybody, he doesn't want to hurt any feelings so he never asks for performance. He himself doesn't participate in all the training missions. He sits in his office and writes us memos asking for more support for his unit, promotions and merit raises; his men love him but they don't perform for him. David and I went over to Virginia, we replaced two of his top men, but it did no good."

David Schultz spoke, "I called the senior officer this morning and told him he was replaced. He begged me to promote his number two, a man named Frank Solly, a good man, but he has missed a number of training missions. We need new faces over there."

Schultz asked Mueller to give more background. "The Nazi army that is coming is slow and ponderous; the leadership is mediocre. They should be perfect for our elite units to engage. When I talked to Mitch and Richie in California we agreed it was the American character to move fast. In every war the secret to the American soldier was speed. To strike the enemy before he is ready."

Schultz had called Mitch at the hotel that morning to tell him the purpose of the meeting and now he asked him if he was ready to go to Virginia.

Mitch had one question. "You okay, Richie?"

"I'm ready to go right now."

Chapter IX

Before World War II started, Europe had a preview of the war—The Spanish civil war. The Democrats and communist Russia supported the elected government of Spain while Germany and Italy sided with the rebels. The dominant personality of Spain, as well as the leader of the Fascist victor, was General Francisco Franco. Called the Caudillo, General Franco was admired by his friends for his almost supernatural ability to weave his way through the pitfall of military and political traps that existed in pre and post World War II. The Caudillo's closest friend was an Englishman, Lord Justin Oliver. The two men shared a mutual respect for each other's ability to make critical decisions, for their own best political interest and for maintaining power in the respective sphere of influence. The latest decision was when Spain was asked by the German army for support during the German civil war. The Caudillo almost gave his support, but pulled back when Justin Oliver told him he would receive little reward from the German army for his support and there was a risk that the Blackshirts could win. When the Blackshirts won, Caudillo knew that once again Justin Oliver had given him good advice.

They shared other interests. Both were dedicated sportsmen. Hunting and fishing was not a hobby; it was more of a passion. Both enjoyed the organization and preparation for the hunt as much as the hunt itself.

Their scheduled hunt was in northern Spain near the French border. From the villa the night before the hunt they spent three hours discussing the guns and ammunition they would use. They would hunt for stags in a deep green forest and the Caudillo had an excellent map showing the stream they would cross, a long meadow that bordered on the forest and the best place for a good shot. The map was marked like a military map for tomorrow's hunt—and both men were delighted that every step was planned.

This was their day and they would enjoy every moment of it.

After a light breakfast they set out in Range Rovers to the place where they would begin. The Spanish people did not see the human side of the Caudillo. They saw a man of medium height, a bit pudgy with a dour, serious personality. A mustache framed his round face that rarely smiled in public. They would have been surprised at his jokes with Justin Oliver that morning—of past hunts, shots missed, fish lost, and the guide that fell off a bridge near Gibraltar and almost drowned. Now the Range Rovers came to a halt and they and the retinue of ten men would be quiet for the next few hours. When they got out of the trucks the smell of the forest and the dark beauty of the tall trees was the opening curtain of the drama.

Five hours later, tired but happy, the two men sat in the shade of a giant oak in two small chairs with a table that held a bottle of brandy and glasses. A small stream ran near by. That and the sounds of the birds were the only sounds from the tranquil forest. The retinue sat a respectful fifty yards away.

Justin Oliver broke the silence. "Excellent shot, Caudillo."

The Caudillo had bagged a stag with an excellent shoulder shot and was pleased with himself. He poured brandy into Oliver's glass. "A good hunt today Justin."

Yes, it was a good hunt despite the fact only one shot was fired all day. But the beauty of the forest and the pond they found off a stream jumping with trout would be visited tomorrow—an excellent new spot.

Caudillo was silent and Oliver knew him well enough from his serious expression that it was time for business.

"Have you heard rumors about Chancellor Lobert?" asked the Caudillo.

Oliver chose his words carefully.

"Yes, I have heard rumors about Albert Lobert. Yes, terrible rumors, but I cannot substantiate them. But, I don't like it that they come from reliable sources." Oliver paused. "Serious men have repeated the rumors to me," including the general who was selling him the ground-to-air missile.

Caudillo sighed. "We are a Catholic country. If it would come out that he had molested children and I supported him with five thousand men for his invasion of America, it would cause unnecessary criticism of me within Spain."

The Caudillo control was absolute in Spain so this kind of talk would not topple his government, but he always balanced the forces that wanted the return of the king—right-wing extremists of his own party and the growing influence of a small group from the Church that wanted more influence from a rubber stamp congress. The Caudillo was always ahead of the curve and did not take the talk about Lobert lightly.

Now the Caudillo took the other side of the argument. "Of

course, if he beats America, such talk would grow dim. Do you think he will beat America?"

Oliver had waited for this question. His judgment would be listened to and remembered. Despite the fact he was a paid American agent, he would give an honest answer to the question.

"I'm not so sure he will beat America. I have contacts in America. They have told me that America's industrial might is surfacing. They have new weapons. I know the woman they have just made chief of staff at the White House, and I have followed the career of David Schultz. These are tough people, they may be more dedicated to their cause than the Blackshirt leadership are supportive of Albert Lobert."

He had not given the Caudillo a yes or no answer, but his judgment of the leadership of the two parties would have great influence on a man who believed that the will of the leadership of a country was a major factor in that country's ability to defend itself.

The Caudillo knew Oliver had American contacts and he had been right about the German civil war. He trusted no man in the world as he trusted this man. The Caudillo did not like the former Reich chancellor, but before he died he had been reasonable with Spain in his dealing. Albert Lobert was a weak man, and perhaps an evil man. The Caudillo had no respect for him.

"I had to give the Germans five thousand men; they wanted a lot more but despite Lobert's attempts to pressure me I said no. If the Americans win, will they blame the Spanish government for Spanish soldiers invading their country?" he asked Justin Oliver.

Oliver answered immediately. "The Americans are aggressive; they are fomenting civil unrest in any country that is friendly to the Blackshirts. If they beat Albert Lobert they will be a great world power and I know they are working on rockets that will carry atomic bombs from America to Europe."

The Caudillo sipped his brandy and looked down.

"And if I gave the American government information that was critical to their national defense and survival would they regard the Spanish government as friendly and also protect the source?"

Justin Oliver knew the Caudillo wanted a direct answer. He was about to produce a bombshell. This was no time to equivocate.

"Caudillo, I have a direct line to senior American officials. I believe they will protect the source and be grateful for information that is critical to their national defense."

The Caudillo began. "Two weeks ago the Germans asked us to widen the gauge of our national rail line spur that runs to their submarine base at Gibraltar. We did and of course our intelligence agents followed the train from Germany. We identified three scientists from the Blackshirt atomic bomb committee. When the train reached Gibraltar two crates were given special handling and loaded onto two submarines. The scientists were clearly in charge of the loading. The submarines are scheduled to leave next week for the Atlantic and the course is obvious—America."

Twelve hours after the Caudillo told Justin Oliver about the German submarines, Susan Tyler told William Allen she had a decoded message from England that said America had friends in high places in Spain.

Minutes later Allen, Tyler, and General Mueller met with the president in his office.

Schultz asked Susan how reliable she thought the message from Justin Oliver was. "He has never been wrong on anything this important and I know he was going hunting with General Franco. His last line, we have friends in high places, I think this comes from Franco himself. We know the Caudillo likes to hedge his bets."

William Allen said, "This would be just like Franco to make sure we owe him on something this important. Also, we hear the number of Spanish volunteers to Lobert's army is small."

Schultz turned to General Mueller. "General, what do you think?"

Mueller stood up. It was clear he intended his words to carry great weight. "Remember Schoenrienst's letter to us. Lobert's army is one of his card tricks. I do not believe Albert Lobert's army is an army of conquest. Half the army is made up of riffraff from Europe; I know the general who leads it. Messinger, he is mediocre. This is not a fighting army. I believe our elite units should stop this army on the border, but I believe this army is a feint and that Lobert intends to destroy two American cities with atomic bombs. He expects America to surrender as happened ten years ago and use the army as an army of occupation. Because of the timing I expect the cities will be attacked just before Lobert's army crosses from Mexico to the USA.

Schultz said, "We know submarines, the approximate time, but we need to know the exact time and the cities. I don't think we can evacuate all the cities on the eastern seaboard and we don't want to tip the Germans that we know their plan."

Allen said to Susan, "We've got a record of all the German code naval traffic because of information you were given by the naval attaché. Can we get his help on the targets and the time?"

Susan pulled out a memo from American code breakers. "I just received this today. I was going to show it at tomorrow's meeting. Two Blackshirt message of the last two weeks have asked the following question. The weather, depth of the water, and US naval surface activity off two American cities, New York and Boston. I think the man in England will help us. I will call our agents in England and tell them to contact him.

American agents in England contacted the German naval attaché and told him it was critical he find out the route and timing of Blackshirts' submarines going to America. He told them he would have to go to Germany, but would return in two days with the information.

Horst Janssen was exhausted from the weeks he had worked on the logistics of the naval fleet going to America. Eighteen-hour days were normal as they prepared the paperwork and supplies for the huge armada that would sail tomorrow. Many naval fighting ships had been converted to troop ships and the details and the work were endless. While today was the last of work, the morale of naval headquarters was low. Naval officers working on the projects were depressed by the work they were doing. Criminals of the worst type were being loaded on their ships for the invasion. Murderers, rapists, and the lowest types were passing through the German ports and even the Blackshirts in charge were experiencing difficulty in controlling such men. Two sailors had been killed before they left, and every man in the fleet had been armed. Many Blackshirts had been at the naval headquarters receiving orders, etc., nasty cruel gutter types who boasted of what they would do to the Americans. Men who were little better than the criminals they led.

As Horst entered his apartment he was startled to see his brother Rudolph Junior sitting in his kitchen.

"You had a key, good, and I see you've had one of my beers, but why didn't you tell me you were coming?"

Horst shook his brother's hand and sat at the kitchen table. "I'm exhausted. We've been working all hours." His voice trailed off. His brother was not listening.

Rudolph said, "Do you remember when our uncle died and Father had his heart attack." Their father adored his older brother Rudolph Sr., and shortly after his death, also died of a heart attack.

The brothers remembered their uncle, a kind gentleman who had only one arm. The hero of Crete and one of Germany's greatest heroes, the heir apparent to the former Reich chancellor and dead just after the civil war started. Horst thought of it as a nightmare. So many had died during those weeks of the war and both their father and uncle died at the same time. Yes, a nightmare.

Rudolph continued, "At Father's funeral General Hindenberg spoke to me. He told me that Albert Lobert had Uncle Rudolph killed."

Horst questioned his brother.

"Why didn't you tell me?"

"Hindenberg said it was dangerous to know but he wanted someone in the family to be aware, and I was the oldest brother. He said that Uncle Rudolph was the finest man he had ever known and someday he would avenge him. Our father died because of his brother's death so Lobert in effect killed them both.

Horst got up. "That bastard. I wish I had known."

Rudolph continued. "After Hindenberg died I decided to exact our family's revenge. I have been passing secrets to the Americans for weeks. They have our naval code books and every bit of information I could give them.

Horst sat down. "Treason!"

"Horst, it is not treason where Lobert is involved; I would do it again."

Horst said, "The Naval Bureau has worked day and night on the invasion fleet. While we hate the kind of people that are going to America, stories are circulating that the top officers of the navy are taking the Blackshirts and the trash to America to get them out of the country. Now a new story. Lobert will lead them; an officer told me the top brass forced him to go. The junta that is staying behind will be led by the navy and our future foreign policy will be peace with the rest of Europe."

Rudolph corrected him. "Peace, if Lobert fails in America and does not come back."

Rudolph took a deep breath.

"We are going to help, to make sure he does not come back. You and I are going to find the destination and timing of two submarines leaving Spain and heading for American waters."

Horst was rocked by this comment.

"You think they have atomic bombs."

"Yes, I do, and I don't think the top navy people know about this."

"Horst, Uncle Rudolph was a brave soldier who killed other brave soldiers in combat. Hindenberg said he planned to make peace with the army, end the civil war, and begin to settle with the rest of Europe, as the navy plans to do now. Albert Lobert killed Rudolph Janssen because he wants the wars to go on. What we do is not just for our family, but for all of Germany. This has got to stop."

The next day Horst Janssen broke into the naval computer and two days later the Americans had the destination of two Nazi submarines, what time they would arrive, and even the names of their captains. In addition, both submarines would have to surface to fire atomic missiles.

Chapter X

Seven weeks to the day Mitch Iberson agreed to take the job, he was riding in the number two seat of a Bell gun ship helicopter going at two hundred miles an hour toward the Rio Grande. The Germans had started crossing the Rio Grande three hours earlier. Mitch's two hundred helicopters carried eight men each, two pilots and six men with two Gatling guns installed in the doorways and grenade launchers in the nose and on the wings. The American force had sixteen hundred men. The Germans five hundred thousand. The odds were three hundred to one.

It was long odds, but the Americans had Mitch Iberson and the Germans had Albert Lobert. The Germans never had a chance.

The day after Mitch arrived at the base he called a meeting of the two hundred pilots. He told Richie the meeting would be short.

"I've been sent here to take over the unit. I've never flown in a helicopter before, so I've got a lot to learn and I'll look for you to help me. The unit has a poor health record; we've got to be ready and in shape to meet the enemy. There will be a two-mile run every morning starting tomorrow at 6:00 A.M."

A groan went up from the pilots. It was not a popular idea. A pilot raised his hand. "Why didn't the president send someone with bird experience?" There was a chorus of approval for the question.

Mitch answered, "I'm a soldier. When the president of the United States gives me an order I follow it and I don't question whether I like it or not."

This did not appease the group.

Next morning at the run only sixty pilots showed up. After the run when pilots tried to go to the mess hall a sign was posted that it was closed for breakfast because of repairs. There was much complaining that Mitch had closed the mess hall out of spite.

The second day of the run the same number, about sixty men, showed up. Just before 6:00 A.M. a staff car pulled up and a tall man got out of the car. The president walked over to Mitch. "I'm used to running at this time, I'm not used to getting up at 5:00 A.M. to get to my run."

Mitch shook his hand. "Thank you for coming, Mr. President."

So they ran. After it was over David Schultz talked to the pilots. He was serious and asked many questions about the training. No one asked him about the Mitch Iberson appointment.

Finally David Schultz turned to Richie. "How about some coffee, Richie."

"Sorry, sir, no coffee. Someone decided to close the mess hall."

The president laughed. "You're running some outfit here, Richie."

Then in a low voice David Schultz said to Richie, "How's it going?"

Richie answered, "Mitch said we're doing great—only half the pilots hate us." They talked small talk for a moment and David Schultz said he had to go. The president moved to his staff car with two Secret Service men at his side. A sergeant came running up.

"Sir, I've got a coffee from the enlisted men's mess hall."

The sergeant offered the coffee, but the president did not accept it.

"Sergeant, that is really nice of you but you don't want me to get in trouble with General Iberson do you?"

"No, Sir."

"Sergeant, I hope the next time I come I can get a coffee and yes, I look forward to having a coffee with you."

Six pilots heard the colloquy between the sergeant and the president. Now the president raised his voice so that no one could be confused about his choice for CO, and his thoughts about the elite unit.

"And if this outfit doesn't shape up there'll be no lunch or supper either." The story quickly went around the base. Next morning, one hundred and twenty pilots ran.

The eighty pilots who didn't run were solidly behind Frank Solly, the number two of the unit, who said, "If he orders me to run I'll do it, but he has to order me."

The eighty who did not run had given Mitch a nickname. They called him Captain Clipboard. Mitch carried a clipboard and would write on it in regards to the answer he got from the questions he would ask the pilots. He was speaking to as many pilots as he could and by the fifth day some of his questions could not be answered by the younger pilots. While Mitch was flying practices and working on administration, Richie was learning to fly.

The pilots, always quick to judge a man's ability, determined he was not a natural pilot. In fact the one thing they did know was he was crazy. Even among the young pilots he was considered absolutely fearless. If the twins were not popular with some of the pilots, Mitch had surprised the crew chiefs by appearing in the repair hangars after a practice day. He asked questions; they had never seen his predecessor so they did not know what to make of it. Next day he was there again and asked the head crew chief why only seventy-five percent of the birds had flown that day.

The chief said, "I put in for replacement parts but they haven't arrived yet." Mitch took the sheet. Next morning at six-thirty when the crew chiefs arrived at the hangar, two large trucks of replacement parts were waiting for them. The driver and assistant driver even helped them unload the parts and carry them into the hangar.

One of the drivers said, "Who the hell do you guys know? My boss got orders right from the top. Some guy named William Allen called and we worked all night. In fact, we drove in just about an hour ago and we were told if this wasn't all of it we had to go back."

In the hangar after practice that day they heard the head crew chief call him Mitch.

It was beginning to bother Richie that many of the pilots did still not like them. He was used to being friendly with men he worked with.

He said to his brother, "Mitch, let's have it out with these guys. I take a swing at Frank Solly and we'll have done with this thing."

Mitch said, "We can't do that, Richie. The Germans have ground-to-air missles, and we have to ask these guys to fly low. I don't want most of the guys flying low, I want all of them to do their job and we have to be a unit to do that. Besides we've got reinforcements coming tomorrow."

There was only one word to describe Sergeant Stretch Carter—magnificent. He was a six-foot-five-inch black man who weighed two hundred pounds and had a thirty-inch waist. Despite riding on a bus for two hours his uniform looked like it had just been pressed. His airborne jump boots shined; he was the finest-looking soldier the headquarters of the helicopter group had ever seen.

He presented his papers and waited until Mitch Iberson came to the office. When he saw Mitch he snapped to attention, saluted, and brought his boots together with a sound that sounded like a gunshot. Mitch returned the salute and shook his hand. "Great to see you, Stretch. Come on in."

Once inside Mitch's office Stretch and Richie began to playfully shadow box. Stretch was giggling, "I've got to bail out the twins again. They called Stretch because they're in trouble."

He was right and the first time he met them he had bailed them out. Stretch was the captain of the city of San Francisco's high school baseball team, called the "City." It was unusual for a junior to be captain of the team but coach Happy Feller would have no one else. The twins were freshmen and when the older boys saw they would be starters on the team they began to pick on them. The older boys were both black and white but quickly backed off when Stretch made it known that no one but Coach Feller and Stretch Carter made decisions who would start on the team. One night Stretch told his parents, "We got these two kids, twins, but I've never seen better young players than them. Next year when I'm a senior, City is going to win the championship of San Francisco and I'm going to be the first black man to captain a baseball team in this town to win a championship and those kids are going to help me."

He was right, and a long friendship was started. When Mitch and Richie attacked the Golden Gate Bridge, Stretch led the attack on the police station.

Stretch said, "I just came in on the bus. You should have heard what some of the pilots were saying about you."

Richie wisecracked, "Those are the guys that like us."

Stretch sat down. "You guys got a baseball team on this post?"

Mitch looked at Stretch. "No, but I think it's a good idea if you started one."

Next day a sign was posted in the mess hall. There would be try-outs for the baseball team, and a game was scheduled with the navy in ten days.

At the practice the first half hour was chaos. Finally Stretch Carter blew a whistle and the forty candidates gathered around the big man. "I posted the notice and scheduled the game with the navy, and it's my bats and balls, so I'm the captain. Anybody have a problem with that?"

No one did.

He directed them. "Take your position in the field and take turns fielding. Everybody gets five swings and we keep working until dark. Same time tomorrow. Pitchers check with me."

By the third day it was obvious who the best players were. You could not throw a ball over or past Stretch at first base. He had great power when he hit it. Frank Solly at shortstop was an excellent fielder, but a weak hitter. Richie Iberson at third base was a good glove man and strong hitter, but the star of the team was the center fielder Mitch Iberson. No pitcher could get him out. He hit the ball hard, no matter where it was pitched.

At the game at navy the helicopter base made short work of the navy team. Leading thirteen to one in the seventh inning Mitch Iberson came to the plate for the fourth time. He had a home run, double, and a single. His fast hands generated great bat speed and the ball rocketed off the bat. When he came up again players from both teams paused to watch. The navy pitcher was hot and tired and he was mad at the copter bench, which was riding him hard. He would put a ball under the chin of the great hitter and see what he was made of. The ball rode in on Mitch closer than the pitcher wanted.

"Look out," he started to yell.

Mitch's bat flew out of his hands, his hat fell off and he was in the dust of the batter's box. As he gathered himself he remembered the words of Coach Happy Feller. "When a pitcher knocks you down, I don't want any of you guys rushing back into the batter's box. I want you to take your time and think. The umpire will always give you time and the pitcher will think he got you. So dust yourself off and remember the next pitch will probably be low and outside."

He settled into the batter's box and thought. Low and outside and probably a curve ball. The pitch was low and outside. He timed it with a great crack of the bat. The ball, a bullet, hit the right field fence. His hardest hit of the day—a double.

One of the pilots sitting next to Stretch said, "God, can that guy hit."

Stretch answered, "You think he can hit now, you should have seen him in high school. Batting champ of San Francisco two years in a row. Our coaches said he was the best hitter in town since Joe DiMaggio." Stretch could not resist. "And a real good guy."

The pilot answered, "He wasn't a good guy to us."

Stretch was tired of that talk.

"What do you want? A pat on the back for a good landing? He's not like that, but wait until we see combat. Of course, that is if you guys are up for combat."

On the bus back to the base all the talk was of the game and Mitch hitting. Sitting in the back a pilot next to Frank Solly said, "He's not Clipboard anymore; I'm calling him Line Drive from now on."

Frank Solly was the classic good field, no hit shortstop. He had never hit four balls that hard his whole life. "He said I'm running tomorrow not for him, for me. I can't hit but I can run."

Next morning all two hundred pilots ran and everyone was early on the flight line for practice.

That day was the best practice the Ninth Cavalry had.

Mitch gathered the twenty wing commanders around after practice. Each wing commander was a leader of ten helicopters.

"Tomorrow we begin to get ready to leave for Texas. All the details will be in a folder on your bunks. I want you to begin to get your men ready. We will go over details until we meet the enemy, probably in ten days. There are two things we all should concentrate on. One, we all know the Germans have ground-to-air rockets. We have to work with our jets to beat them. We can do that.

Two, intelligence says the Germans have raped and murdered their way through Mexico. They think these are not regular soldiers. They won't like the taste of gunfire. We can stand off and fire rockets at them, but we're not going to do that; we're going to take it to them. That's why we've been flying so low. We are going to ram it down their throat. Exact maximum casualties; I think they will fold. Tell your men we're going for a knockout—first day, first hour, first wing."

Ten days later, the morning of the battle, Mitch walked into the hangar with the crew chiefs. It was the same each morning. Five minutes of jokes, who made the coffee, and then Mitch would ask, "How many you putting up today, Chief." The last practice it was ninety-five percent.

Mitch asked, "How many you putting up today, Chief."

The chief pulled on his cap. "All two hundred, sir."

Mitch looked up from his clipboard.

The chief repeated. "They all go, all two hundred fly today, sir."

Deliberately Mitch switched the clipboard to his left hand and shook the chief's hand. Men who had not changed their clothes in two days shook his hand. Men who had not had a hot meal or slept for the last thirty hours shook his hand.

One of them said later, "I had not changed my clothes for two days. He didn't say anything, but when he shook my hand I would have worked for another two days if he asked me."

The hangar door opened and the pilots saw the crew chiefs running. It was the first time they had ever seen them running to the copters.

Mitch swiftly walked to the wing commanders waiting for him. How many times had he heard Coach Feller say bring it on before a game. It meant the players should gather close. The strongest sharing their strength with the others. Mitch laid the clipboard on the grass. The chiefs were his friends but their men would face death with him in the few hours. They were his brothers.

He said, "Bring it on." They gathered close. Mitch raised his right hand and made a fist. He looked at Frank Solly, who raised his right arm and made a fist with his right hand. Mitch touched his fist to Frank's fist.

"Victory, Frank."

Solly answered, "Victory, Mitch."

He repeated to the others, "Victory."

They repeated to him, "Victory."

Then the wing commanders ran to their birds. The sixteen hundred men waiting in their copters saw the leaders running to lead them in battle.

General Mueller was right. Mitch Iberson was a man that captains would carry ammunition for.

The American jets saw the top cover of German jets over the Rio Grande as the army was crossing the shallow river, in some places less than two feet deep. Flying higher and faster they shot down twenty of the enemy in ten minutes.

The rest of the German jets turned and ran.

The leader of the jets called to Mitch, "The cover is gone."

Mitch, flying, could see the vast panorama in front of him. Thousands of men in green uniforms had crossed the river. American jets were faking dives, but staying above ten thousand feet. The German ground-to-air guns were on the wings. Not as many as he expected. They were firing rockets at the jets. They did not expect a ground-level attack. All their rockets were set for high attacks. This was the front of the column—almost one hundred thousand men. The center of the column was many miles back with three times the ground-to-air missiles to protect Albert Lobert.

In a deliberate, almost monotone, voice Mitch directed his men. It was like practice. "First wing take the left; second wing take the right."

On the left ten helicopters swept in low firing rockets at less than one hundred yards. All aimed for the missile launchers. Not a single rocket was fired at the birds. There was not time to adjust the height. The copters swung around and the men at the doors were firing Gatling guns at the German gun crews. Some infantry were firing at the copters but most were keeping their heads down.

Mitch could see he did not need a second attack. The copters were crisscrossing the wings looking for targets. No German ground-to-air were firing back.

Mitch called the jet leader.

"This is the Ninth, I'm pulling my guys out; you can come down now."

He ordered the two wings of birds to rejoin the main group five hundred yards hovering north of the river.

The jet came down strafing and firing rockets at the center of the column. When the battle started the German army was perhaps four miles wide. As the jets came down the wings expanded. Men were running to escape the hell in the center. Now the jets were climbing and the leader spoke to Mitch.

"We're going home; we'll be back in thirty minutes. I'm leaving ten for cover so no bad guys show up."

Mitch knew he didn't need all two hundred copters. He called Frank Solly.

"Frank, Plan B."

Solly led his one hundred birds in a wide arc to the right. They were to avoid the middle of the German army and Lobert and all his ground-to-air. They would attack the rear of the army twenty miles south, mostly supply trucks. Mitch saw Richie, second from Franks lead, wangle his bird. It was a well-done signal to Mitch. Mitch smiled. Richie was not only a good man, he was a good brother.

Now, Mitch directed his eight wings to go straight ahead. He would hold back the first two wings. There was more ground fire now, but not much.

On this side of the river Mitch saw a German officer trying to rally his men to fire at the copters. Two men raised their rifles and shot the officer. They threw their guns down and joined a group running for cover under a set of trees. This was reported all day. Officers being shot by their own men. It was rockets for squad car and tanks. Gatling guns for infantry. With no ground-to-air the copters were flying very low. Suddenly he saw a copter on fire one hundred yards south of the river and to the west. It landed and six men jumped out. He called the first wing.

"Copter down one hundred yards south and west of the river. Three go in and rescue. The rest fly cover."

The leader of the wing replied, "We got him, Line Drive. We'll be with them in a minute."

A German tank was racing parallel to the river. The copters were told the engines in the rear would go on fire if hit. A bird put two rockets into him, and saw the tank disappear in flames. Now the men of the downed copter were rescued. The copters were ranging further south. There were low hills and ravines and the Germans were using them for cover. The Americans began firing grenades from launchers. Still very low ground fire. Lobert's soldiers of fortune were not fighting back. Mitch saw a bird smoking, but moving north.

He called, "You okay? Want a rescue?"

The pilot said, "I can make it several miles north. I can make the tanks. I don't want to walk home."

American tanks were ten miles north of the river. They had set a perimeter to help downed copters, but already hundreds of Germans had surrendered. Mitch saw to the east and south of the river perhaps ten German tanks had formed a circle and were keeping individual copters away with machine guns and cannon fire. He called wings three and four to form up. He recognized Ted Marchall in wing three.

"Ted, hold on; I'm calling down jets. You follow them in after they strafe. The Nazis will have their heads down."

Mitch called the jets. "Just make one run, my guys will follow you in."

The jets came down and strafed the tanks, then the copters were behind them. Six tanks were on fire. Two raced away. There was so much smoke Mitch could not see the rest.

Marchall called, "Line Drive, we have no rockets left and no bullets."

Mitch said. "Okay, Then go home."

He called around. Half the copters were out of ammunition and he sent them home. Copters were now crossing the battlefield looking for targets. The jet leader called, "Ninth, we'll be with you in five minutes."

Mitch said, "Okay, I'm pulling my guys out. You have the field to yourself. We'll be back in an hour."

Mitch ordered his men to return to base. He saw thousands of Germans walking north, most with hands up. None with weapons.

At the base, the head crew chief raced to meet him. Mitch took off his helmet, "What's it look like, chief?"

"Five birds down, sir. Only one crew not rescued. Maybe five percent casualties, mostly door gunners. Not one copter hit by ground air."

Mitch had three wings gassed and ready to go. He debated whether to send them ahead or wait for the rest. They had started together. They would go back together. For such a one-sided battle five percent casualties was high. The American birds were flying low.

An officer came running up. "I've got the president on the radio in my jeep."

David Schultz was at his conference table with General Mueller, Susan, and Allen. "How's it going, Mitch?"

"Good, we've broken the front of the army. Lots of prisoners. General Mueller was right. The men are shooting their officers when they attempt to rally them."

Schultz, sitting next to Mueller, squeezed his wrist.

"How are our casualties?"

Mitch said, "It's a shooting gallery out there. We've got five percent casualties and five copters down, but I can report this is an elite unit, sir, and the jets are great."

"Great job, Mitch; all our prayers are with you."

"Sir, I've sent Frank Solly to the rear of the German army. I can see him coming back. I better see how that went."

"Mitch, we're proud of you and the men. We'll be watching and may God be with you."

The president slumped in his chair. The jets and elite unit had justified his faith.

Mitch watched Solly land his bird. His wingman Richie was not with him. Solly raced to Mitch. "It's going good, but Richie is down. I saw him and his crew on top of a hill. We left two jets to fly cover. You've got birds ready to go. I'll take them.

Mitch stood quiet as Solly gave his orders. "We're taking the birds that are ready. You two go in for the rescue; I'll fly high cover." High cover was more dangerous since it was a big target. As the birds took off Mitch saw Stretch Carter climb in one of the rescue ships. He had a bar.

Mitch was numb but he had to snap out of it. Returning to the Rio Grande there were fires and wrecked vehicles and tanks and birds throughout the landscape. For miles he could see Germans trying to get to the river. They were not being attacked if they crossed the river with their hands up. Beyond the hills men were hiding and columns of men were walking south to the main body of the Germany army. The copters circled and loudspeakers said, "If you cross the river with your hands up we won't fire on you." Most turned and walked north with their hands up.

Those hiding in the hills brought down two copters with their fire. After the crews were rescued, Mitch ordered them all back to the base.

They prepared to land and Mitch could see Richie. He was all right. His arm was in a sling. Mitch jumped out of the copter and ran to the group taking out Sergeant Carter on a stretcher. He was covered with blood. The big man had a large hole in his side. His eyes were glazed. He was going into shock. A corpsman was holding a plasma bottle. He shook his head to tell Mitch it was bad.

Mitch got down on one knee. He thought my, God we're going to lose this guy. He leaned over and whispered in his ear. "The first black man to captain a championship team at the City cannot die." Stretch looked at him, tried to speak, but couldn't. Then, with Richie at his side, they took him to the hospital. Mitch began to talk to the men. Some were jubilant; others just glad to be alive. All were relieved they had done their job. He walked through the hangar. One of the crew chiefs was crying. His cousin, a pilot, was dead.

Mitch finally got to his hut. He was too exhausted to take off his flight suit. He sat on his bed. He wanted to forget today, but too many events had happened. He began to think about tomorrow.

Frank Solly came in. He had two beers. "I spoke to the hospital. Your brother is fine. The sergeant has lost a lot of blood. They'll know better tomorrow, but I sense he's out of danger." Solly sat in a chair and put the beer on the desk.

"You're gonna have to give the Sergeant a medal. He jumped out of the bird before it landed, firing the bar. He charged about one hundred of them when he ran out of ammunition. He used the Browning as a club, I saw him hit two of them. The rest ran away. I don't blame them, I would have run away too."

The beer made Mitch lightheaded. It was good; he wanted to relax.

Solly wanted to talk, which also was good. Mitch did not want to be alone.

Solly said, "For the first hour it was fun, then I was on adrenalin. And you know what, I just wanted to fly low and get this thing over. The brass was right. Take it to them, don't drag this thing out."

Mitch finally spoke. "Tomorrow will be different. The group we didn't touch today will be ready and they are better soldiers. They have more ground-to-air. Tomorrow we have to probe."

Solly said, "I just want to get it over, and I'm thinking what am I going to do when it is over. I love flying. I'll stay in the army or get into commercial copter work. My wife is great; she'll stick with me whatever I want to do." Solly was the best pilot in the outfit. He should continue to fly.

"What are you going to do, Mitch, when it's over?"

Mitch said, "Frank, for ten years everything I've done is based on the Germans. The revolution and now the war. God, I want to get rid of these people. Since I was in high school they have dominated my life. I don't know what I want to do." Solly said, "I hear they are starting a baseball league. You should think about that; you can play."

Mitch thought it would be great to play baseball every day for a living.

Frank said, "Where'd you learn to hit like that?"

"We had a great coach in high school."

Frank looked at Mitch's hand holding the bottle. They were the same height and weight but Iberson's hands were twice the size of Solly's. That's where he got his power from.

Frank spoke. "One of the pilots that got killed today was my bunkmate. I can't go back and sleep in that hut. Can I sleep here?"

Mitch was glad he would stay; he didn't want to be solitary tonight. This man was his brother too.

Sergeant Fritz Paulus crouched lower in the hole he found. The American helicopters were going away but they struck so fast he would not stand up until dark. He tightened his hold on his submachine gun. He was almost out of ammunition. He had shot an American gunner standing in the door of a helicopter. It showed how low they were flying. The submachine gun was only good for close range. The lieutenant had said for weeks the Americans would not fight, so when two of his own men shot him, Paulus did not go after them.

The lieutenant was stupid; the Americans were spying on them. Planes, helicopters and once he had even seen two men on motorcycles in the distance. This was not a sign they were going to surrender. He peered over the rim of the hole. German tanks, trucks, and equipment were burning, and thousands of men in green uniforms were on the ground dead or wounded. He had not seen such close fighting since Russia. The Americans struck with such speed and the operation was insane to put all the ground-to-air on the wings. No one had told them about the helicopters. The troops were paralyzed when they attacked. He also knew too many of the ground-to-air were guarding Albert Lobert in the center of the army. He heard his friend Sergeant Typper say about Lobert why was he not leading the men. "Why doesn't the Fuhrer travel with us."

"*Warum Fahrt, Der Fuhrer Nicht Mit.*" At the beginning of the battle Lobert's conquistadors had thrown their guns away and run like rabbits. He thought most of them were rabble like the corporal from prison. Why they made him a corporal he did not know. He was the worst soldier Paulus had ever met. Sergeant Typper and Paulus had tried to make a soldier out of him, but failed. On the second day of the campaign he disappeared and returned two days later, blood all over his sleeve.

Probably some poor Mexican, he refused to obey orders and stole from the other men. The final insult, he beat up and stomped a much smaller man. Paulus had gone to the lieutenant and demanded a court-martial, but the lieutenant refused. Typper and Paulus took the corporal out in the desert to hunt for wood. Typper put a bullet in his neck and Paulus finished him off. Discipline in the platoon improved a great deal after that.

The Americans' helicopters and jets had worked together. Paulus saw the command helicopter always circling, not darting in like the others. One time Paulus was close enough to shoot at the command helicopter, but he did not. It reminded him of someone, Rommell, yes Rommell, always in the thick of the action. He was with Rommell in North Africa, a real fighter.

Yes, the American leader made them fly low and he thought, I didn't shoot at him because I didn't want to expose myself. No, because he wanted to be with them, real fighting men, men he could respect. Sergeant Paulus would wait until it was dark and then he would walk north and surrender. One year later he became an American soldier.

If Sergeant Paulus knew what he wanted, Albert Lobert was confused and discouraged. As his army crossed the Rio Grande he radioed again and again to Gibraltar, trying to confirm his submarines had committed atomic attack on American cities. The only answer he received was, "No confirmation of attacks. We cannot contact the submarines." He did not believe this was a double-cross since he had promised the naval officer in Gibraltar they would be put in charge of the navy after the war. Lobert could not have known that both submarines surfaced as planned, but one did not even get its crew on deck before two torpedoes from an American submarine sent it to the bottom. The second met the same fate. Its captain startled when he came to the cunning tower to see a torpedo hitting his bow. He was thrown into the water and dragged under when the front of his boat rolled over on him. From the whole operation only five German sailors were rescued.

The second blow to Lobert was the sight of his jets fleeing south just as the battle started. To his urgent calls to the air base in southern Mexico he received an answer they would be back tomorrow. But because of major losses they would not return today. The general in charge was told by his best pilots that to fight the American jets was suicide. The commander refused to attack again today and began to prepare to retreat to his home base in Venezuela.

Then Lobert and General Messinger began to hear cries for reinforcements for the army at the river. They were not prepared for the American helicopters and Lobert knew the battle was lost. He couldn't go back to Germany, and he couldn't stay here. Albert would need a new deck of cards.

Chapter XI

Mitch slept until 6:00 A.M., took a shower and felt better. General Quotious was on the radio. Great job, Mitch; yesterday went the way we practiced." General Quotious was fifty-five years old but his enthusiasm and energy made him sound twenty years younger.

He continued. "The main body of the German army has formed a great circle about twenty miles south of the Rio Grande. They wised up, putting the ground-to-air in clusters, some for high attack, some for low. I think they have almost two hundred thousand men with the main ammunition dump in the center. They don't have a perfect circle, the terrain forces bulges and hills and water makes for gaps, so we'll attack the gaps." The general had large helicopters that carried 105 artillery guns and rocket-firing jeeps and infantry.

"My jets attacked their air bases in southern Mexico at dawn. We did a lot of damage, and my boys think some of their jets already pulled out last night.

Now the army we attacked yesterday, we've got almost fifty thousand prisoners. Our tanks are crossing the river and we'll attack about noon if we can soften them up. The tanks will be carrying

American flags, so tell your pilots that not all the tanks south of the river are Nazis. So we coordinate jets and copters again today. At eight o'clock I'm going to show the Germans something their fathers saw, B-17 bombing. Tell your boys to look up. We'll be coming over your base in about thirty minutes."

Mitch thought, "How like Archie to go off course to show off his B-17."

The flight line and breakfast was quiet. A lot of empty seats. The men were ready for today, but the electricity of the previous day was gone.

Then someone yelled, "Here they come." The B-17s were at six thousand feet and starting to climb to ten thousand feet. A good head wind over eight thousand feet was against them so Archie would be five minutes late to target. The planes were painted silver, they were beautiful. Four-engine giants, majestic and regal, climbing to announce "America is coming; try and stop us."

The men at the base started to cheer and wave.

"Give them hell!"

"Go get them!"

"Bomb it right down their nose!"

A crew chief came out of the hangar. He was playing "America the Beautiful" on a trumpet; the men started to sing. Mitch felt a chill down his spine. The electricity was back. He knew his men would fly low again today.

The crew chiefs would put up one hundred and eighty today. Frank Solly had gone ahead with ten as reconnaissance. Twenty minutes from target Mitch heard thunder. The pilots did not like lightning.

Mitch's pilot said, "I don't see any clouds. Where did that come from?"

A series of claps, not thunder, but explosions.

Frank Solly came on the radio. "Mitch, you should see this; it's like the Fourth of July. Rockets going off, explosions. Archie hit the German ammunition dump." A series of loud explosions followed.

Solly came back on. "We're at the west side of the enemy. No straight lines, the topography won't allow it. Just ahead of us the Germans have set up guns, tanks, ground-to-air on a plateau that juts out into the desert. One of Archie's big helicopters unloaded two 105s and they are firing from cover. I don't think the Germans can see them. The jets are diving on the plateau but not coming down low. One guy did dive below ten thousand. They shot a missile at him. He waited until the last minute and dove away. The damn thing missed him, and he attacked the gun crew. I think the Germans are trigger happy; they are firing at planes too high to hit."

"There is a ravine with tree cover to the north of the German positions. I'm going to sneak five copters up that ravine. I'll be back in five minutes."

Ten minutes later Solly was back. "We did it—caught them flat-footed. Came over the rim firing rockets. Set two tanks on fire, splatted the ground-to-air with the Gatlings. We stayed for about four minutes. As we pulled out three jets came down and tore them up. They can't react to combination attacks."

Solly was right. The Americans had two weeks of practice and the ultimate practice combat the day before. The Germans had no practice and hearing of the disaster the day before were very nervous and trigger happy. Today a new ingredient, artillery fire. The Americans would probe a weak spot. The Germans would rush reinforcements but always too late as big copters would pull the attackers away.

As Mitch's copters moved to the east of the circle the jet leader called down. "Ninth, do you see that low mountain range with some cloud cover jutting into the desert?

"Yes, I do."

"They've got five or six ground-to-air at the end of the range. I bet they've got a couple in the tree line by the side of the mountain. I'll fake coming down. Watch the side of the mountain and see if we get fire from them."

"Roger."

Mitch ordered Ted Marchall to take two copters into the cloud cover. The American jets started to dive and immediately pulled up. Rockets from the end of the range and two from the side of the mountain spiraled upward. One exploded and caused minor damage to a jet.

Mitch was about to order Ted to attack, but he was already firing from two hundred yards away. The German guns blew up in a loud explosion. It was the best shot Mitch had seen in two days.

Marchall was euphoric. "Now, Line Drive, I call that a home run."

Normally, Mitch didn't like such banter but this was a great shot.

"Ted, I call that a home run with the bases loaded."

The Americans set up a new base just north of the river so jets and copters were in continuous action with gas and ammunition supply. As the morning wore on they grew bolder and bolder, always working together. Now the jets would begin a run from five miles out, strafing and firing rockets. The Germans almost always fired high; they misjudged the speed and the height of the jets. As soon as the Germans fired, copters would drop out of the low clouds and finish off the ground-to-air crew. After four hours the Germans started to withdraw from the perimeter; slowly at first then a large group from the north broke. They had taken a pounding and then American tanks appeared.

The rout was on.

"The east perimeter urgently needs reinforcements." It was General Runstendt's adjutant. He was on the verge of panic. General Runstendt was missing.

At the German command post General Messinger instructed the operator to say we'll call back. He had no reinforcements. His last ten tanks had just been sent north. The explosions from the ammunition dump had finally stopped but the smoke continued to drift in the direction of the command post choking all the radio operators. General Messinger's shoulder hurt. He had been knocked to the ground when the bombs hit. The Americans used World War II bombers, but they flew too high for his ground-to-air. They knew the top range for his weapons, and the bombing was very accurate.

There were continuing calls for reinforcement and the commanders wanted to know where the Nazi jets were. After the bombing was over Albert Lobert took off in a small plane. He said he was flying to the jet base in southern Mexico to get help. American tanks had broken through in the north. The ten tanks he sent could not hold them. Messinger thought, "Am I in command or not." Lobert's orders to him were so vague he did not know what he should do. Lobert's orders were always a problem. Messinger wanted to keep a mobile reserve, one hundred of his best Panzer tanks and crews with ground-to-air following in trucks. This way if the Americans broke through he could gain a local victory and perhaps turn the battle. But Lobert insisted they be scattered around the perimeter. They were being destroyed piecemeal. Messinger had thousands of casualties, but some of his men were still fighting back. In the south an entire division was missing; ten thousand men had disappeared. He assumed they'd run away, finding cover in a deep swamp with large trees and safety from the air attacks.

The plan for ground-to-air to be clustered had not worked. They were too inexperienced. Lobert had not let them practice together before the battle. It was a great weapon; Messinger saw it work against conventional planes, but Lobert didn't understand its limits. The Americans knew exactly how to exploit the weapon. They must have practiced, but how could they know so much when the Germans didn't even know the Americans had helicopters? Messinger had warned Lobert that if Mueller was advising the Americans expect attacks with great speed. Mueller was a devotee of Rommell; he would always emphasize speed. Lobert said, "I beat Mueller at Berlin; my soldiers of fortune will be more than a match for the Americans." Messinger had been at the military academy with Mueller, who had always been first in his class, while Messinger had been at the bottom. Messinger knew Mueller would have no respect for him and Lobert and that's the way the Americans fought. They attacked in a manner that suggested the Germans would have no answer.

Runstendt's adjutant was calling again. Runstendt was dead; he had been leading charges against the Americans on the east perimeter. Three times his tanks attacked the artillery of the big copters, but each time they flew away before he could destroy them. Finally assisted by the helicopter gun ships they cut him off from his lines, surrounded his tank, crashed through a small wood, and two American jeeps firing rockets turned his tank into a burning ember. Without Runstendt the infantry began to leave their trenches and many surrendered. The east was lost.

Messinger could see on the frightened faces of his radio operator the army was coming apart. Even if they held today, there would be no ammunition for tomorrow.

He told his radio man to call the American leader. After five minutes Mitch Iberson came on the radio.

"I am the American commander."

"I'm General Messinger. I want a truce."

"No truce, general, unconditional surrender and we want Lobert."

Mitch saw the Germans were leaving the trenches. He saw an officer shot by his own men; his copters were flying into the circle with no opposing fire. It was beginning to look like yesterday.

Messinger said, "Albert Lobert is not here. He flew away this morning. I am not authorized to surrender."

General Mueller had warned the American leaders to expect Lobert to flee. Mitch made a decision. He knew Messinger couldn't get all his men to surrender at once and that with the circle getting smaller Americans were going to get killed by friendly fire. He had six copters down in the east and saw two jets go down. Perhaps one hundred infantry were casualties in the east. It was a shooting gallery. If he could stop it now he would save lives.

"General, we'll pull back for twenty minutes. Send out trucks with white flags telling your men to give up. If we see men moving north with their hands up we won't begin again, but get moving, and if it begins again we'll finish it."

Mitch called the copters and the jet leader. "Their general is sending out trucks with white flags. Don't fire on them. We're pulling back for twenty minutes. Wait for my command."

The American tank commander in the north had just fought off a weak counterattack. He was prepared to drive through the German center to the great fire and cut their position in two. Then he saw men with hands up—a trickle, then a mob. A German squad car with a white flag was driving perhaps a mile away and clearly ordering men to surrender. Gradually the firing stopped and the battlefield grew quiet. German troops who did not get the order could see other men in green uniforms with their hands up walking north and put down their arms. The more experienced soldiers knew it was over two hours ago.

The architect of this disaster, Albert Lobert, landed at a small airport on the west coast of Mexico. They had flown very low and had not been seen by any American planes. Lobert was joined by four men and escorted to a dock and a waiting submarine. The Reich chancellor of Germany was now the Reich chancellor of thirty men and one submarine.

Chapter XII

The German government sent a representative to Washington to ask the American government if they would consider exchanging ambassadors and normalizing relations between the two countries. William Allen attended the meeting for the Americans and presented a list of demands by his government before the Americans would consider the German requests.

Germany must withdraw all its troops from all foreign countries.

The Blackshirts in South America must surrender all their weapons and return to Europe.

Germany will attempt to convince the Japanese to return all American prisoners. If they do not, Germany would break off all relations with Japan.

If either nation captures Albert Lobert, he will be put on trial as a war criminal.

Germany will have free elections in three years.

Neutral Spain will be the seat of a peace conference and Germany and America will sign a peace treaty.

Lord Oliver and General Franco were delighted that Spain would enjoy the prestige of hosting the conference.

Lord Oliver, always sensitive to changes in diplomacy, said to the Caudillo, "The Americans have proved to be fair and generous to the help we gave them, but they are a great world power now and as such expect everything they do will be to maintain such power. I expect you will be approached to join some kind of a European defense community. The Communists have gained solid control of Russia. They have taken over the government of some small Baltic states and I expect Communist parties in Hungary and Poland will dominate those countries. The Americans will not let the Communists dominate western Europe.

Susan Tyler was the driving force in organizing the victory parties in Washington. She told the president and William Allen that so many Americans had worked so hard and so long and that the administration had to say thank you. There would be a victory parade in the morning, medals would be given in the afternoon, and five parties that night, including one at the White House, would be held. The president would visit each party, ending with a ball at the White House.

The victory parade was splendid with great weather, and millions visiting Washington cheering the soldiers. At the White House, David Schultz pinned the Congressional Medal of Honor on Sergeant Stretch Carter. General Mueller congratulated the sergeant and the two exchanged ideas. Neither one understood the other's point, but each knew that something very deep was exchanged.

The general said, "I am a great admirer of your friend Iberson. In fact, I recommended him to the president for leadership of the helicopter unit. I told him that Iberson was a man who could get other men to do extraordinary things."

The general was about to tell the story of the battle of the Meause River when Carter said, "He saved my life in Mexico. I was hit hard and about to give in to the pain when he said to me, 'The first black man to be captain of a championship team in San Francisco can not die.' I hung on."

Before he could explain, Susan Tyler was waving them to come to the Oval Office. "The president is going to give General Quotoius a medal. Can you come in?"

Neither man had a chance to explain his point, but both were right.

The same day a German submarine crawled into Tokyo Bay. The former Reich Chancellor Albert Lobert was carried off the submarine on a stretcher, sick from the trip. His low spirits were made lower when he found a captain was in charge of the Japanese official party that greeted him.

General Togo, military ruler, was informed that Lobert had arrived in Japan.

He asked one question. "Did he bring plans for atomic bombs and scientists with him?"

Informed he had, the general said, "Put him on the military base as I have instructed. Make sure he is under guard, we may trade him to the Americans later."

Lobert had joined the friends he deserved.

Susan Tyler had arranged a date for Mitch Iberson. Mimi, a young woman who spoke four languages, had replaced Susan at the State Department. She was as petite and sweet as anyone Susan knew. Iberson, always a decision maker, would marry her four weeks later.

At the White House, Mitch and Mimi entered the main ballroom. When the crowd saw them they started to clap. Some pilots grouped to the right started to whistle and cheer. Mitch saw Frank, his brother, Ted, and the head crew chief. He waved.

Ted, who had two drinks, yelled, "Hey Mitch, way to go, Line Drive."

The clapping grew louder. Mitch, always poised and knowing what button to push, knew he could not quiet the crowd, but he could share it. He walked over to the president of the United States and shook his hand. David Schultz, a man who also understood what motivated people, lifted Mitch's arm in the air. The crowd on the left began to chant.

"Iberson . . . Schultz . . . Iberson . . . Schultz!"

General Mueller, a full American now, was stamping his foot and clapping. He was yelling "Iberson . . . Schultz!"

The president and Iberson faced the center of the crowd and raised their arms in a salute.

"Iberson . . . Schultz . . . Iberson . . . Schultz!"

Susan Tyler wiped her eyes with her handkerchief, tears of joy streaming down her cheeks.

* * *

The president raised William Allen's arm.

"Iberson . . . Schultz . . . Allen!" the crowd cheered.

The Americans were with the friends they deserved.